The Letting

by

Cathrine Goldstein

The Letting

Cover Art by *Angela Anderson*

The Wild Rose Press, Inc.
PO Box 708
Adams Basin, NY 14410-0708
Visit us at www.thewildrosepress.com

Publishing History
First Climbing Rose Edition, 2014
Print ISBN 978-1-62830-662-0
Digital ISBN 978-1-62830-663-7

Published in the United States of America

"What if the Devil doesn't know he's the Devil?" I ask.

Phoenix shakes his head, confused. "What?"

"Why? Why does the bad I've done have to define me?"

"Because you're a murdering sadist," he snaps back at me.

"No, I am not." I clench my teeth, standing my ground. I am tired of these labels I am suddenly wearing. "I never, I mean never knew what happened to those girls I led to the Lettings. I am so very sorry I played any role in this vile enterprise in which we exist, but I was clueless. Maybe I'm ignorant, or downright stupid, but I would rather have been dead than be responsible for hurting anyone. And before you go throwing malicious names around, maybe it's time you consider maybe you're wrong...? What if you kidnapped and tortured me in the name of a revolution that is wrong?"

"It's not," he argues.

"But I didn't think I was wrong, either." I am exasperated. "Don't you get it?" He takes a step back away from me, but I go on. "We are completely turned around. The only information we're fed is from a corrupt enterprise. What makes you think your information is any more accurate than mine?"

For the first time ever, he looks terrified. I let a moment go by before I gesture for Raven to come over, and she hurries to my side.

"This is Raven," I say, slowly, talking to Phoenix. "She's your sister."

Praise for *THE LETTING*

"Cathrine Goldstein's *THE LETTING* offers a chilling vision of the not-too-distant future. Idealistic and patriotic Veronica Billings discovers to her horror she's been the New World's most successful executioner. In Goldstein's pulse-pounding thriller, the fearless seventeen-year-old races to save humanity, and those she cares for, before Veronica becomes her own next victim of The Letting."

~Michael Murphy, NY mystery author

"*THE LETTING* is *The Handmaid's Tale* meets *The Hunger Games*, a tense ride that slowly squeezes you between its fingers until you cry mercy, and beg to find out how it will all end."

~Kristen Rutherford, head writer of The Nerdist Show *on BBC America, host of #parent on Geek & Sundry*

Dedication

For Jay, Penelope, and Pickle.
Thank you.

Chapter One

The hot summer night is so oppressive the heat clings to my body like a dead weight I'm unable to shake. Mosquitoes buzz by me, dive-bombing my head, circling my ponytail, hovering at my ear. I lift a heavy hand to swat them away, but to me they are little more than a noisy nuisance. For some reason, they never bother to bite me. I wonder if I've grown immune to them, spending so many long summer evenings here in the deep woods where the mosquitoes thrive. But no, when I think about it, I can't recall ever having one single mosquito bite. Ever. I guess they just don't like me.

Trudging across campus, I will myself to think about what it's like to do these bed checks in the middle of winter, when the snow is past my calf, and I'm certain I'll pull my foot clear from my boot as I lift it, slogging my way from cabin to cabin. On those nights, the cold is biting, and it whips my cheeks until they are raw. Tonight, as the perspiration dots my forehead, I realize my imagery isn't working. It's still hot as hell. I have to laugh when I think of how, on those bitter nights, I do my best to imagine nights just like tonight, nights when the sun has mercifully gone down, but the temperature still hovers over ninety degrees. Come to think of it, imagining didn't work then, either. Frankly, it never works, but imagining another time and place comes naturally to me. To all of us. It's what we've been taught since birth.

As I stomp across the grounds, I make little dust clouds with my boots. Thankfully, this summer has been blissfully dry. But because of it, our landscape is little more than large patches of brown dirt. I reach the cabin and slowly, arduously, raise my hand to knock. There's no real reason. The girls love it when I visit. They look forward to it, and it is my jurisdiction. But I do it anyway, out of courtesy and politeness. After all, when these girls "blossom" and leave me, they are moving on to the New World, and who knows what manners they will be expected to know. The least I can do is help prepare them.

The thought of them leaving me makes me sad, and I take a long, labored breath. I watch my hand rap on the rickety cabin door as if I am watching it move through water. The amount of effort it takes to do even this small action astounds me. I feel a drop of sweat trickle down my spine. The cabin door rattles in response, but even it seems too tired to shake and wobble as it usually does. I hear small squeals of delight from inside, and I peer through the ripped screen on the cabin door. Almost all of the girls in cabin O are already in bed, but they're waiting for me to tuck them in, tell them a story, and kiss them good-night. All the things their mothers would be doing if they were still at home. No matter how difficult home was, it's still devastating to leave your mother behind.

Cabin O has always had a soft spot in my heart, perhaps because I am an O as well, or maybe it's because these girls are just so young. "Ronnie," one of the girls squeals. "Come in. Come in."

I let myself glide through the door, and it slams shut behind me. No matter how often I have complained to management and asked them to come fix it, no matter how hard I tug on it, it never closes completely. Because of this, there is no feasible way to keep the mosquitoes out, so I have devised a way to tuck all of my campers in at night, covering them with sheets of mosquito netting I found in one of the old, unused buildings at the far edge of camp. It was one of the buildings in use when we were busy, but no one has stepped in there in years. I have all of my campers sleep in sleeping bags in rows, on the floor, and I pitch "peaks" with tent poles. Then I drape the netting across the poles and it falls gracefully over the top of the sleeping girls. I do this in every one of my cabins, cabin A, cabin B, cabin AB and this, cabin O. I have already been to the other cabins, and they are set for the night. I wipe the sweat that's dripped onto my brow and enter into the darkness of cabin O.

"Ronnie?" the tiny voice repeats itself.

"Lulu?" I ask. Of course, I know it's Lulu calling my name. The eldest of this little group, she has made herself my honorary sidekick. Although I love all my girls, there is a special place in my heart for her.

Through the darkness, I smile at her. This is the smallest group of girls I've ever had in cabin O, but I'm not surprised. Once prevalent, O is now almost extinct. These girls are also the youngest I've had at my camp, ever, and they attached to me immediately. I was ten when I came, but that was because I was so tall they thought I was older. They used to wait to bring the girls to camp until they were eleven, but now they come as young as eight or nine. Just babies. But as sad as it makes me that they're here at such a young age, I'm also glad I'll be able to spend more time with them before they blossom and are sent on to the New World. Every time a group of my campers leaves me, it breaks my heart. I know when these girls go, it very nearly will kill me.

"What story tonight?" I sit cross-legged on the floor, at the foot of their sleeping bags and yank on my sticky tank top, pulling it away from my body.

"Tell us about the New World." Lulu doesn't miss a beat.

"The New World?" I tease. "Aren't you tired of that story?"

"Nooooo." Four tiny little voices speak in unison.

"Shh…" I say quieting them, good-naturedly. It's not that I'm doing anything wrong, but it is past curfew, and Margaret, my superior, looks for any reason she can to reprimand me. I smile at my girls. I know I'm safe here, no one will check up on me. Sometimes Margaret will do the midday inspections, but she tries never to come into the cabins at night. She acts as if it's beneath her, but I know the truth is that she's afraid of the dark. The other Leader, my best friend Gretchen, does the morning inspections, and so I handle the night all on my own. I like it that way.

"Quiet voices," I tell my girls. Although I know no one is going to double-check my work, I don't want to be too loud and risk getting any of us into trouble. The Letting is in two days, and the girls are all supposed to be rested and well fed. And for these girls in cabin O, this is their first Letting. Each day that draws closer to the eventful day, their adrenaline increases. Tomorrow night, it will be nearly impossible for any of them to sleep. I'm sure I'll spend the night in their cabin consoling them, but I don't mind, especially since I may not see them for days after the Letting.

"Okay, lie down and close your eyes." The girls try, though the heat seems to make even this impossible. Slowly, I feel calm make its way into the cabin. It lingers, hovering above the girls, but patiently pushes past the oppressive heat and falls quietly on top of us all. Sitting there next to four little girls, all missing their dolls and their mothers, my heart aches for them. The least I can do is keep their minds occupied. Besides, I like talking about the New World. It's where my own mother is, and it makes me feel closer to her.

"Once upon a time," I begin, "the world was a different place. It was a world where people were not obligated to help one another and so they didn't. Where words like 'charity' and 'altruism' were used only by a minority group, the 'Good People,' or the 'Givers' as we call them. They were the only ones who bothered to help."

I hear a small yawn from the tiniest of the girls, Lilly, who has been enjoying her past few months at camp, thinking she was still too small to be called to the Letting, and much too young to be sent to the New World. For her, this had all been pure entertainment, until now. But this time around, they have summoned even her. I stare at her thoughtfully and think, maybe she was on to something. Maybe at least some part of childhood should consist of simple pleasure.

"Sorry." Lilly assumes I stopped telling the story because she yawned.

"It's fine." I try to reassure her. "It's bedtime. It's

okay to yawn."

I look around, and through the darkness, I see tiny shapes moving underneath the mosquito netting. Some flip onto their sides or tummies. I go on.

"Those people, the Givers, were the forefathers of our world." I know this because back before I was sent to camp, when I was still in school, my history teacher had told us this in class.

I look around the room of cabin O and am gripped with the simultaneous, paradoxical feelings of immense gratitude and deep melancholy, when I realize that once these girls move on to the New World, they will receive educations I can only dream about. My enthusiasm for their educations is what makes me so confident about bringing these young girls to the Lettings. No matter what shape they are in when they come back to me, I know fairly soon, once they have paid their debt to society, they will be reunited with their mothers and given stellar educations.

I hear a faint snore, but I go on remembering my history textbook, my story almost verbatim. "The rest of the people, the 'Selfish People', or the 'Takers' as we call them, spent their time working with the sole intent to make money. They were involved in hedonistic rituals, useless recreational activities, and the constant pursuit of happiness. The most wasteful of all of these things was the time they spent on small machines they carried with them day in and day out— machines they claimed connected them to the rest of the world."

"They didn't?" asks a still wide-awake camper. Straining through the darkness, I see it is Violet, Lilly's older sister, who's asked the question. The fact that she's asked this, and not the meaning of the word hedonistic, proves they are now prepping these girls at a remarkably young age. Lilly sleeps now, curled up next to Violet, snoring faintly.

"No," I answer. "These people spent more and more time in isolation, asking these machines to do more and more things for them. Soon the machines were everywhere, and they had taken over. Schools as we know them ceased to exist. All students learned their schoolwork at home, staring into one of those machines that would connect them to their classroom. All adults worked from home too, and soon social interaction became passé. They were a civilization of lazy, greedy people who relied entirely on machines. Soon, their once overpopulated world began to die off because there was no social interaction left between people. Within a few generations, they forgot how."

"But social interaction is mandatory." It's Lulu. She sits up and leans forward, waiting for my response. I look at her, stunned. I had no idea they were now informing girls this young about the Couplings. She can read the look on my face. "I'm the oldest."

Through the darkness, I can see her shrug. "I overheard the Collector telling my mother she was due."

I nod. I look at Lulu's bright blue eyes and long blonde hair, and I know her mother must have fought hard to free Lulu from the life of a Coupling. For some reason, tonight I can't help myself.

I glance at the little girl. "Lulu, if you're the oldest, do you know how many brothers or sisters you have?" I realize I'm whispering, and clear my throat.

"I know of three for sure," she answers quietly.

"Two were boys and my sister, Clara, who will probably be coming here soon. Hopefully. I've told her all about the New World. And all about you."

"Me?" I ask, surprised. "How did you tell her about me?" I wonder if Lulu has some secret communication going with the city.

"I told her before. I told her we could have a better life if we were a good match. We all know about you. It's a big honor to come to your camp."

I am floored by the prospect of anyone in the city knowing me, but still it makes me smile. I know I am a good government worker, and one of the main reasons Margaret hates me so very much is because I have been highly decorated as a Leader. One whole wall of my cabin is filled with plaques and documents honoring me for my excellent service. I have singlehandedly brought more girls to the Lettings than anyone else, ever, in the history of the world. And what's more, I have succeeded, time and again, from keeping the rebels, who want to steal the young girls, far from our camp.

Yet, despite all that, there is some question in my mind. Some seed my mother planted, all those years ago. But tonight, like every night, I push that grain of uncertainty away and focus on my accomplishments. It is hot tonight, but the sense of pride I feel is comforting. I look over the bodies of my four little girls, wondering about them. How many have siblings they know nothing about? What were their lives like back home? Only one, Raven, the singular one of them with dark hair, seems wide awake. She stares at me with watchful eyes, trying to anticipate my next move. Lilly wakes with a start, and the other two stretch and yawn, and then, once again, Lilly begins to doze.

"The Old World was every man for himself," I explain, trying to get back on track.

Something about the way Raven looks at me is unnerving, so I concentrate on the words I am saying. I see them laid out on the pages of a textbook, in front of me.

"Since they were a violent people, they eventually broke out of their confines and brought their basic human needs to the streets. Ironically, once they finally had the one on one contact they so desperately needed, it was too late. Total anarchy began, and they depleted resources until there was nothing left. Thankfully, our forefathers were there to save those few people who survived, and since then the New World has triumphed.

"But the damage done by the selfish people was not completely eradicated. The Takers of the Old World left us in the dire straits we are in now, barely surviving." My words come faster and louder. "Food and happiness have become commodities that are rationed by our knowledgeable guides." I suddenly realize I went off script. I look around quickly, avoiding eye contact with Raven, my eyes darting up and down the row of girls, wondering if any one of them was awake enough to notice. Especially Raven. "Food and happiness rationed?"

Rationed? Those few words are the words of a rebel, not the calm, strong Leader that I'm supposed to be. That I am. No matter what else, I am true to my civic duty. There is no question I am here for morale. I believe in our government and what we are doing more than anyone else. I know human beings were near extinction. I know it is a privilege to be released from the factories and squalor of the city and to be brought here to camp, with its beautiful lake and picturesque woods, to prepare for the Lettings. I know how lucky I was, me in particular, to be chosen for the Lettings and not for the Couplings. What I do is a civic duty, but it is also an honor. And when these girls blossom, they move on to the New World where they share in all of its glories and riches. My one regret is that I was never chosen to donate. But at least I can prepare those who can. No, I am certainly not a rebel. I am far from it. I am the girl who has willingly led hundreds of young girls to the Lettings.

I want to reiterate, to explain what I meant to say, but try as I might, I am tongue-tied. Suddenly, I feel young, and the image of my mother sitting at the edge of my bed is so vivid it takes my breath away. In the darkness and safety of the night, she told me stories of her mother's great-grandmother who was part of the generation that lived in the Old World. She spoke so softly I strained to hear her words, and often wondered if they were truly meant for me to hear. I remember my mother dipping her small, white hand into a tin containing oil taken from sheep's wool, and rubbing the calluses on my hands that formed from hours spent toiling in the factory. Quietly, in those moments only a mother and daughter can share, she told of a magical place where young girls were brought to dance classes and horseback riding lessons. Where they played in backyards littered with dandelions and not trash. Once, to show me what they looked like, she drew me a picture of a dandelion, which I still have to this day. I knew she had the impulse to crumple it up and throw it away, but instead, she gave it to me. She told me if anyone ever found that picture, I must tell them it is a picture of a flower in the New World I am eager to see. But these are not things I can share with these girls. These are things I should not even know. These things my mother said, confuse me still.

I clear my throat, snapping back to the suffocating heat of this night. "So, we are here today thanks to a few good people."

"The Givers," Raven whispers, sounding in awe of the word.

"The Givers," I repeat back to her, solemnly. "Thanks to the Givers, we are all here today. And you girls, all chosen to participate in the Lettings, are so very special, because you will one day be able to cross into the New World."

Soft spontaneous applause erupts. I smile at them, glad for their innocence and excitement, but somehow in my blood tonight, I feel it's just not…right. I blame my odd feeling on the heat and try to push the thoughts out of my head. "All right girls, it's lights out." I start to rise.

"But the New World," Lulu says quietly. "We didn't hear about the New World."

I can hear the ache in her voice. It is a young girl's ache, brought about by loneliness. The way she speaks, the way she asks, I know she is holding on by a thread. She is waiting for her reunion. She is waiting to be back with her mother. I know that ache all too well. I've felt it for the past seven years.

"Okay," I agree, feeling the tightness in my own throat. I am shocked I still feel this way after all of this time. Although I tried to let go of hope years ago, it seems hope won't let go of me. Maybe that's why I still sneak out every night, way past Leader's curfew, to go deep into the woods to eat those mushrooms my mother insisted I eat when I was young.

"Veronica," my mother had said that night. There was no impatience in her voice, though I could see the intensity in her eyes. "These are very special mushrooms."

We were somewhere in the middle of our city, deep inside an old park. A place I had never been before. It was overgrown with weeds, and I remember the feeling of the weeds, hard and strong, brushing against my leg. One weed cut me slightly, but I could tell from my mother's expression, it was not the time to tell her. It was time to concentrate.

"These will help you grow strong, but you must, must eat them every day. Do you understand me?"

I was too overwhelmed to speak.

"Now watch me," my mother said. "These mushrooms are poisonous." She pointed to another patch of mushrooms. They grew right next to the safe patch, and they looked remarkably similar.

"See how these grow in clusters?" she asked. "You have to avoid these. Veronica, listen to me."

I looked up at her, feeling the urgency in what she said.

"The poisonous mushrooms will kill you."

I felt myself take a step back from the mushroom patch. "But these others," she said, squatting down and scooping up a single mushroom, "these will save your life."

I only nodded at her that day, unaware of what any of it meant. She offered me the mushroom, and I bit into it, dirt and all. It tasted bitter, musky, and the grit ground in my teeth.

"Pew," I exclaimed, spitting the mushroom onto the ground. I looked up at my mother. "It's horrible."

"I know." She stood there stiffly for a few moments and then took the remainder of the mushroom out of my hand and dusted off all the dirt. "This should help." She handed it back to me, and I took another bite. It still tasted bitter and musky, but there was less grittiness.

"Are you sure these are the right ones?" I asked, chewing as quickly as I could.

"Yes," my mother said, never cracking a smile. She stepped forward and held out another. And you must be sure, too. Look." She turned the mushroom upside down. "Look under the cap."

"Here?"

"Yes. This part is called the gills. In your mushrooms, the spores hang onto the bottom of the cap. They are shaped like large round circles. This is how you know your mushrooms."

"But they look like so many other mushrooms," I remember saying, exasperated. My mother stepped forward and took me by the hand.

"These are your mushrooms," she said, softly. And still holding my hand, we walked off together, through the tall weeds and past fallen bridges, until we saw the ancient clock with the animals, lying on the ground. This was to be my marker, my way in and out of the old park alone.

"You'll be tired now," she said to me. "Sleepy. The mushrooms will make you sleepy until your body gets used to them. That's why you must remember to eat only one at a time."

They tasted so vile, there was never any concern

about me wanting more. That's all I remember of that day.

And here, now, seven years later, I can navigate my way in and out of these deep woods alone. I can find my mushrooms in the pitch black of night with the stars as my guide. Still at seventeen-years-old, I steal away every night, though my reason for eating those mushrooms has dissolved. Certainly, by telling me the mushrooms would save my life, my mother meant they had nutrition I would never receive elsewhere. And she must have been right, because standing next to the other Leaders at camp I am nearly a foot taller than any one of them.

My jet black hair is long, too. It hangs down my back with a soft wave at the bottom. My skin is shiny, the color of maple syrup. Everything about me is strong. My arms, my long legs, even my facial features are prominent—my nose, high cheekbones, and dark brown, almond shaped eyes. I don't know if I'm attractive, because frankly, it's never mattered. My mother told me once some of my father's ancestors were the first people to live on this land. The "Natives," I think she called them. The other ancestors came from an exotic place on the other side of the world, a thriving place that once was painted in the color red. He was a perfect mix of both of them, and she said I am the spitting image of him. I like that, because although I've never known my father, we are still connected. And now, although I'm nearly grown, and I'm no longer in need of nutrition to help me grow, I still walk the woods nightly, telling myself it would make my mother happy. My mother whom I haven't heard from in four years. This ritual is the only other connection I have to my family, and it is one I cannot lose.

I need to shake my growing malaise and let these girls be hopeful. Looking over them, they seem no larger than the porcelain dolls I once made in the factory in the city. Is it possible that in only two days these tiny wisps of people will be hooked up to a complex system of machines far bigger than they are? Is it really their duty to allow the blood to be drained from their tiny, emaciated bodies? Even if it is all for the greater good? Yes, I tell myself, shaking my head. What they do is important. Someday, when they are old and living in the New World, if they need blood, a new crop of fledgling girls, just "ripe," will supply them. It is the natural progression of life. And with that, I settle down to concoct a story of sweet candy drops hanging from trees and bedrooms filled with toys as far as the eye can see. And, of course, families who will be right there, next to them.

"In the New World…" I barely speak the last word when there is a hurried but faint knock on the cabin door. One of the girls shrieks and I can see those who are awake cower, climbing into their sleeping bags despite the stifling heat.

Without thinking, I am up and at the door. My lanky legs get me there within a second. Gretchen stands at the door. She is breathing heavily and drenched in perspiration. It looks and sounds as if she has just gone for a mile swim in the lake—something Gretchen would never have the strength or stamina to do.

"Gretchen?" I ask, confused. She almost always is asleep by this time. She's out at nine at night, but up at four, so she can take a walk and meditate before we start our day. I have known her for the past five years, and we are as close as two friends can be.

"I need to come in," she whispers.

She pushes past me and into the cabin. "Why are you here?" she asks, trying to make out the shapes in the dark.

"Nerves. They were nervous about the Letting."

Gretchen nods, as if her thoughts are miles away.

"Ronnie, listen, you need to get back to the cabin, fast. When I went to the mess hall tonight to help clean, Margaret was on the walkie. I overheard her saying she wanted to tell you something 'herself' and 'in person.' She seemed really jumpy, Ron. Agitated. I don't think she'll wait 'til morning."

I feel my stomach drop. I don't know what this is, but I'm certain it's not good.

"Do you have any guess?" I whisper. I hear my breath, hurried and shallow.

"None." Gretchen shakes her head. "But this is Margaret. She's had it in for you for…well, forever."

She is right, and obviously, I wasn't the only one to notice it.

"You'd better get back to the cabin."

I nod, turning to the door. Then I remember my girls. "I need to say good-night," I tell Gretchen.

"Forget it," she snaps. "You'll see them in the morning."

"No," I insist, with more force than I intend. "I'm not going to let them think I forgot them." I turn and storm away from Gretchen.

I love Gretchen, but sometimes I think she really misses the point. She never seems to grasp what's right there in front of her eyes. Even though we live together and work together, there's something about her that remains a mystery to me—like those nights she is sound asleep calling out someone's name. *Günter*, I think she murmurs in her garbled, sleepy voice. He must be someone left behind, as most boys are, to work the factories. I asked her about it once, but she refused to speak about it. I can't blame her. Remembering things from the past can be too painful sometimes. Or maybe the mysterious aura that surrounds her is her illness, eclipsing her beauty, eclipsing, her. I feel for Gretchen, but there's little I can do for her. Here, in cabin O, at least I can ease their fears. I go over to my sleeping dolls and stare down at them.

"Ladies," I whisper. "You can come out." Two little bodies wriggle their way out of their sleeping bags, trusting me implicitly. I wish I trusted myself that completely. "Good night, girls." I bend down and touch each one briefly on the head for just a second. Even if they're sleeping, I know they can feel the connection. Although we are a civilization that has survived the complete depletion of human connection, and should know better, we have such little of it here. If it's all I can give them, at least I can give them this.

****

Gretchen is waiting for me, and in the darkness we walk side by side, quietly. She has no idea what this is about either, but I can tell by her quick pace and her stolen glances up at me, she is concerned. I find this even more unsettling. We are walking much too quickly for the heat, and both of us are sweated through by the time we are halfway to our cabin. Neither of us slows our pace, and I know Gretchen must be struggling to keep up. I look down at Gretchen, and in the faint moonlight, I can see her blonde hair shining. She is beautiful, and at sixteen, she is so very delicate, like a tiny ghost-girl with pale skin and deep violet rings under her large blue eyes. With her petite frame and soft voice, she doesn't look or sound much older than the girls in cabin O. I think even if Gretchen was well and had been able to attend Lettings, they still would have kept her here at camp, rather than sending her directly to the New World. The girls are supposed to feel comfortable and bond with her because she looks like one of them. But for the most part, I haven't seen that happen. I think it's because poor Gretchen always seems worried, and it frightens the girls. I've just never ascertained what she's worried about.

Through the darkness, our cabin magically appears before us. It's still many yards away, but there's no light on, which means Margaret isn't there, yet. Margaret is terrified of the dark. I can't even imagine how hard it must be for her here in the woods at night.

Gretchen and I let out a sigh at the same time. Without a word, I switch on the lamp in the corner and the fan in the window, and Gretchen and I make our way to our cots. We each sit, Gretchen, ladylike, on the edge of the cot, legs crossed at her ankles; me, cross-legged in the middle of my bed. We sit in silence for a few moments listening to each other breathe.

"Oh, all right," I say finally, uncrossing my legs and standing. "Whatever it's going to be, worrying won't help."

"I know." Gretchen looks at me, and through the dim light, I can see the tears welling in her eyes.

"What's wrong?" I ask.

"Oh Ronnie." Gretchen falls forward, burying her

face in her pillow. She lifts her head to speak. "It's so selfish of me…but I can't help but think they're going to send you on to the New World. And what will I do here without you?"

The New World? The words sit heavily in the room. Of course, we talk about the New World nearly every day, but it's always with the campers. Never each other. The thought of one of us heading to the New World…well, we always hoped we would someday. But now? Have I served my time? It's almost too much to imagine. What will the New World be like? I mean, really like? I'm too old to believe in candy trees and toys, so what will be waiting for me? Then I let myself think the thought I try never to think. Will my mother be there, waiting for me? Or has she forgotten all about me?

My thoughts are interrupted by Gretchen's small hand squeezing mine. "Ron? I'm sorry. I didn't mean to worry you. Who knows what's really going on? It could be some change in protocol, or something."

I nod and we are startled by a knock on the door. Neither Gretchen nor I move. Neither of us speaks. We sit there, the silence palpable. The knock comes again, louder this time. The door rattles.

"Ronnie?" Gretchen whispers. I nod my head and cross to the door.

I pull the door open as if I'm yanking off a plastic bandage. The action startles Margaret who steps back as soon as she sees me. I have to admit I enjoy the moment of power over her. Although she is only one year older than me, at eighteen, Margaret runs the camp. Of course, she has orders and superiors, but I've never met them. Here, at this camp deep in the woods,

Margaret is the law. And unfortunately, the law doesn't much like me. I never really understood why. Margaret pulls herself together, visibly smoothing her shirt over her waistline. With long sleeves and long pants, she must be sweltering. She looks up at me. "May I come in?" she asks.

I step aside to let her pass.

Once she is inside the cabin, I see the eagerness in her eyes. Her eyes are a muddy green, and she is so happy about something, she is nearly giddy. She looks around for a place to sit but there isn't one. And neither Gretchen nor I are going to offer up a cot, that's for sure.

"Oh out with it, Margaret," I snap, realizing how bossy I must sound. "Whatever you came for, I can tell you're beside yourself with excitement. Just tell us." I am careful to say "us," not to tip my hand.

"I have wonderful news." Margaret has a huge plastic smile growing wider on her face.

Outside, the world is quiet except for the cicadas. Their cries grow louder and louder until the sound has morphed into a cyclone inside my brain. I wish I could rip open the top of my head and force them out. I am heady, and dizzy. I reach my hand out to steady myself, but I grab only air. Behind me, I hear Gretchen's shallow, hurried breathing.

"What is it?" I ask, breathless.

I pray Margaret is moving on to another camp. I know they must exist out here, somewhere. The woods are too vast for it to be only us. Or maybe she's been given a higher rank, or a bigger command. Maybe she's moving on to headquarters in the New World. If that's the case then maybe...just maybe...maybe someone has noticed me? Maybe someone will leave me in charge of the camp? Margaret interrupts my thoughts when she wheels around on her ballet flats, facing me directly. Her hands fly up, unable to contain her mirth.

"You have been summoned to the next Letting!"

Chapter Two

The room goes black.

The next thing I know I am being roused, my head in Gretchen's lap. She is trying to get me to drink a glass of water.

"You need to hydrate," she tells me.

I look into her eyes, but there is no fear there, no worry. This relaxes me a bit.

"To have a successful Letting, your veins must be plump." Her hands busily stroke my hair and hold the glass. She looks at me then away, over and over as she speaks. "At least four quarts of water tonight and tomorrow eight quarts minimum. You'll have to pee like the devil," she smiles, "but it will make the draw easier."

I reach for the water, but instead of taking the glass, I grab Gretchen's arm. My action surprises her, and for just a moment, I see a spark of something deep inside those blue eyes. Then as quickly as it appears, it fades again.

"You need water," she repeats, calmly.

"No." I shake my head. "I need to know what's going on."

She nods delicately, and I catch the smallest tear escape the corner of her eye, betraying her carefully controlled emotions. So she is scared, after all.

Unlike me, the Lettings terrify Gretchen. The

Gretchen she was showing me a moment ago, the efficient, soft, yet confident Gretchen. This is the girl she shows our campers—this is the front she wears. She is always warm and caring to the girls, but she's somewhat standoffish. She never bonds with any of them. I'm sure she's concerned she'll betray her fears and terrify them.

I let go of my grasp on her arm and sit up, next to her. I take her hand in mine. "You don't have to be afraid," I whisper.

"I'm not." She is clearly trying to be brave. This time her lie is so transparent even she doesn't believe it.

"This is what we do," I assure Gretchen, trying to allay her concerns. She nods again. "This is what I do." Saying these words calms me as well. This is what I do. I am a Leader. After the Harvester has brought the ripe girls to me, I prepare them, and I lead the girls to the Letting.

But why have I been summoned? I blossomed early and haven't been ripe for nearly six years. In those early days, when I was ripe and they first checked my blood there was something they didn't like. Something didn't fit. But they kept me on at camp because I always looked so much older than the others, and I was a natural Leader. I needed to pay my debt to society in some way. So that someway was to stay here. In my early days, I was a Leader-in-Training, but as I've grown and the older Leaders have moved on to the New World, I have become Head Leader of our camp. No one has brought more girls to the Lettings and subsequently, the New World, than me. And there is no one above me, except Margaret.

Margaret. As I sit here in the dark staring at

Gretchen, both of us scared to move for fear we'll have to act, my mind races with questions. Why is Margaret happy for me? She has never made it a secret she dislikes me. But why she dislikes me is a mystery. Gretchen thinks Margaret is jealous because I have a better rapport with the campers and I'm well liked. She thinks Margaret fears for her job. I have a wall full of awards from the government, and I would be the next in line to take over running the camp. But even if that were true, Margaret would move on to the New World, and her life would be wonderful. Maybe she's scared of change. Or maybe she loves her career. Or maybe Gretchen's not right. I look up at Gretchen, and her hands are trembling.

"Why are you so scared?" I ask. "The needles? The machines? The Caretakers?" She only nods. I would imagine all of this would seem unfathomable to a girl who can't run a quarter of a mile without running out of breath. Then Gretchen stands, seeming suddenly powerful and competent. She looks much bigger than her petite five-foot-tall frame. She looks me dead in the eyes.

"You need to drink." She pushes the glass of water into my hands. "Tonight and tomorrow. Then you must eat. The real food, not the food bars we eat to survive. You need to eat red meat and spinach and drink gallons of the algae drink they force on those girls. You must do this because if they have summoned you, they must be in desperate need of an O. And you must offer them enough so you…" She seems to be choosing her words carefully. "…so you are healthy enough to be summoned another day."

****

I toss and turn for hours. Partly because it's much too early for me to be in bed, and part of it's the heat and my concern over having been summoned myself. I see the silhouette of Gretchen, her chest rising and falling. Occasionally, her small body convulses slightly as she fights for a breath. Her hands clench and then relax when her breathing is restored to its nice, easy flow. I squeeze my eyes shut but all I see are images of machines, the size of my cabin, attached to me, sucking the very life from my body. When the girls come back to me, exhausted and anemic, it's easy for me to carry them off the truck and into their beds where Gretchen is waiting with a warm nettle soup to rebuild their blood. But who will carry me? And more importantly, how will I help my girls if I'm too exhausted to help myself? I can't take it anymore. I rise from my bed and silently steal across the room and out our door.

Once I feel the warmth of the night, I remember that with all the craziness that happened tonight, I never picked my mushroom. Somehow, just realizing this makes me feel better. Now my wandering has a purpose.

Despite the pitch black of night, I walk my usual path with no fear of getting lost. I have walked this way so many times I have forged a trail for myself. I can feel my way, the tall weeds, already broken under my feet. Occasionally, one will still stand tall and fight back, scratching my leg, reminding me this is his turf. Inevitably, the scratch makes me think of my mother and the first time she showed me my mushrooms. This drives me forward in search of my mushrooms and my mother.

I reach my usual patch, but tonight I don't want to

stop. I don't want to do anything the same way I normally do. Instead, I push ahead, feeling soggy ground, new reeds cracking under my boots. I am immediately sorry I didn't stop to change from my shorts and tank top into long pants and sleeves, something that could offer me some protection. But it's too damned hot anyway. As I walk, my mind is reeling. I try to understand my thoughts. I am uneasy, that's for sure. But I came to this camp seven years ago to be called to the Letting, so what has changed? I was so confident then, so sure.

I remember leaving on the day I had been harvested, a tiny bedroll in my hand, my mother's picture of the dandelion tucked safely inside. I remember being self-assured as I climbed aboard the long, open-backed truck. I remember my mother's eyes, lighter than mine in color but far more intense. I remember her fierce gaze, and despite the chaos and all the crying children, she never once let me out of her sight. She was boarding another moving object, larger than mine, and nicer looking. It was taking her to the New World. There she would work a government job for a period of time, helping those in need before she would be released into paradise to do as she pleased. And then, once I had blossomed and she had fulfilled her obligation, we would be reunited. I knew this was the right move for us, to be away from that city riddled with crime and pollution, to never again be starving or have to work ourselves to exhaustion. Thanks to the fact that I am an O, we were the chosen ones, the lucky ones. It could have been so much worse. We could have waited a few more years, and then I would have been called for the Coupling. I knew I was lucky, and I tried to make every other girl who got on that truck with me feel the same way. I never cried that day. I knew my small breasts were swelling under my t-shirt. I knew it wouldn't be long until I blossomed. I just never expected to have toxic blood that would cause me to wait seven long years for our reunion. I never cried the day I left my mother. And I will not cry today.

On and on I push, my arms pumping, sweat running down my legs and dripping into my boots, my blood almost painful as it courses through my veins. I think of the calisthenics I put the girls through—the jumping jacks, the jogs we take, the games we play. Anything to keep the blood moving.

Between the heat of the night and the exercise, I am probably an easy stick now. On and on, farther and farther I push, until when I turn back, I can no longer see even the outline of the small cabins behind me. I am caught somewhere in limbo, with camp behind me and the unknown before me.

For a moment, I panic. What if I can't find my way back? What if I am lost out here? Lost, somewhere in the middle of these six hundred acres of woods? Or what if my carelessness causes me real trouble? What if a bear finds me before I find my way back? Who will take care of my girls?

All of these thoughts are legitimate concerns, yet I cannot will myself to stop. It is as if I am being pulled by some invisible force, and no matter how hard my brain tries to resist, my feet will not stop. They move faster and faster until I break out into a run. Soon, panic and fear are the fire fueling my run, but I keep running the wrong way. I am now so far from camp I wonder if I can make it back before Gretchen notices I'm missing.

I run swiftly and easily, farther and faster, half-expecting to see the slight glimmer of light from the sunrise breaking before me. Thankfully, I am sure-footed, even when I leave the weeds and run over the slickness of ankle deep, pine needles.

I run straight up an embankment, trees growing thicker with every step. Higher and higher I climb, my brain unable to stop my feet, wondering repeatedly why I am doing this. Where am I heading? What am I running from? And more importantly, what am I running to?

The sweat pools on my back and in my boots. My palms feel wet. I am climbing higher and higher, wondering how and if I will ever get back.

Then I am face down on the pine needles. I feel the impact my body makes, but I am somehow distanced from it. I hear myself gasp, and I feel the air rush from my body. I know it must hurt, pine needles stick deep into the fresh cuts on my hands, one knee crashed against a large stone, and the other is skinned open. I do feel a gash on my cheek while I wait for the rest of the pain to register, but it never does.

I need to get myself up, but I can't. All I want is to lie still in the thick pine needles and cry for my mother. But my mother is not coming. And I don't know if she ever will. So, I need to lift my head and focus. I put my bloody hands under my shoulders to push myself up and—

Wham!

Something hits me on the head. Hard. The pain radiating through my skull is excruciating, and yet somehow I know it is only a harbinger of more pain to come. In this one moment, I feel everything I thought I should have felt moments ago. Every part of my body is in agony.

Bam!

There is a blunt impact right between my shoulder blades, and with a grunt, I am down again.

"Ugh," I groan through clenched teeth, squeezing my eyes shut. The darkness has me completely discombobulated, and I have no idea what is happening. Then I hear the voices.

"Got it," a voice screams. Then a bigger, even heavier weight is on my back, pinning me down. It must be a knee digging in my back.

I try to speak, to tell the voice I am not a bear or whatever creature he's trying to trap, but nothing comes out. When I attempt to explain, dirt fills my mouth. I spit the dirt out, trying not to choke. Within seconds, I hear more footsteps and voices growing louder. They are the voices of boys. But boys out here? In the middle of the woods? This cannot be good. It can only mean rebels.

I have no time to process anything. Suddenly my hands are pinned behind my back, and I am pulled to my feet. I can barely walk because of my blown knee, so I hobble, trying to keep up with the mass of anger and energy forcing me forward. We climb higher up the embankment and I slip on the needles.

"Grab her," one voice yells. And suddenly two hands are there, one on each arm, dragging me on. My head is throbbing now, and my body feels broken. My neck goes slack and my head drops forward.

"Don't let her black out," a voice warns. And suddenly a hand slaps me, trying to keep me conscious.

How I wish they would just let me go, just let me

slide away, to a better, more comfortable place.

They drag me and slap me for what seems an eternity. Finally, I am in the middle of a grass field, in a makeshift camp, far from my home base. My head is still throbbing, but I do my best to take in my surroundings, in case…in case I ever have the opportunity to escape. Best I can tell, there are small tents pitched in a semicircle around a pile of logs. Obviously, the logs are for their campfire. Next to the tents are various forms of weaponry: long guns, spears, and bows and arrows, all piled in neat piles. Diagonally placed near the back of every tent is a torch, burning. They are obviously hunters, waiting to trap… something.

I am thrown into the middle of the camp, and I lose my balance. Unable to catch myself, I fall, landing a fraction of an inch from the campfire. Thankfully, it's unlit.

"Get up," a voice roars, and I know it is talking to me. Carefully, I force myself to my elbows. "Get up," the voice repeats, louder. I try, I really, really try to stand, but I make it to one foot and fall over again. "GET UP!" the voice screams at me. I stagger to my feet, my head ringing, and turn in the direction the voice is coming from.

The glow from the torches allows me to make out the shapes of the people standing there. There are two, no, three of them. One is average height, one is very tall, and another is quite tiny. No matter what, I am completely outnumbered. I feel a tremor run through my body and know this is the end for me. No matter what they do or don't do to me here, I will never come out of it the same.

The tallest one steps forward. He is remarkably blond, so blond his head is like a beacon in the night. The tiny bit of moonlight reflects off his near-white hair. He remains mostly a shadow to me, but I can make out his slight features: a small upturned nose, close set eyes, cherub shaped lips. Most of all, I see a large scar shaped like a crescent moon that starts just below his eye socket and travels down until it is hidden away by his t-shirt. Despite the terror I am feeling now, something about his face is familiar, though there is no way I could ever have seen it before. "Well, if it isn't Veronica Killings," he taunts, with an amused look on his face.

"Billings," I choke out, spitting blood as I speak.

"Tomato—tom-ah-to," he says, smiling. His words confuse me.

"How do you know who I am?" I hear my words, choppy and agitated.

"Everyone knows who you are." He smiles again. He turns to his comrades and one of them nods, appreciatively. "But not everyone knows where to find you."

"It's a secret?" I want to ask so many things but this is all that comes into my aching mind. I put my hand up to my throbbing cheek. The warmth from my hand stings the open wound, and I pull it away. The oppressive night and my aching body become too much to bear.

"What's going on?" I ask, genuinely confused. "Who are you?"

The tall one continues to smile.

"Who are any of you?" I begin to feel the panic settling over me. In just a few hours, my girls will be waking up and preparing for the biggest day of their young lives with no one to guide them. Gretchen will be there, but she can't appease the girls the way I can. I hope she remembers to hold their hands and not just force them to drink their green algae goo.

My face stings, my leg throbs, and I have grown incredibly itchy from the pine needles that remain stuck to me. Worst of all is my head. My head is pounding.

As I look at my assailant, I see the cruelty pouring out of his expression. I can tell he would love nothing more than to see me dead, or worse.

I strain to see if the other figures are as terrifying, but I see merely shadows.

"The least you can do is tell me who you are," I yell. "You, you, cowards!" I spit the words at them. "You attack me three to one, and you have the gall to be smug about it?"

The tall one takes another step toward me. The look of humor on his face is replaced by anger. Pure, unadulterated anger. I see hatred in his beady, little eyes. He takes another step and another, trying to force me to back down. But I won't. Looking up slightly, I am able to stare him straight in the eyes.

I feel his breath on my skin, and he looks at me like I am a complete mystery to him—like he is trying to crack some ancient code and the answer lies in my face. At this distance, I see his scar clearly. It is ridged and jagged on the edges. Some parts are still red, others, a deep purple. His eyes scan my face, up and down, up and down, trying to take in every detail. Suddenly, without warning, he grabs my arm and spins me to face the others.

"Step forward," he commands, and they do. The

average height boy walks up directly beside the tall boy. He is slightly heavy, with a buzz cut and a round face. I don't like his look. The other lags behind. The blond boy raises my arm into the air. "Here is the face of pure evil," he declares. "And we have stopped her."

Buzzcut raises his fist into the air and lets out a loud "whoop!" The other figure remains quiet. I wrack my aching brain, trying to imagine what any of this means.

"What are you talking about?" I ask, terrified and confused.

"What am I talking about?" The blond boy looks directly at me. "What am I talking about?" he asks again, turning to face the others as if he was rallying troops. "I am talking about you, Veronica Killings." He spits the last words at me.

"Why do you keep calling me that? I don't know what you're talking about." I am exhausted and exasperated. I want nothing more than to fall down and wake up in my bed, to find all of this an impossible dream.

"Really?" the blond boy asks.

"Why don't you prove it's lying?" Buzzcut suggests.

"Good idea." The blond boy speaks in a tone that sounds like they're discussing a science project. In the faint moonlight, I see they may only be a few years older than me. "So Veronica Killings, let's see what you really know, shall we?" My stomach clenches, knowing this is about to become a very violent game of truth or dare. "How many has it been, Veronica? Hm?" he asks.

"How many has what been?"

"Wrong answer," he growls, punching me in the stomach. The ache I feel radiates from the inside out, and I am certain I will vomit all over him. But I have no food in my stomach and the best I can do is dry heave. The blond boy and Buzzcut laugh.

"Looks like it's trying to puke up its own guts." Buzzcut laughs harder.

"Let's try again, shall we?" the leader asks me. I shake my head no, violently. "You've got a lot of nerve," he hisses. He grabs my arm and pins it behind my back, wrenching it upwards.

"Ow," I moan, my arm throbbing.

"What's the matter," he asks, "uncomfortable?"

"Please," I plead. "Please let me go."

He only laughs and yanks my arm tighter. I feel the blood leave my hand and my arm tingles through the pain.

"You're mistaken!" I cry, fighting for my breath. "I'm not who you think I am."

"Really?" He jerks me harder. My knees give out, and I dangle in midair with just his viselike grip holding me up.

"That's funny," the blond boy counters. "Because I know exactly who you are. Now, we must decide what to do with you."

"Nothing," warns another voice. I hear another set of footsteps approaching quickly. I raise my head and see a dark figure emerging from the shadow of the night. "Nothing you have planned. Let her go."

"But Phoenix," the blond boy protests.

"Let her go," Phoenix repeats. Phoenix wears a shotgun across his body. He reaches up and pulls the gun to the front, holding it in one hand. The blond boy drops my arm. I crash to the ground.

"Who did this to her?" Phoenix asks, looking at my injuries as he crosses to me. He puts out his hand and helps me up. His hand is rough and warm, and although he represents everything I have been taught to fear, I am incredibly grateful for his kindness.

"She came to us this way," the blond boy lies.

"Oh really?" Phoenix asks. "And if I asked her, she'd agree?" Phoenix looks me dead in the eyes, and I am suddenly not afraid.

"I fell. In the woods," I mumble, unable to explain why I lied to this kind boy to save the awful one.

"I see." Phoenix looks at me. The heat I feel racing through my body is no longer caused by the stifling night air. I stare back at him, and though I am certain his attention lingers on me merely to assess my damage, I am drinking him in. He is tall, a few inches taller than me, and his eyes...his eyes are the color of a moment. That fleeting moment when the summer sky is so perfectly blue you know everything must be right in the world. His hair is short, black, and tousled in a way that hides his shy waves. The slight scruff growing over his lip and on his chin is black as the night as well. He wears a sweat-stained, olive green t-shirt that is tight across his arms and hangs perfectly over his lean body. It falls just over the top of his jeans. I am painfully aware of my damaged face, and that I have been staring at him for much, much too long.

He doesn't smile. Instead, he turns away. "Whoever did this," he announces, "is as much of an animal as she is."

His words hurt worse than the beating.

"Do not touch her again, Gunnar," Phoenix informs

the blond boy.

Gunnar. Gunnar. Despite my aching pride and stomach, the name Gunnar sticks with me. It means something to me. Why do I know the name Gunnar? I run through the names of the very few men I have ever known personally. My history teacher, my boss at the factory, the man who sold my mother our protein bars. There were too many boys working at the factory to know all of their names, but still…Gunnar, Gunnar, Gunnar…

"Günter?" I speak too loudly, and they all turn to me. "It's not Günter, it's Gunnar. I know why I know that name." And suddenly I realize what is happening. "No," I whisper, devastated, taking a step back from all of them. "No," I repeat, quietly defeated.

My eyes scan each of them until they land on the smallest figure in the group, still hovering in the background.

"Gretchen?" I ask. "It was Gunnar you were saying, wasn't it? All those nights I woke up to hold your hand through your nightmares. Come on, Gretchen. The least you can do is come forward and face me."

Chapter Three

Gretchen steps forward but is unable to look at me.

"Why are you doing this?" The anger I'm feeling makes my blood boil. My heart is pumping faster, making my fresh wounds throb in response.

She doesn't answer. At this moment, Gretchen's weakness repulses me. I can't help but think if she was stronger, mentally and physically, she wouldn't have fallen into this, whatever this is, and she would not be a traitor.

"For what?" I am incensed. "A boy?" I ask pointedly, looking at Gunnar. "You know that's illegal." They all seem to smirk at me at once. "And besides, you could do so much better." I hope to wipe the smirk off Gunnar's face. It works. He sneers at me like a wild dog, but she doesn't answer. "Come on," I implore. "You're my best friend, Gretchen. We live together. How? How could you do this to me?"

"How could she do this to you?" Gunnar asks, shaking his head. "You have got some nerve," he shouts at me, walking straight up to me. He is standing directly before me. His spit splatters my face when he speaks.

I reach up and wipe it away. Then I can't help myself. I smile at Gunnar and it enrages him. "Do you see this?" Gunnar asks, fuming. He turns to Phoenix. "She's smiling at me. After everything she's done.

Let's just kill it now." He grabs a machete from the pile of weapons closest to him.

In that instant, I don't know why he hates me, but I know how much he hates me. Being hacked to death by a machete must be one of the worst possible ways to die. Out of the corner of my eye, I see Gretchen has turned away, squeezing her eyes shut. So she really believes he'll do it.

I hate this boy.

"We're not killing her, yet," Phoenix tells them. Despite the word *yet*, this makes me feel a little better. I feel the tension in my body lessen. But as my adrenaline drops off, the pain intensifies. I feel my knees buckle, and I drop to the ground.

"We need a plan." Phoenix turns to Gunnar and Buzzcut. "After all of the months spent hunting her, it's ironic she came to us. And now we have no idea what to do with her."

"Why would you hunt me?" I ask, genuinely confused. Phoenix looks at me with profound sadness in his eyes. I don't expect them to answer me. I was taught that rebels are fiends and if we are caught, and can somehow escape, we are to run deep into the woods. Never, under any circumstance, do you lead a rebel back to your camp. They will steal your supplies, kidnap the girls, and leave you dead.

"Let's get her over there." Phoenix points to a long pole next to a basket of weapons. "We can tie her to that. In the morning, we can decide what to do with her." Gunnar and Buzzcut each take me by an arm and lift me to my feet.

"You can't." Gretchen finally breaks her silence.

"What do you mean we can't?" Gunnar asks,

indignant. "Since when do you make the rules here? You had one job, and as I remember, we wasted a whole lot of time waiting for you to decide the time was right. I'm not waiting any longer." He shakes me as he speaks and pain radiates through my body.

"Yeah," Buzzcut says, his head nodding intensely. Phoenix holds up his hand to silence them.

"Why not?" Phoenix asks Gretchen, calmly. "Why can't we hold her here for the night?"

"Because she's been summoned to the next Letting." Gretchen's words have a deep impact on Phoenix.

"Well how do you like that?" Gunnar asks, clapping in appreciation. Buzzcut whoops and claps along with him.

"But I don't understand." Phoenix's voice is soft. What he says is meant only for Gretchen. "She must be eighteen years old."

"I'm seventeen," I clarify, and I'm not sure why I speak. Phoenix looks at me, confused and yet, curious.

"You're only seventeen?" he asks, obviously surprised.

"Yes," I answer, softly. "I'm just…very…tall." For a moment, I think I see a smile try to dance across his lips, but it disappears as fast as it came.

"Who cares how old it is?" Buzzcut asks.

"Imagine the damage it'll do when it's eighteen?" Gunnar adds. So they've been listening to everything.

Phoenix turns his back to the boys and in doing so, he has created a small semicircle with Gretchen and me. The boys walk away, and I watch their animated speech pattern. I know they're talking about me. Phoenix looks at Gretchen when he speaks. "Even at seventeen, still, she must have..." He looks down at the ground now. Even in the dark of the night, I can tell he's embarrassed. He looks young now. Almost sweet. At this moment, it's hard to believe he's a crazy, kidnapping murderer.

"I have," I confess, trying to gain control of the situation. "Six years ago."

Phoenix looks up at me, nodding.

"Then why do they want her?" he asks the two of us, and for a split second, it feels almost as if he's on my side. I give myself the luxury of staring at the dimple on his right cheek, concealed beneath his scruff. But no. I force my eyes away. It doesn't matter how handsome he is, he is still bad. And besides, any feelings for him would be forbidden and therefore, suicidal.

"What I imagine is that there must be an extreme shortage of O." Gretchen speaks in her calm and clinical way. Gretchen would be an excellent Caregiver if she was ever allowed to have an education beyond fifth grade.

Phoenix nods, trying to make sense of the situation. The exact same thing I've been trying to do for the past several hours. "Or else...," she adds, "or else they're summoning her to the New World."

"Veronica?" Phoenix asks with complete surprise. He speaks my name with a familiarity that makes my insides tingle.

"Yes." Gretchen nods solemnly.

"But why would they take her?" he asks. "She's their top performer."

"I know," Gretchen agrees. "We can't let that happen."

"Why not?"

We all turn to see Gunnar has made his way back to our little group.

"Gretchen?" he asks. "Why not? Why can't we let them take her? Gretchen, are you getting soft on me?"

At that moment he takes the gun he holds in his hand and prods me in the stomach with the barrel. I lose my breath and fall backward. Phoenix puts out his hand for me, and I grab it instinctively. Once I am steady, he shakes free of my grasp.

Gretchen does not even flinch. "We could have some fun with her, guys," Gunnar continues. "Put our mark on her tonight so we get the credit. Make her a no-show for the Letting and deliver her straight to the doorstep of the Inferno ourselves. Good riddance, I say."

"No," Phoenix declares definitively.

"Why not?" Gunnar asks, standing toe to toe with Phoenix.

"Because the point is to destroy their perfect system. And if they are planning to take her to the Inferno, and we deliver her to them, it wouldn't so much as cause a ripple in their system. After all of this time, after all of these plans, we will not let them win. Even if their win would be a victory for us as well."

"Fine." Gunnar backs away from Phoenix and paces, clearly agitated. "Then let's do her in right now."

"Yeah," Buzzcut chimes in. "Let's do it, now." The two of them point their guns at me.

"No," Phoenix repeats, even more calmly. I am suddenly aware the only thing keeping me alive is an unformed plan of an untrustworthy boy who hates me, and a girl who's betrayed me.

"Why not?" Buzzcut asks, bouncing up and down on his toes.

"Because we need her," Phoenix blurts. Once he's said it, I can tell he is as surprised as the rest of us.

"What?" Gunnar asks. "Need her? For what? Are you insane?" Despite the terror I am feeling, I laugh at the irony of this question. They all look at me until Buzzcut breaks the silence.

"That's bogus, man," Buzzcut argues.

"We don't need her, Phoenix. That wasn't part of the plan." Gunnar's breathing is shallow, and I can tell he is angry. He is speaking through his teeth, trying to remain calm.

"Neither was the fact she just stumbled into our camp," Phoenix snaps. "And besides, the best plans adjust when the circumstances change. And none of us, none of us, thought she would be called to the Letting. There has to be a reason. We need to find out why." Gunnar and Buzzcut grumble to each other, unhappy, but I can tell they are resigned to follow Phoenix's lead.

"So what's the plan?" Gretchen asks, softly.

"I don't know, yet." Phoenix runs his hand through his hair. "But no one hurts her until I figure out the best way to make this situation work to our advantage."

"All right," Gunnar succumbs. "But I hope it's our situation and not your situation you're worried about." He points directly to Phoenix, looking from him to me, and back again. Phoenix straightens himself and stares at Gunnar.

"After all of this time, Gunnar, I would assume you, of all people, would trust me to do the right thing."

Gunnar nods sheepishly and looks away.

"She'll stay over here, now," Phoenix indicates

where he wants me, "until we have a plan. How long do we have until she's missed?" he asks Gretchen.

Gretchen looks out at the moon lingering over the mountains. "Three, maybe four hours. Any longer and she will definitely be missed. Especially the day before her Letting."

Phoenix nods, takes my arm firmly but gently, and leads me to a pole anchored deep in the ground.

"Put your arms behind you, please," he instructs.

I do and he carefully ties my hands together first, and then to the pole. I feel him purposely trying not to touch me.

"Gretchen?" He calls her over. "Please keep an eye on Ver—her." He stops. It's as if he suddenly does not want to use my name. "Call us if she gives you any trouble."

Gretchen nods. Phoenix stands and walks away with Gunnar and Buzzcut close behind.

Gretchen and I sit in silence for a long time before she asks, "Are you hungry?"

I don't answer her.

"Thirsty?"

Again, I do not answer. I look away into the black of night.

"I understand. Really. But what if you make it to the Letting? If you're dehydrated it won't be successful."

I roll my eyes at her, knowing there is no way these maniacs will deliver me to the Letting so I may do my job. I'm so angry with her for thinking she can patronize me by playing to my patriotism like that.

"No?" she asks.

I keep my head turned, stubbornly.

"Doesn't matter?"

I still don't speak.

"Well, let me tell you something. If they need O, they will do anything they have to, to get it from you. Heck, they'll probably even find you here in the absolute middle of nowhere." She looks off into the night. "And when they do find you, they'll drain the blood from your arms, legs, between your toes, the backs of your hands—all the places you've seen bandaged when the girls come back to us. But they won't stop there. They'll get it out of you however they have to, even if it means sedating you and draining from multiple sites. Multiple, Ron."

"Don't call me that," I hiss.

"Fine." She tosses her ponytail over her shoulder and bites down hard on her bottom lip. After a moment, she speaks again. "Do you know what multiple draw sites can mean, Veronica? Do you? They can kill you, Ronnie." She speaks much more softly now. "They can kill you."

"They wouldn't do that." I am disgusted with her.

"Why not?" Gretchen asks, plainly. "Why not?" she repeats. "Because you're the great Veronica Billings—the girl who's brought more young girls to the Lettings than anyone else in history?"

"No," I reply, confused, "because they wouldn't kill me." She looks at me for a moment. Her eyes are sad and tired.

"Yes, they would, Ronnie. Yes, they would. Just the same as they would kill any of us."

"But that's the thing," I protest. "They wouldn't kill any of us."

"Oh Ronnie." Gretchen pats my uninjured knee.

She suddenly seems the older, stronger one now. "Do you really believe in a magic world with candy drops on trees and rooms filled sky-high with toys?"

"Of course not," I reply, my breath coming in short shallow gasps. "But I know there is a better world. Where my mother is. A place where we'll all be going."

"Of course there's a better world." Tears fill Gretchen's normally milky eyes until they look like two buckets of crystal clear water. "It's called Heaven, Ron. When they take us to the New World, they take us to our death."

Chapter Four

Her words are so absurd, so ridiculous, I burst out laughing. Sitting here, tied to a stake, tethered to the earth, laughter pours out of me. It begins as if I've just heard a funny joke and then quickly escalates to hysteria. As swiftly as the laughing started, it morphs into tears, and I fight to take in even small gulps of air. I am trembling now, laughter shakes my body as tears stream down my face. My normally strong body feels weak, exhausted, as rolls of laughter and buckets of tears release from me simultaneously. I laugh and cry for minutes more, until I finally begin to calm. When I can see straight, I look at Gretchen and realize she is sitting there quietly.

"I knew you didn't know." She offers me a small, sad smile. "They said you had to know, but I knew you didn't."

Staring at Gretchen, I know she is telling me the truth. Shame radiates through my body with such force I cannot bear to hold my head up. I cannot bear to breathe. Slowly, I sink down, arms still pinned behind me, until I am parallel with the earth. The position I am in causes immense pain in my arms. Good, I think. Just good. I close my eyes to escape into darkness and lessen the guilt I am feeling, but instead of a reprieve, I see the face of every girl I have ever led to the Letting, of every girl I have ever promised a better life. Instead of trees with lollipop branches, I see mass graves of tiny bodies with their blood drained from them, one thrown carelessly on top of the other. It is unbearable. But I still have to know.

"Why?" I ask, certain now Gretchen will tell me the truth.

"Because the world that was supposed to develop, that altruistic, wonderful place where we all help one another, it never happened, Ron."

"What did happen?" I can't look at her, the mental and physical anguish too much to bear.

"It is worse than it was. We are a two-class system. The very wealthy people live in complete luxury. The rest of us serve them, body and soul."

"But it's so much blood," I challenge, the prospect of something so horrific not making any sense to me. "Why would they need so much blood?"

"The wealthy people live their lives in the constant search for hedonistic pleasure. You remember that. It all started because they are involved in all sorts of activities that can harm them. Things we could never even imagine. They race against each other on small two wheeled vehicles, crashing into each other. They jump from bridges and flying objects, high in the sky, risking death. All for fun. And they get injured, and need blood."

I pull myself up to a seated position, appreciative for the conversation that momentarily keeps my mind off who I am and what I've done. My arms are relieved once I'm in an upright position. She goes on.

"But more than anything they are a culture obsessed with youth and beauty. Once Principal Leader Farnsworth the First discovered the blood of a young girl can keep people young and help them live forever, well, there was no stopping them."

"They do all this to stay young?" I ask, my eyes shut, disgusted at the prospect.

"Yes." She nods. "All in the name of youth and beauty. They hope to live forever."

"So they drain the life out of a young girl to prolong the life of an elderly woman?" I ask, breathlessly.

"We call them Leeches." Gretchen faces me squarely and bites her lower lip. Then her mood changes a bit, and she seems to soften. "They don't think of it like that." She looks at the ground while she speaks. "They...they really don't think about it at all. And the ones with the supply of blood that keeps the wealthy young, they make a fortune."

"So they keep the money in their tight little circle."

"Exactly." She faces me again and her eyes harden.

"But what did they think would happen when they run out of young girls to Let?" I ask.

"Being driven solely by pleasure makes one forget about preparing for the future. So right now, there is an unbelievable shortage of girls. And too many boys. That's why they increased the frequency of the Couplings. So much rides on very few women."

I shudder at the thought, glad my own mother is free from her duty as a Coupling.

"Why aren't they taking the boys to the Lettings?" I ask.

"They say it's because they'll have no one to work their factories and make their goods."

I nod, finding it hard to swallow. I remember seven years ago when I was working in a factory, there were an inordinate number of boys to girls, even then.

"But the truth is whatever is in the blood of a ripe girl is the thing keeping them young. It doesn't exist in boy blood. Phoenix thinks they'll move on to the boys next. Desperation will lead them to try anything."

"They'll destroy an entire population."

"Yes, it's genocide," she condemns. I hear the disgust in her voice. "Just a slow genocide that's masked as something else entirely."

"But why?" I ask. "Why do they bother to mask it? Why don't they just take us all and do what they want with us?"

"It's easier this way. Everyone is contained, and no one fights them. And as long as we have people like—" Gretchen stops herself and turns away.

"People like who?" I realize why she paused. "People like me? As long as they have people like me who are ignorant enough and evil enough to do their dirty work, well then, why rock the boat?"

"Something like that." She looks down at her feet.

"We know why they want you."

I turn, startled to find Phoenix standing at my side, less than a yard away from me. I never heard him approach.

"Why?" Gretchen asks, jumping up to stand next to Phoenix.

"Yes, why?" I ask, my curiosity winning out over my fear.

Phoenix looks at me with a pained expression. He lifts his arm as if he's going to wave Gretchen on, away from me, then something changes his mind.

"It doesn't matter now," he mutters quietly, deciding to tell us both.

"What is it?" Gretchen asks, yanking on her ponytail impatiently. He speaks slowly so I'll understand everything.

"Our...well their leader, Farnsworth, is a hemophiliac. Something they've kept secret and have never been able to cure. He takes regular blood transfusions, weekly. And he's in desperate need. He thinks the transfusions will cure his condition. He's terrified of dying and wants nothing more than to stay young."

"And he's an O," I say, certain of it without Phoenix having to tell me. He just nods. I crane my neck to look at Phoenix, who is still standing at my side. "My girls? Wouldn't there..." I feel sick as I form the words. "Wouldn't there be enough...blood from them?"

"No. These tiny girls aren't offering enough," Gretchen explains.

"But the Harvesters...?" I ask.

"They've run dry," Phoenix divulges. He shakes his head and kicks an innocent stone.

"You're telling me, our cities have no more young girls who are O's?" I ask, both stunned and skeptical.

Phoenix just looks away. I feel the rage growing inside me, and I struggle to turn to look Phoenix in the eye. "Are you saying they have already depleted an entire population of a blood type of young girls?"

"Young and adult both," Gretchen whispers.

"Well, why haven't you done anything about it?" I ask, nearly yelling at Phoenix. He looks surprised. "You seem to have all the answers," I shout. "You tell me you know it all. You have the grand plan. So why didn't you stop it before?"

Sitting there, staring up at him, I am disgusted with him, with me, and especially with the world we live in.

"I'm trying to do that, now." His voice rises as he speaks, and he paces uneasily.

"But I've been there for seven years." The tears stream down my cheeks. "I am personally responsible for killing hundreds of young girls. F-for…nothing… And you could have done something. You could have stopped it."

"How?" he asks, and I hear the genuine question. I see the genuine pain in his eyes.

"You should have killed me," I blurt. "You should have walked right into camp and shot me and Margaret, and Gretchen." I glare at her. "And you should have taken those girls and run."

"And where should I have gone once I had them?" Again, I hear the honest question in his voice. "Back to the city, where they'll be harvested once again? A new camp will open. It will start all over again."

"I don't know," I shout. "You're the mastermind."

He looks at me with so much hurt in his eyes it is painful to watch. But I cannot force my eyes away. Instead, my anger dissolves and instinctively, I want to reach out and touch him. I am eternally grateful my arms are tied.

Gretchen can tell we've gone way off track. "So they've turned to you. The only O they know of and can count on. I'm sure they think you'll appreciate being the direct donor for Farnsworth himself." Her words make me nauseated.

"But Gretchen, I can't donate." I'm still enraged. "You know that. My blood is toxic. Why would they want me?"

"They must think they've found a way to clean it." She shrugs and throws up her hands.

I nod, understanding if I had made it to the Letting without interference, it would have been my job to serve Farnsworth until such time as I was no longer able to perform. I would have been the sole supplier to an atrocious dictator. To a man who tricked me into being his accomplice to murder. After years of using me indirectly to bring him wealth and fame, he now wants to use me directly to stay alive. I have never hated anyone this much. Not even Gunnar.

Thank God I have been caught by this small band of rebels. Now they can stop him by stopping me. I take a large gulp of the hot night air, grateful to be tethered to the earth.

"So these girls are the last?" I ask, thinking of my four little endangered waifs, asleep in their sleeping bags. "There are no babies after them?"

"None." Gretchen shakes her head. "And there are hardly any young women to Couple."

"What about where Farnsworth lives?" Then it dawns on me. "Is that the New World?"

"They call it that. We call it the Inferno."

I nod along.

"What about the Inferno then? Couldn't people there supply one another?"

"They could, I guess. But they don't. They are the privileged ones. Even way back when blood donations first became mandatory, they somehow avoided it. Now they have laws and rules keeping them exempt. And they believe the stolen blood running through their veins is all that keeps them young. I doubt they'll give it up willingly. Who knows." She looks away, wistfully.

"Maybe they'll turn on each other one day."

Out of the corner of my eye, I look at Phoenix. He has been remarkably quiet.

"Why don't they keep the girls longer?" I ask, my body shaking even as I ask this question. "Blood renews itself. Why don't they let them grow and create more?"

"Because they're pigs," Gretchen retorts, looking directly at me. "They are spoiled and rich. Every one of them. And they take everything they can from a girl. Young blood is riper, purer—blood filled with life. So they take what they need and they don't think ahead. They just assume there will always be more. There always has been."

"So they force the older girls who weren't chosen to donate to more frequent Couplings, trying to create new blood," I say, understanding. "And when I see a Letting girl is near blossoming and I report it...I send that girl to her death."

"Yes," Gretchen whispers, her eyes cast downward to the grass and dirt beneath us.

"And the law doesn't allow cross vocations," I state. "That's why everyone wants to be a Letting so they're sure not to become a Coupling. It's just because no one really knows what happens to these Letting girls."

"Yes. The truth is the Letting girls are too young and too weak to Couple and mother a child, but Farnsworth instated that bogus law about no Letting becoming a Coupling to make it sound like he cared. Really, up until now, he's had a glut of girls so it was no problem. And now he's afraid that if he pushed girls from the Letting to the Coupling, those in the city would revolt, and even the Leeches in the Inferno would begin to ask questions."

"Why didn't you ever tell me?" I ask, softly. "Why didn't you let me know?"

"Would you have believed me?" Gretchen asks, looking straight into my eyes. "You are so damned…patriotic." She stares angrily at me.

"I thought that was a good thing," I say, flabbergasted.

"I know you did," she responds, softly.

"But why didn't you explain? Why didn't you tell me what was happening? Why did you let me be so damned proud of the horrible things I was doing?"

"Because we couldn't risk compromising the revolution."

"Revolution?" I ask. "There's a revolution?" Then the absurdity grasps hold of me. "But who's revolting? The four of you?" I can hear the sarcasm in my voice, and I am immediately sorry for it.

"Yes," Phoenix snipes, breaking his silence. "The four of us."

"But how will you stop them?" I ask Phoenix. "It took you God knows how long to get to me, and when you did, it was merely by chance."

I laugh a small, hysterical laugh. This is beyond ridiculous, and Phoenix, this fearless leader of four, needs to understand that.

He looks at me. His eyes are now hard and angry. He's not my friend, nor is he on my side, and I need to remember that. I know I've overstepped a boundary, but I don't know what the boundaries are in the case of kidnapping, planning a coup, and conspiracy. He must understand that. But I don't think he does, because suddenly the comfort I've been feeling around Phoenix changes and I feel…uneasy.

He steps over to me and sits down directly in front of me. His look is pensive, and it's because of me.

"I was twelve when I was told I lost my mother to the New World. I was working in a factory and hadn't seen her in nearly four years. I never got a chance to say goodbye. I swore then and there I would stop Farnsworth and anyone else who was involved in his twisted operation." He looks at me pointedly as he speaks. "No one is sorrier or more embarrassed than I am that it has taken me all this time to get even this close to Farnsworth. But if you were really as naïve to all of it as Gretchen believes you were, then how can you be so judgmental toward me?"

His question is honest and pure. Once again, my heart aches.

"Phoenix, I—"

He puts up his hand to silence me. "Now, after waiting six years, I refuse to miss my opportunity."

Phoenix stands and hovers over me. I am certain he will kill me now. And why not? I acted as the enemy for all this time, and then I had the audacity to make fun of his rebellion.

He moves behind me, and I feel the light breeze he creates as he walks. I close my eyes for a moment, enjoying the reprieve from the heat of the night and the heat of the situation. I feel him stop behind me. So this is how he'll do it, strangulation, or if I'm lucky, maybe he'll just snap my neck. He is tall enough and strong enough for either. I keep my eyes closed and prepare for my end. I think of my mother, and of my four little souls who will be terrified without me.

He squats down behind me, and I can feel the warmth radiate off his body. I prepare for the instant of pain and my trip to the New World, but instead of his hands clasping on either side of my head, I feel them start to untie the ropes that have me bound to the stake.

The rope falls away. I turn and look up at him, dumbfounded.

"Let's get you back to camp so you can go to the Letting."

Chapter Five

I sit on the floor of cabin O, rubbing my tender wrists. I look at my still-sleeping girls and think how easy it would be to pretend all that happened was nothing more than a horrible nightmare. To pretend it's a day just like any other day. To think life is once again as I believed it was. How wonderful it would be to be the one to bring these little girls to their family reunions instead of their deaths.

Despite the stifling heat, I shudder.

Then I begin to wonder. What if Phoenix and Gretchen are wrong? I have spent seven years of my life building an impeccable reputation as a Leader, and I am heralded by my government. Who are they to tell me everything I've done is wrong? Who are they to say I'm evil? They are the rebels. The very people we have been warned about. What if they are lying, trying to turn me into a traitor? What if they plan to use me to overthrow a bogus corrupt government and I do nothing to stop them? What if? What if? What if…?

Try as I might to convince myself otherwise, I know in my gut Gretchen is not lying to me. And I don't know why, but for some reason, despite it all, despite her lies and my anger, I still trust her.

And then…then, there's my mother. She is the thought I have not allowed myself to have until right this moment, as close to alone as I will ever be in the darkness of cabin O. My mother, whom I haven't heard from in nearly four years.

Thinking of her—her creamy skin, her black hair, her candy red lips, her belt pulled tightly around her tiny waist, her hips, large and comforting—will never be the same. It can't even be as it was yesterday.

Yesterday, I was able to imagine the woman she would be now with gray streaks in her flowing black mane, her brow creased with worry over me, and her eyes still bright and smart. And just yesterday, I allowed myself the luxury of imagining what she'd think of the young woman I'd become. But today?

Today, I can only picture her as she was. And I am aware, more and more often of my past. I am remembering only snippets of my life with her—her white hands, the bitter mushrooms, the cold air as I walked by the clock at the entrance to the park, my cot shimmying slightly as she sat down on it gracefully, the stories of the New World and the secrets of the Old.

Maybe that's what life is, an empty scrapbook, waiting to be filled with these moments—these frozen snippets—that, strung together, make up a life. You can't hold or touch today, yet you know it's here. And maybe I can't feel her anymore, but I know she existed. So today, with memory replacing imagination, I am certain she is gone.

And also, I am certain I have done much wrong.

My aching sorrow is interrupted by a faint moan. I rush to my sleeping campers and discover it is Lulu having nightmares again. She thrashes back and forth until I put my hand on her arm. Once she knows I'm here, she slips back into a sound sleep. Her blind trust in me, coupled with the realization of the loss of my mother, is too much to take. I step away from her and push the side of my hand into my mouth to keep from screaming. I bite down hard on my knuckle, tears wetting my face. I have cried so much tonight tears feel normal against my cheek, so I don't even bother to wipe them away.

All I want to do is get up and run, to make myself free of everything, but I know Phoenix, Gunnar, and Buzzcut are all waiting in the woods, waiting for me to bolt so they have a reason to shoot me. And I would never willingly leave my girls. Not now. Not the day before the Letting. And yet, all I want to do is get away to the woods, find my mushroom, and consequently, my mother. My empty soul aches as my brain reminds me that this is the first night in seven years, I haven't eaten a mushroom.

I draw my legs up tightly to my chest, trying desperately to come up with a plan that keeps us all alive: the girls, Gretchen, me, and even Phoenix. Perhaps it's because he spared my life, or maybe it's because of his belief in my importance in the revolution, but for some reason, I do not want to let him down.

After hours of sitting here trying to devise a plan, I realize Phoenix had been right. There is no easy answer here. It is impossible to solve this situation. All I know is I must save these girls: for who they are, for who they could be, and for all of the girls who've come before them. And if I'm going to save these little souls, I had better survive the Letting myself.

****

I must have fallen asleep, because the next thing I know, I am startled by the sound of the bugle. Reveille is here way too early this morning. I watch the tiny shapes move under their mosquito netting, and I am suddenly paralyzed. I don't know what to do. "Ronnie?" I hear a tiny voice ask. It's Lulu. Her voice alone brings me to tears. "Ronnie? You okay?" she asks, sensing something is not right.

"Of course," I manage to croak out, my throat tight. I imagine how they are seeing me: beaten, exhausted, tear-stained, and defeated. "I'm just thinking about how proud I am of all of you." I speak with as much excitement as I can muster. Then Lulu looks directly at me, and I see the terror in her face.

"What happened?" she asks, shrinking away. Instinctively, I reach up and touch my sore cheek.

"It's nothing," I lie, trying to reassure her. "I had a bad fall when I went running."

My answer seems to appease all of them except Raven. Raven eyes my injuries suspiciously. My lie makes me feel like I'm going to vomit. Instead, I force the bile down and do exactly what Phoenix has told me to do. I act as if today is any other day.

But it's not any other day. It's the day before I'm sent to the Letting, and more importantly, it's the day before the beginning of the end for these four tiny people. I pray my smile masks my terror. I stand up and stretch as tall as I can. My arms reach the exposed beams along the ceiling of the cabin.

"You think I'll be as tall as you when I grow up?" It's Violet this time. She is obviously satisfied with the excuse I gave for my appearance. I can't help myself. I pull her to me and begin to sob.

"Ronnie?" Lulu asks. I hear the alarm in her voice. Raven hangs close by, just far away enough, looking at me out of the corner of her eye. Just then the cabin door slams, and I turn. Gretchen is standing there, staring at me. She raises an eyebrow.

So this is it. No matter what I wanted to think, this is real. This is truly happening.

"Ronnie?" Gretchen asks in her soothing voice. "Is everything okay?"

"Of course." I muster all my courage and strength. "I'm just so proud of our little campers in cabin O."

Lilly and Violet turn to me, smiling. Raven is her usual quiet self, but Lulu is not convinced.

Gretchen eyes Lulu and then looks at me.

"You okay Lulu?" I ask, as calmly as I can.

"Yes." She nods her head. "I'm just not feeling all that well."

"What is it?" I ask her, glad for the distraction.

"My stomach feels a touch queasy." I exhale, happy to focus on a case of butterflies.

"I get it," I tell her. "But I promise there's nothing to be nervous about."

Lulu nods again.

"Now," I say, rubbing my hands together. "We have a big day of training ahead of us, so what do you say we all head to the mess hall?"

The girls are still sleepy but eager to please me. One by one, they fold up their sleeping bags and take turns going to the latrine. Each is now wearing her regulation white and red ringer-tee and a red pair of shorts. They line up behind me and follow me out, like lambs to the slaughter.

****

Breakfast the day before the Letting is always a big deal. The usual daily breakfast of powdered milk and a protein bar is replaced with a veritable feast. Although our breakfast doesn't change, the girls eat fried eggs with buttered toast, steak, and hash browns with spinach tossed throughout. And of course, there is the green algae drink.

I stand in line at the kitchen window and wait as each little person before me has her plate filled. Lilly has trouble seeing over the pile of food she carries. When it's my turn at the window, I hand Willy, the cook, my cup for my powdered milk.

"Not today, Ronnie." He sounds genuinely happy for me. "Today you get the real stuff." He hands me back an empty cup and a loaded down plate.

One whiff of the food makes me realize I am ravenous. He smiles a warm smile at me, and I once again feel horribly guilty. I don't deserve his warmth, and I don't deserve this breakfast.

"Don't even think about it." Gretchen walks up next to me. She holds a cup of milk and a protein bar. "If you're going to have a successful Letting," she whispers, "you had better eat." She hands me a glass of the green algae goo.

"And what if I don't?" I whisper back. "What if I simply pass out and die on the table. What difference would it make?"

"Well," she says, looking thoughtful, as if she's really considering the option. "It would matter to Farnsworth. And it would matter to those four little girls over there." She points at Lulu, Lilly, Violet, and Raven.

Gretchen is right. The girls would be lost without me to guide them. At least the three of them. Raven, I'm not so sure about. They are all devouring their breakfasts as we speak. I smile at them, happy to see the girls eating heartily.

"I know you love them, Ron." Gretchen is staring at me. "Now we have to find a way to save them." Her voice is so low it's barely perceptible.

I nod. Then for some reason, with everything else that is happening, I wonder if it would matter to him. I ask the ridiculous question.

"Does he hate me?" I turn to Gretchen. I can hear the vulnerability in my own voice.

Gretchen looks at me, confused. She tilts her head and narrows her eyes.

"Of course he hates you," she states, matter-of-factly. "Now let's eat before the horn blows for first period."

I nod, the smell of the food on my tray making me sick.

****

We sit in silence and I am amazed at how each of my girls has nearly cleaned her plate. Nervous little Lulu has eaten the most of all of them. I'm glad her nerves have calmed enough to let her eat, but the guilt I'm feeling is nearly paralyzing me.

"Eat," Gretchen whispers and I obey.

I stuff in bite after bite of egg and steak, knowing it's the only thing I can do to help at this moment. When I finally stop for a breath, my plate is empty. I can't believe how hungry I've been.

Gretchen smiles, handing me my glass of algae goo. I chug it back as quickly as possible, wishing I had just one more bite of steak to wash the taste of algae out of my mouth.

"You can thank the Inferno for this one too."

Gretchen waves her wafer cracker breakfast bar. I just nod, fighting hard to keep the rich food down. I see some of the girls struggling with it, too. Lilly and Violet have both run off to the latrine. I follow them in, hoping they're able to keep the food in their tiny bodies.

"Oh," I hear coming from a bathroom stall. Since the bathroom stalls are separated by curtains, I can't knock, so I whisper through the divider.

"Violet?" I ask. "You okay?" Before she can answer, Raven and Lulu have joined us. They stand next to me, swaying back and forth slightly, in desperate need of their turns. Lulu looks green. Maybe she's really coming down with something. I try to banish the thought. That would be another hurdle we don't need to face.

After I have collected my girls who have all managed to hold on to their breakfasts, the horn sounds for first period. Today is not a normal activity day for these girls. This is a day meant strictly and only for preparation. Today we'll exercise at the waterfront. Stretching their muscles in the lake will be great for blood flow in all areas of the body in case any one of them is a tough stick. To head to their morning exercises, we have to walk a good distance down a giant hill, guarded by deep woods on both sides. I know Phoenix and the others will be hidden there, somewhere, with a rifle aimed at my head, only too happy to pull the trigger and take me out of the picture. The thought makes me shiver, even against the heat of the morning. I wince from the pain in my knee, and quietly, my little lambs scoot down the hill after me, our feet kicking up stones as we go. The girls are too quiet, and I know on a normal day, I would be working hard to keep their spirits up. I try a song.

"My country, my country, I do declare. My person, my body, I do swear." The girls begin to join in, quietly.

"To give them to help you, and in return, you let me live happily noon 'til noon. I'm honored to do for you what I can, and in return, I do see your greater plan. My country, my country, how I love you. My country, my country, will see me through."

When I look back at my campers, I notice Lulu is lagging behind. The Letting is affecting her way more than I thought it would.

"Lulu?" I ask, slowing my stride so she can catch up. "You don't want to sing?" She just shakes her head no. "Still your stomach?"

"Yes." Her voice is small, faint.

"Lulu, is this the first time you've ever eaten food like this?" I feel my own breakfast, heavy in my stomach.

She nods.

"I know. It hurts your stomach at first. Just give it some time. It'll get better."

Lulu looks up at me and smiles.

I can't imagine what she's going to do with the stuffed artichokes and beans for lunch, and the mandatory dinner of liver and spinach. The poor kid.

We make it down to the waterfront for our exercise. Luckily, today is as hot as yesterday, and although it's uncomfortable, it means the girls won't have to spend their night soaking in warm tubs to improve circulation. I step into the lake, ankle deep, and they follow. Tiny sunfish shoot by my feet and I wonder, just for a moment, what it would be like to be them, free to swim away from all my problems. Soon enough, all four girls are laughing and splashing; all four forgetting what tomorrow means. Tomorrow. But I can't forget what tomorrow means. I sit on the gray beach at the edge of the water, feeling the dirty sand make its way into my cut-off denim shorts. I stand up and slide my shorts and tank top off, revealing a black one-piece swimsuit with an open back. It's my only one, but I like this swimsuit. It allows me to move in the water, and sometimes I swim for miles.

The sun is strong, but not yet oppressive, and I bask in the feeling of the warmth on my body. I lean back and let the sun drench my entire being, feeling, momentarily, relaxed. Then something in the woods grabs my attention and like a shot, I am on my feet. Lulu watches me, as does Raven, but Lilly and Violet are oblivious to any change in me. Lulu and Raven watch me watching the woods.

"Ronnie?" Lulu asks.

"Shh," I quiet her. Lilly and Violet join the other two girls, and the four of them huddle together, knee deep in the lake. I strain my eyes and my ears to see what or who is out there, but I see nothing. But I can't shake this feeling there's something…

One thing is certain, whoever or whatever it is would be unwelcome. There is no reason for Phoenix and his group to show themselves to these girls, so it may be a wild animal, or another small faction of rebels. I'm not taking any chances.

"Girls," I speak in a hushed voice. "Let's go up the hill. We're changing our plan for today." No matter how upbeat I try to sound, they know better.

Quickly, the four of them wrap themselves in

towels and scurry up the hill as fast as possible. I am right behind, rushing them, but there is no way they can move fast enough to make me happy. My long legs would have me to the top of the hill in less than five minutes, but as a group, it will take us nearly fifteen.

Fifteen minutes is plenty long enough for a band of rebels to come and snatch up any one of these girls to sell her on the black market for private blood donations. I never really worried about it before. I was always careful, but I figured my girls were safe in my camp. Were safe with me. But since learning Phoenix and his gang are out there, so close to us, it's feasible to think another group may be as well. And since I've learned I'm the biggest danger these girls face, well then, nothing is as I thought it was.

I scan the woods with every step I take, listening for a snap of a twig or the stomp of a footstep. I push my girls a bit harder. "Come on, girls. Let's get that blood pumping."

I'm trying not to scare them, but they are already terrified. The huddled mass that walks in front of me proves that. Looking at them, I think of Gretchen and me, all those years ago. How I thought we would always be lifelong best friends. How I could never have imagined she would become a traitor.

We make it to the top of the hill, and I have never been so happy to see our cabins. I exhale, a sense of peace finally winning out over panic.

"Okay, girls, how about a rest time?" Their limbs are still shaking, and I can tell they are genuinely frightened. I need to fix this.

"Girls," I say, trying to regain control. "There is nothing to be scared of. Do you remember last night, when I told you to be quiet in case Margaret was nearby?"

Three of them nod. Raven just stares.

"Well, I thought I heard her today, too." I know it's a pitiful lie, but it's all I have. "And if she has special orders for me, today, the day before your"—I stop myself midsentence—"our Letting, I need to hear them. That's all."

I speak as soothingly as possible. I hope at least a couple of them buy my excuse. I know Raven won't, but I'm hopeful for the other three. "So, what do you think of some playtime in the cabin?"

The girls nod and head off to their cabin. I would love nothing more than to crawl into my own cabin and hide, maybe even fall asleep, but I know my adrenaline would never allow it. Besides, I can still feel something. Someone. And I need to get to the bottom of it. If we're going to be attacked and raided, I had better be prepared.

I look around the campgrounds for a weapon of any kind, but I find we are abysmally unprepared. If Phoenix and his gang or an even more unscrupulous bunch were to come our way, I would have no way to stop them. In the past, I've lit fires to scare the rebels off, and none ever infiltrated our camp. But this is different. This time someone is on our turf. After more searching, I decide on a poker from an old, nonworking fireplace in the mess hall.

Armed with that, I begin to walk to the perimeter of the camp. I know this is a bad idea, but I also know I have to stop whoever is there. Maybe, just maybe, whoever it is will be happy with obtaining me, and leave the girls alone. The girls could very well survive the Letting tomorrow, and by the next time they are summoned, maybe Phoenix would have found a way to free them from their horrific fate.

As I walk on faster and faster, I know this is a completely inane thought, and if Phoenix, Gunnar, or Buzzcut are anywhere nearby, they may very well shoot me on the spot. But I have to know. After all of the years of being a closet danger myself, I now want to know when I am facing one.

I walk to a far area of the campgrounds, past the old tennis courts, crossing the invisible border of our camp. I push through the trees about three layers deep, but I find nothing. I do this again by the arts and crafts cabin, and then on the opposite side of the camp, over by the old Infirmary. Again, there is no one. I walk toward the one entrance into the camp, the dirt road, and still I see no one. Finally, I know I have no other choice but to head back down toward the water.

Slowly, fireplace poker in my hand, I start the descent down the hill. Naturally, downhill is so much easier than uphill, so I prepare myself mentally to run back up the hill if I need to. With my aching knee, it will be nothing short of a challenge. But it would be a challenge to anyone chasing me as well. With every slip I make on the hill, I grab myself, steadying myself, trying not to appear weak or feeble, just in case someone is watching. In a matter of minutes, I am back at the waterfront.

Looking around the giant lake, I see how easy it would be for anyone to hide anywhere. There is no way I can canvas the entire area, so since I have nothing left to lose, I offer myself up.

"Okay," I shout, holding my hands out and turning

in a circle. "Come out. Whoever you are, come out and show yourself. You want someone? Then don't go after a child. I am one of the last remaining O's. Here I am."

I hear a twig snap, then another. Then there is the sound of footsteps, rushing in my ears. I think of closing my eyes and bracing for impact, but instead I steady myself and lift my fireplace poker. Maybe, if I'm lucky, I can catch an eye or lame someone, even if only temporarily. Maybe I'll be able to get away into the woods, though I have no idea what I'll do when I get there.

Then, not far up the beach, I see a figure dressed in camouflage. He walks swiftly toward me carrying a gun in front of him. He holds it pointing upward, away from me, but I feel my heart pound and my palms begin to sweat. I recognize him. It's Phoenix. I brace myself for his approach. He walks up, right next to me. He narrows his eyes at me.

"Are you really this naïve?" he asks. He looks disgusted with me.

He purposely looks away, and I realize I'm still in my swimsuit.

"Here." He hands me the denim cut-offs I left lying on the beach. He still won't look at me. "It's not smart to leave things lying around. Especially your things. Some of the rebels have dogs trained to find you." Again, his words feel like a slap in my face.

"Why?" I ask. "If everyone knows where I'm stationed, they can get to me any time."

"Not everyone knows where your camp is. It's not common knowledge. And I don't know what anyone else's motives are." He straightens up and tightens his grasp on his rifle. "All I know is it would be easier to grab you when you are away from the safety and protection of your camp."

I nod, remembering I am a wanted person because I have committed horrible crimes. I shrink back from Phoenix.

"Uh, you should put them on." He points to the shorts, his eyes still avoiding me.

I nod again, my cheeks burning red, wondering if I look that bad in my swimsuit. I slide my feet into the shorts, one leg, than the other, thinking I'm thin and nearly six feet tall with long legs and tan skin, so it can't be all bad. But apparently, whatever I look like repulses him. He doesn't turn back until I'm covered.

"Thanks," I squeak out and he nods. We stand there, the two of us, quiet for whole minutes. There are so many things I want to ask, like, why can't we become partners in his revolution? But the words don't come. Instead, our attention snaps to the gravel road and the sound of footsteps approaching. I raise my poker, and he looks at me for one moment before stepping in front of me, holding the gun. Finally, we see Gretchen on the path. She looks at us, quizzically.

"You're missing lunch," she pants, winded from her walk down. Gretchen never makes this trek down the hill, because she'll have to go back up. She takes a deep breath. "And Lulu's sick."

I suddenly forget everything else.

"What's wrong?" I ask.

"Don't know. She won't talk to anyone but you."

I turn to Phoenix. I'm certain there is something to say, but instead I leave him and sprint up the hill. I feel his eyes on me as I go.

Within minutes, I am in cabin O.

"Lulu?" I ask, quietly. I am huffing and puffing from my run. I fight to calm my breath as I step in, closer to Lulu. Raven blocks my way.

"Raven, honey. Let me by, please." She does, but even in the midday sun, the cabin is dark, and it's difficult for me to see. "Why aren't you at lunch?" I ask Raven, realizing the time.

She just shrugs.

"Go to the mess hall," I tell her, and she walks out, closing the door quietly behind her. When I am sure I see Raven walk through the lunchroom door, I turn to Lulu.

"What's wrong? Lulu? Honey? Is it your stomach again? Are you scared?"

In the shadows, I see Lulu shake her head. Somewhere, deep inside, I have that horrific sinking feeling. "What is it then?" I ask. I walk closer to her cot where she is curled up in a tiny ball. I reach down and stroke her back. "Lulu? Please tell me. I can't help you if you don't tell me."

"You can't help me anyway," she whimpers, and I can tell she's been crying.

"Why not? There's nothing that we—"

"I'm no good anymore." Her voice is shaky and barely perceptible.

"What are you talking about, Lulu?"

"I'll never see you again." She reaches out and grabs hold of my arm. It sends a chill down my spine.

"But Lulu, what are you talking about?"

"Oh Ronnie." Quiet tears wash over her delicate cheeks. "I just blossomed."

Chapter Six

I sink down onto the floor next to Lulu's bed. It can't be, I decide. She has to be wrong. It is not feasible that a nine-year-old girl…The exhaustion I'm feeling from lack of sleep sends a tremor through my body, but my adrenaline keeps me focused. I turn myself to face Lulu and stroke her hair, softly.

"Lulu, honey, how do you know?" I ask as carefully as I can.

She doesn't speak, she just points to a small pile of soiled clothes on the edge of her cot.

I nod. "Does anyone else know?"

"No," Lulu whispers.

"That's good." No matter what, this needs to stay between us.

I rack my brain for an answer…for anything. But the answer doesn't come. Instead, the tears do. I chide myself for crying so much. I am usually the girl who never cries. I wipe the tears quickly. The last thing I need to do is instill more fear in Lulu.

"I don't want to leave you," Lulu cries, and I force a smile.

Many of my campers have given me this same teary goodbye, but it's never before been this difficult.

"I don't want you to either," I agree, softly. Usually, I follow those words with, "But you're going to a wonderful place where you'll see your mother."

The thought of those poisonous words brings a bitter taste to my mouth. Today I say nothing more.

"And I don't want to go," Lulu whispers.

"Where?" I ask, just as quietly, understanding now there really is nowhere for her to go.

"To the New World."

"Why not?" I am unable to say more. Unable to concoct a lie about trees dripping with candy. Unable to shake from my brain the image of streets littered with limp, lifeless children.

"Because it just doesn't feel right." The words she speaks are poignant and important, yet they come out of a tiny body, huddled up into an even tinier ball.

How I wish I had followed my instincts any of those times I had wondered. If I had...if I had, would it have made a difference? Could I have kept any one of those hundreds of little girls from being sent to the New World? Did I get caught up in the praise and accolades, and did I refuse to listen...to really listen to my heart? Guilt radiates through me like a searing pain. It is so much worse than the wounds I received from my beating. But there's no time for guilt. Now there is only time for action.

"Well you're not going," I state definitively, standing up next to her. I realize I must look like a giant to this tiny person. And if I'm a giant, I had better come up with a giant plan. Quickly, I snatch Lulu's soiled garments and stash them into her backpack. Then I grab two pairs of undergarments, shorts, and t-shirts and stuff them into the same bag. I cram the backpack under her cot. Then I take my personal stash of toiletries and secretly, I lead her to the latrine to explain everything she needs to know. Soon we are back in the cabin, and I grab her bag. I know there is only one place for her, but I'm not sure how to get her there. And first, I'll need to clear camp and the watchful eyes of Margaret.

****

Luckily, when we leave the cabin I hear sounds coming from the mess hall, and know I have a bit more time until the campers leave their lunch and head back to rest period in their cabins. This is what I need to be most careful about. There is a head count at rest time that is usually done by Margaret. Today, I'll need an excuse to do it myself, which means I need Gretchen.

It's strange hearing the sounds of more voices than the four tiny ones I've grown accustomed to. I have been so busy with being kidnapped, beaten and insulted, all the while preparing myself and my girls for the Letting…well, I very nearly forgot there are other campers here. And I will have to earn each one's trust and respect as well. I will be expected to lead each one to the Letting and then to the New World. Well, I would be if circumstances were normal. But now, who knows? Just the thought of our situation sends panic reeling through my body.

I cannot let panic take over. I must keep control.

Quietly, I sneak Lulu from the door of the cabin to the outside wall farthest from both the mess hall and the camp office where Margaret eats her lunch. I've never known why she eats there, but I've always assumed she likes the peace and quiet. Hovering at the side of the cabin, my palms flat against the wooden planks, I hear Lulu panting beside me. There is no time even to try to pretend this is a game. She knows as well as I do, this—whatever this is—and its outcome, are deadly serious. My immediate dilemma is how to move us from the cabin to the hill without being spotted.

We both take deep breaths and start quietly, past the cabins and toward the path, but I have to be extremely careful of our pacing. If it's too fast, it will be obvious, but too slow and we'll be spotted. Steadily, we walk across the grass fields when all I want to do is break out into a sprint, carrying Lulu along with me.

As we walk, I see Lulu grimace from the newly acquired pain she is feeling. I see the path clearly in front of us, the place where the grass meets the gravel, and it's so close I can nearly touch it. We'll have about ten yards to walk to get to the gravel and then we must move very quickly and carefully, because there is no reason to be on the gravel path except to go to the waterfront. And what could possibly be my reason to take her to the waterfront now? At this time? At this hour? Alone? And even if we were to get there successfully, will he even be there? And will he take her?

Step, step, step, her tiny legs and my long legs find a rhythm, until finally, we touch gravel. Then we hear the bugle play, signifying the end of lunch period. Lulu's weary eyes dart up at me, terrified. Damn. I was hoping to be clear of camp before the bugle. Everyone will be leaving the mess hall and here we are, in plain view, trying to break away.

We must press on. We walk a few steps more and I hear footsteps fall in time behind us. They are heavy steps and they grow faster and faster until I feel a hand on my shoulder. I know who it is without even looking. I wheel around and look down at Margaret's round, shiny face, staring up at me. Her lips are pursed, and she stands like she is wearing a suit of armor three sizes too small. I need to think fast.

"Margaret?" I sound as disgusted as I can. "Do you have a good reason for stopping us?" She looks at me first with surprise, then with hatred in her eyes.

"I don't need a reason." She speaks through clenched teeth.

"No?" I stand tall, staying as strong as I can. "Well I hope you remember to tell them that tomorrow when I sign her in at Services and they see what I see..."

I allow my voice to trail off. Lulu eyes me with a panicked look. It is a huge gamble I'm taking, but it's the only chance we have.

"Come on, Lulu," I sigh, trying to mask my terror with ambivalence. "Let's go." I turn Lulu around toward the cabins and can tell she's genuinely confused. But then, so am I. I have no idea what I'm doing.

"I'm sure you're right to send her to rest time, Margaret." I speak with every undertone of sarcasm I can muster. "You would know better than me what the Lettors want. Me, I'm just responsible for prepping more successful draws than any other person in history."

As soon as I say it, I feel nauseated and dizzy. I feel the ground want to come up but I force myself to stand strong. Is it true? More than any other person in history?

I grab Lulu by the hand and begin to pull her back toward the cabin. I see the tears flowing from her eyes and feel them building in mine. No. This is not the time to falter. I must stay strong.

Margaret lets us walk quite a distance back toward the cabins, and despite my fear that she won't stop us, the space gives me a tiny reprieve. I need this time to concoct my bogus story.

"Wait," Margaret blurts finally, and I feel the rigid muscles in my neck relax a tiny bit. I turn slowly.

"Are you talking to me?" I ask, and she nods. "What?" I stand perfectly still, trying to remember to breathe.

"What is it you see?" she asks, nodding toward Lulu as if she didn't even exist—as if she were only a number—which may be exactly what she is to them. What all of us are.

"Margaret." I walk straight up to her. "If you can't see it…" I turn my head to look at her sideways. I read the expression of disappointment in her face. I have to be careful not to lead Margaret to Lulu's real "condition," but I'm banking on the fact Lulu looks way too young for anyone to think anything of the sort. But still, to be safe, I can only toy with Margaret for so long.

"What is it?" Margaret asks. "I-I'm not with them like you are. I'm busy running a camp. Just tell me, Veronica."

I can tell she's genuinely frustrated, and deep down I'm glad to have pushed her this far.

"Well she's dehydrated, of course." I say it like I'm reading medical stats about Lulu's tiny body, and like any of it is true.

Margaret stares at Lulu, trying to see something…anything that will give her a clue.

"Oh for goodness sake," I exclaim, grabbing Lulu's arm and holding it up. I turn her hand upward to reveal her fingers. "Shriveled up skin." I drop her arm.

Next, I cup her chin with my hand and turn her

face upward toward Margaret.

"Sunken eyes. Stick out your tongue please." I instruct Lulu in a voice as cold as I can make it.

She obeys.

"And just look at her tongue…" I turn away, as if disgusted.

Margaret nods along as if any of it were true. Of course, I would never let any of my girls get dehydrated. It's something I would watch, especially in this heat and especially the day before a Letting. But I, on the other hand, am starting to feel very thirsty.

"Why is she wearing a backpack?" Margaret asks, eyeing the bag. "And why do you have her out in the heat, walking?"

"Really?" I ask. "The backpack is carrying water and she's out walking because I have to keep her moving to make sure her veins haven't collapsed."

Lulu shrinks back slightly and gasps.

Margaret looks surprised as well.

"Well," Margaret barks, obviously out of her element. "She's your charge. You had better know what you're doing. And remember, tomorrow's your first Letting, too." She speaks with such syrupy sweetness I want to slap her.

"Are we done?" I ask and she nods.

"Okay, Lulu." I turn back to her. "Now we need to walk with knees touching elbows. Can you try it?" I do the ridiculous action that will get her blood pumping and she copies me. Then we jog in circles a bit as Margaret walks away. "Okay, now up and down the hill, pumping your arms."

"No." I'm hoping Lulu's refusal is for good measure.

"I'm sorry." I sound as cold and professional as I can. "A lot is riding on you tomorrow. Your country and its leaders are relying on you. Your job is to show up prepared, and my job is to prepare you."

Lulu nods and I walk her down the top part of the hill and back up again. We repeat the action until I am certain Margaret has gone back to her office. I am fairly sure Margaret will never venture to the waterfront, so we're safe for the moment. I just pray all of this is not in vain.

We begin our trek to the waterfront and Lulu gives out at the halfway mark. "I can't," she whimpers. "I just can't." I recognize the terror and exhaustion in her. I sit down on the ground next to her.

"We have to go." As much as I want to keep moving, I know if I push too hard she will resist. I speak as gently as I can. "There is someone down there, at the waterfront. He's a friend of Gretchen's. He is a good person, and he will help you."

"He's not your friend?" she asks, her bright blue eyes wide with fear. I shake my head.

"No. Sometimes I wish he was. But no...he's not. I do trust him though. And I want you to trust him, too. Okay?"

As soon as I say the words, I realize they're true. And they'd better be. And I'd better be right for trusting him, otherwise I am handing Lulu over to a dangerous, rebel lunatic. And who knows what he might do? Despite the heat, a chill runs through me. I shake it off and stand, stretching myself up as close to the beating sun as I possibly can. Maybe it will give me the power I so desperately need.

"Okay." Lulu looks up at me, nodding. I reach my

hand out to help her to her feet. Then in one big swoop, I pull her onto my back and we move swiftly and much less carefully down to the waterfront. The only thing that matters now is speed. When we make it to the bottom Phoenix is there, as if he was waiting for us, and he does not seem the slightest bit surprised to see us.

I ease Lulu off my back. She stands close to me, her body tight up against me. The sweat pours from my forehead as I struggle to catch my breath.

"How did you know?" I ask.

"I don't know," he shrugs. "I just had a feeling I should be here."

As much as I want to believe him, something in the way he says it makes me doubt his answer. Instinctively, I scan the woods for any sign of Gunnar and Buzzcut. Phoenix watches me. Regardless of my doubt, I still have to do something with Lulu, before they do.

"Phoenix…" I speak as carefully as I can, trying not to upset Lulu. "Lulu cannot have her blood drawn tomorrow. She's…no longer ripe."

His eyes give away surprise, but he only nods.

I turn to Lulu whose cheeks have flushed a bright pink, obviously mortified I am sharing her biggest secret with a strange man. "You don't have to be afraid. Remember, he's friends with Gretchen. You stick with him and do everything he tells you to do. After the Letting tomorrow, I will find you."

"Pinkie promise?" she asks, holding up her tiny little finger. I stare at it and then look at Phoenix, hoping for some type of guidance, but he looks away.

"Pinkie promise," I say, locking my finger with hers, caught in the absurdity of a child so young she still asks for a "pinkie promise," having to be protected from the New World. It's disgusting.

I begin to walk off, but Phoenix catches up to me. I know he's going to tell me to forget the favor I'm asking, that it's too much. But instead, he grabs my arm to stop me. I look at his hand on my elbow and my eyes search his face, and I have never felt so…lost. I expect him to ask me if I'm certain. To tell me that she's so young. But he doesn't.

"I don't know what you're planning." He points at Lulu but keeps his eyes focused on me. His voice is low and even. "But this is my show. And my plan. You are only free right now because I need you to go to the Letting. You're not some kind of savior, Veronica." His face turns red with frustration, and he leans in close to me. "You're the enemy."

He drops his hand from my elbow, and despite his words, I'm sorry when he does. I don't understand what's going on. I don't know when I became the bad guy, and more importantly, I don't know how to save these girls. And selfishly, I-I don't understand why the feeling of his hand on me was so comforting. I was raised to believe he is the enemy. But I just can't see him as such. Sadly, the truth is this boy hates me and no matter what I try to do to fix it, I cannot. I can never undo what I've done. I am a monster, and he needs to stop me. But at least Lulu will be safe, if only for a little while.

I turn away from the two of them with such an ache in my heart it hurts all the way to my toes. I force down a sob that wants to explode from my chest, and draw in as much oxygen as I can.

"Ronnie?" I turn back to see little Lulu, trying to

smile at me. "Good luck tomorrow." I turn away from her and run up the hill.

****

When I get back to the cabin, Gretchen is sitting with the three other girls. "Where have you been?" she asks. She doesn't raise her voice, but I can see a vein in her temple, throbbing. I know she is angry.

"I had to keep Margaret from doing the head count as soon as I realized Lulu was missing. Believe me, it wasn't easy." She doesn't even leave me time to mutter an apology. "Where is she?" Gretchen demands. I'm amazed Gretchen asks me this. She must understand I'm trying to keep this secret.

"I thought she was with you..." I speak deliberately, trying to read her mood.

"No...the last I heard you were taking her to the waterfront to help her circulation." She rolls her eyes, and it's obvious she doesn't believe my excuse or my motivation.

"Yes, but I sent her back up." I speak slowly, loading my words with subtext, trying to tell Gretchen what I need to say. "I had to take care of some...things...at the waterfront."

Gretchen understands me, but she shows no sign of recognition. She will not let me off the hook. "Gretchen?"

"I hope you know what you're doing, Ronnie. Because after all this time, I would hate to jeopardize an operation like this."

I look around at three sets of tiny eyes, staring at me. I am confused. I'm exhausted from lack of sleep and sick from food, and I cannot get a handle on what is happening. I am about to ask her what she means by any of it, when there is a panicked knock on the door.

"Veronica? Gretchen?" We hear a terrified voice from outside yelling. "We're being attacked!"

Chapter Seven

As fast as I can, I get each of the three girls in cabin O hidden under their cots, and I try to get to the others in the remaining cabins. I rush to the window to decide which way to go, but I see I'm too late. Crying girls are being forced out of their tents at gunpoint. That's all I'm allowed to see before Gretchen forces me away from the window. She motions for me to squat down low, and stay in a corner of the room, mostly in shadow. Now the best I can do is hear the interaction. My girls are so terrified there is not a sound within our cabin.

"Where are they?" someone outside yells.

"All you girls make a circle," another voice shouts. This one belongs to a woman. The whimpering and crying grows louder.

"Shut up." It's yet another voice. So far, there are three of them. I inch to the door, but Gretchen holds me back.

"If you go, they will find these three," she whispers. I nod. She's right. My body aches, wanting Gretchen to let me pass so I can do my job and try to fight off the rebels, but I remember I am not a free person. Although I am in my camp, I am still Phoenix's prisoner. And he is doing me a favor by guarding Lulu. I can't screw this up.

The thought of Phoenix distracts me for a moment,

and then I am startled by the sound of a lone gunshot. I am on my feet before I realize what I'm doing, but this time Gretchen uses a jump rope she finds lying on the floor to physically restrain me. I am stunned by her sheer strength, and she motions for me to squat down again. I close my eyes and pray the shot was fired into the air. I look at Gretchen, and she signs that everything is okay. The woman speaks again.

"Where are they?" The gunshot didn't accomplish anything, the crying grows louder and more hysterical, but then suddenly, a hush falls over camp. Although it irks me, I know exactly what is going on without being told. I know that Margaret has stepped up. I hear her tight, throaty voice clearly.

"I am Margaret Stephens." There is not so much as a hint of tremor in her voice. "And this is my camp. I do not appreciate your approach, but I will help you in any way possible, to see no one gets hurt."

Despite the hysteria, I am utterly shocked by Margaret's calm and smooth demeanor. For the first time ever, I realize why she is in charge. I hope I'm this competent if I'm ever in her situation.

"What is it you are looking for?" she asks.

"Don't play with us." The first man speaks.

I reprimand myself for the relief I feel that none of the voices belong to Phoenix.

"I assure you I would never do that." Margaret is obviously trying to placate him. "But you need to give me more information. Please. I truly do not know what it is you want."

"We want the same thing everyone wants," the woman urges. "We want the O's."

"What makes you think we have O's?" Margaret

asks, calmly.

"I'm ready to pop her now," the second male threatens.

"Cool it." It's the woman. "Look. We don't want to hurt anyone. But we've come for the O's. And we're not leaving without them."

"But you know O's are extinct," Margaret clarifies.

"We know you have her," the first man barks. "The Leader."

I wish I had the physical and mental strength to break free of my binds and inch my way back to the window to see who we are up against. But somewhere deep inside, I am worried that even if I were free, fear would keep me glued to my spot.

"Veronica Billings," the woman adds. The sound of my own name sends a shudder through my body. Gretchen turns to face me. I look at her for an answer but she shakes her head.

"Oh," Margaret responds, sounding surprised. "I had completely forgotten Veronica is an O." I hear murmuring from the rebels. "I have no love for Ms. Billings. In fact, I would happily turn her over to you. But she is not here. She took a camper to the waterfront to prep her for the next Letting."

"When is the next Letting?" the woman asks.

"In a week or so," Margaret lies smoothly.

"She's lying." It's the first male. "The Letting's tomorrow. I heard the rumor. That's why we've gotta find her now."

"Tomorrow?" the woman asks. I can tell she's surprised. "Where is she?" Her voice is urgent, desperate even.

"I told you," Margaret repeats. "She's at the

water—"

"You'd better hope she is," the first male snaps. "'Cause if we get there and find you're lying to us again…I wouldn't want to be you."

"I'm not lying." Margaret is still calm but I hear an edge creeping into her voice. "If you don't believe me, why don't you go and see for yourself?"

"Wait, wait, wait…" The first man speaks again. I really wish he would just shut up. "She is the last remaining O and you're just going to give her up?" Thankfully, it sounds like they don't know about my four little girls.

"My job is to protect this camp," Margaret explains, "not one girl. If you want her and you find her, she's all yours."

"Don't you know what she's worth on the black market?" he asks.

"I am a worker for the government." I can hear the pride in Margaret's words. "I know nothing about a black market."

"This is bull," the first man yells. Then every one of the campers outside gasps collectively. It can only mean one thing: that awful man must have pulled a gun on Margaret.

It's too much. I can't let Margaret die for me. If I'm heading to the Letting anyway, why not let a group of rebels capture me. At least the girls will be safe. I pull at my binds, but they grow tighter and tighter the harder I pull. As if she can read my mind, Gretchen puts up her hand to quiet my thoughts and she creeps forward even closer to the window to peer out. I can tell by the tension in her body that I am right. There must be a gun pointed at Margaret. Everyone is so very quiet all I hear is the sound of my own shallow breath. But what do I do now? Harder and harder I pull on the rope holding me, trying to break free. Maybe, if I walk out, maybe they will take me and just disappear. But a nagging voice inside me tells me they will kill all of the remaining campers just so there are no witnesses. Their desire for me may be all that's keeping any of us alive. Or, on the other hand, maybe that's what I want to think because I am such a coward. It doesn't matter anyway. Gretchen has tied this knot in such a way that I can't break free. There's another skill I never realized she had—knot tying. Where did she pick that up? I stare at her, her long blonde hair pulled back in a hurried ponytail, her petite frame struggling to see out the window. In this light, with this expression of fierce determination on her face, I hardly recognize her. It's like she's the mysterious twin of my best friend. Someone I really don't know all that well. Come to think of it, Gretchen has so many secrets I'm beginning to wonder if I ever really knew her at all. The commotion starts up again outside. Someone begins shouting.

"Put it down." I hear the words and immediately recognize the voice. It is undoubtedly Phoenix. Gretchen frowns slightly and then looks at me. She looks confused.

"He said drop it." This time the voice belongs to Gunnar.

"Drop the gun." It is Buzzcut. So my fantasy of Phoenix suddenly becoming a solo act is just that, a fantasy. Why, in the middle of all this am I having fantasies about Phoenix...? I shake my head and a chill runs through my body. I am both terrified and thrilled.

Then I remember: Lulu. If all three of them are here, where is Lulu? I pray she is okay, knowing if she is alone, she will be terrified.

"Well, if it isn't Phoenix rising from the ashes." It is that second man's voice again.

"Bryce." Phoenix's voice is slow and even. "There is no need for this. Drop your gun and get lost."

"Oh isn't that your thing?" So the second man is named Bryce. And obviously, they have a history.

"My thing?" Phoenix asks. "My thing hasn't changed. You're the one who jumped ship."

"Because you weren't getting it done," Bryce answers.

"I have her," Phoenix boasts.

"What?"

"Veronica Billings. I have her."

"What do you mean have her?"

"At a camp. Not far from here. I am holding her there."

"Bull—"

"Believe what you want." Just the sound of Phoenix's voice calms me. "But look around. Don't you think the great Veronica Billings would come charging out from wherever she was hiding, waving a sword, just to save her camp?" He's right. I should have done exactly that. I didn't think it was possible, but I have disgusted myself even more. I watch the drama unfold through Gretchen's body language. She looks down, momentarily.

"Veronica's a coward," Bryce scoffs. "She's hiding."

"She's not a coward." Phoenix challenges Bryce with his words. "She's a prisoner."

"How'd you finally get her?" Bryce asks.

"Luck. Look Bryce, even if you captured Veronica today, what would you get but some money? And what would that do for you? Do you really want to go live in the Inferno? Selling her wouldn't make any difference in the world. It wouldn't change any of those things we wanted to change—"

"You wanted to change, Phoenix. You wanted to change."

"You did too, Bryce. Once upon a time. So be smart here. Put the guns away. Raid the mess hall. Stock up on some food and head back to the city."

"There's nothing left there for me."

"Jeannie?" Phoenix asks. There is no answer. "Jeannie's gone?" Phoenix sounds doubtful and brotherly. So Bryce must have had one of those "relationships" they say existed once upon a time. A partnership where two people choose to be together— something that is highly illegal in our world and carries with it a hefty penalty. I know it's taboo, but my brain can't help but flash vivid pictures of what that must have been like—to be with someone because you want to be with him. There is a long pause before anyone speaks.

"They called her to the Coupling. To the Coupling, Phoenix." Then I hear some kind of commotion and loud, uncontrolled sobs. But they are not from the girls or any one of us. They are from Bryce. I can't hear the exact words Phoenix says to Bryce, but I believe he says he's sorry.

When the crying stops, Phoenix speaks. "Just go, Bryce. Head back home and wait for my message. I will call on you when the time is right. But that time is not now. Selling Veronica to them would make you no better than Veronica herself." Those horrible, vile words make Gretchen nod and must work magic on Bryce because I hear heavy footsteps marching away. Then the footsteps stop, maybe just a few feet from my cabin door.

"You really have her, Phoenix? You really have that...that...monster?"

"I have her." And the steps march on.

Gretchen unties me and gives the all clear. I stand, stretching, working out the kinks that are becoming familiar to my body. Suddenly there are three sets of eyes staring at me from underneath their cots. "You'd better explain," Gretchen advises. "You've all got a long road ahead of you." I nod, but before I can say a word, the cabin door is yanked open and Lulu comes storming through.

"Did you know?" she asks.

"Lulu," I exclaim. "You have to be careful, Margaret may still be—"

"Margaret is in the Infirmary with cold compresses on her head. I want you to answer my question. Did you know?"

"I..."

"No," she snarls, sounding more like a woman than a girl. "Answer me. Did you know what was going to happen to all of those girls?"

I shake my head. "Of course not, Lulu. I didn't know anything. I never would have done this job if I knew." She nods at me. Thankfully, I think she understands me and believes me. How I wish he would too.

Moments later, he walks through the door of the

cabin. "Thank you," I whisper.

"I didn't do it for you," he snaps. He turns away from me and holds out his hand for Lulu. She slips her tiny hand into his, and he holds onto her protectively. The other three girls watch, in complete shock. Phoenix and Lulu walk quickly and quietly out the door, leaving me with a longing, a yearning that runs through my body like a strong electric current. My body aches in response, and it is suddenly impossible to stand. I sink to the floor, at once jealous of both of them. I am jealous of their ease together, I am jealous of Phoenix taking my place as protector of Lulu, and mostly, I am jealous of her proximity to him. All I want is to walk in the middle of the two of them, holding both of their hands, loving both of them. Gretchen must understand.

"Ronnie," she warns, walking to me. "I don't know what you're thinking but it can never happen between you two. He has spent his entire life on a quest to topple you. Even if he wanted to be with you, which he doesn't, he never could. Too many people are relying on his hatred for you. The entire rebel movement is based on it. You need to understand how this will work. He will take you to the Letting himself tomorrow so he can get his foot in the door. Then he will bring down the Letting and everything around it. He will starve the Inferno of the blood they so desperately need. Then he will get to Farnsworth. And when it is all over, Ronnie, he will be our new governing leader, and you will be dead." I step back from her, horrified. "It is the one way it can go, Ronnie. You and I both know with your toxic blood, you should have been dead seven years ago. The fact that you lived this long is a gift. You should be thankful you've had this much time."

I nod my head, knowing she is right. Tomorrow, I will be drained and left for dead. I will die a slow and painful death and yet, I deserve much worse. But she is wrong about one thing. These past seven years have not been a gift. They have been nothing short of a curse. I nod again and turn to walk out of cabin O to compose myself and prepare for tomorrow's Letting as best I can.

"Wait." I turn, startled by a voice I barely recognize. It is Raven.

"I'm sorry, girls," I stammer. "All of this...You shouldn't have heard any of it."

"I knew all of it anyway," Raven admits.

I watch as Gretchen moves closer to Raven, hovering over her like she might try to silence her at any second.

"Phoenix would never let you die," Raven states, in her simple, childish way.

"Of course he would," Gretchen snaps, laughing at Raven.

"No," Raven protests. "No matter how much he hates you, he would never let you die."

"Oh really?" Gretchen asks, sounding exhausted from the conversation. "And how would you know?" Gretchen is too possessive when she talks about Phoenix. There is...something there.

Raven stares up at Gretchen with two piercing blue eyes, and I see it immediately. Raven no longer needs to explain, but she says it anyway.

"I know, because Phoenix is my brother."

Chapter Eight

I stare at Gretchen, dumbfounded. Is it true? How did Gretchen not know? Does Phoenix know? He couldn't. He saw Raven just a few minutes ago and said nothing. This is a precarious situation. Everything will change if Phoenix is suddenly fighting for blood instead of just a rebel movement. I look back at Gretchen, and see the thought reflect in her eyes. She has realized exactly this, at precisely the same moment as I.

"Ronnie…no," she shakes her head.

"You've got to be kidding," I respond, the pitch of my voice rising. "Of course he needs to know."

"No," she snaps at me. She walks right up to me and we stand toe to toe. She cranes her neck to look me in the eye. I feel bulky and cumbersome standing close to her tiny, sinewy body, but I also feel powerful. Short of tying a mean rope, what can Gretchen possibly do to me? And to tie me up, she has to be able to catch me.

"Don't even think about it, Veronica."

I'm not sure if she's telling me to stay mum or to stay put. It doesn't matter anyway, because I'm not going to do either one. I hesitate for a moment, and then decide I can go and leave the last two girls with Gretchen. No matter what, Gretchen would never hurt these girls, even if it's only because they are too valuable. That thought makes my stomach ache, but I decide to push past it and concentrate on the good things I know about Gretchen, whatever those may be.

I look at her again. After all these years, do I really know her? Well, if my instinct is right about her feelings for Phoenix, she would never harm his sister. Even a sister he doesn't know exists.

"You should stand back." I quickly grab a canteen of water and make my way to the doorway.

"Why?" Gretchen asks, not moving and standing her ground.

"Because I'm leaving. And I'm taking this one with me," I grab Raven by the arm. It doesn't take anything to convince her to come with me. Her body falls naturally in step with mine.

"You're not leaving," Gretchen commands. "And you're certainly not taking that one."

"Yes, I'm doing both. I'm leaving and taking Raven with me. That leaves two girls for each of us. At this point, they are safer if they're separated. Who knows how many more rebel factions have found us and are just biding their time?"

I can tell by the way she narrows her eyes the idea of competition from a rebel group annoys Gretchen. "Girls…" I turn to address Violet and Lilly. "You two stay with Gretchen. She will protect you for now, and I will be back for the Letting tomorrow. I will not leave you alone."

The girls nod.

"You're insane," Gretchen warns me. "He will kill you the second he lays eyes on you."

"Maybe so, but he didn't the last time. And he won't kill this one," I say, moving Raven in front of me. I place my hands protectively on her shoulders. "Look at her, Gretchen. She's the spitting image of him."

Gretchen carefully assesses Raven's long dark hair and piercing blue eyes. But the look on Gretchen's face is not the look I'm expecting. There's no longing in her gaze, no softness. If Gretchen is in love with Phoenix, I would have thought there would be at least a small spot in her heart for his sister. Maybe I'm wrong about them. Maybe Gretchen doesn't have those feelings. They're illegal anyway. But I would have thought she, a literal rebel, would not have cared about a law. Not like me, the rule follower.

I'm wasting too much time. I stuff the canteen into an old green canvas backpack. I toss the bag over my shoulder and walk to the door. Raven is right beside me. I open the door and Gretchen speaks. "If I had a gun, I'd shoot you."

"No you wouldn't," I challenge, turning back to her. "My blood is too expensive to let it spill out all over a cabin floor. And besides, you know he has a plan. And that plan gets me to the Letting."

"If anyone else finds you, you'll suffer a fate worse than death." Somehow, she seems almost happy about it.

"Better me than her." I point to Raven. "Better me than any of you."

"Oh spare me the Saint Veronica spiel," Gretchen whines. "I have lived with it for way too long and it's nauseating."

I stare at her for a moment, wondering if deep inside there is any glimmer of the friend I once thought was mine. Her eyes are cold and unyielding. Sadly, they tell me what I need to know. I take Raven's hand tightly in mine, and together, we storm out of the cabin.

Halfway to the waterfront, I stop for some mushrooms. Suddenly, and like always when I pick my mushrooms, I am overtaken with thoughts of my mother. Could I have been wrong about her, too? Could she still be alive? And if so, where could she be? Does she know who I am and what I've been doing? Could she possibly forgive me? Then the big thought hits me. Could she possibly know how I feel about him? And could she ever explain to me why?

I look down at Raven who waits patiently for me. She turns her face up and smiles at me. One look at Raven's blue eyes and I know I would do anything for those eyes. They are so much like her brother's. I am too confused to trust food in my stomach right now. I stuff the mushrooms into my pocket, and we press on.

We make it to the waterfront without incident. Once I step foot on the sand, I feel my body relax and my breathing slow. Somehow, for some reason, I feel safer here. It is mere moments before he comes running forward.

"I am not shielding another one of your charges," he yells at me. "I am trying to lead a revolution."

He turns his back on us and begins to storm away but I'm getting really tired of all of this. I chase after him. Within a few steps, I am able to catch him. I grab his arm, and he spins around. His eyes meet mine, and I expect to see fury, but instead I see only passion. Passion for the revolution he is leading. And I know he is supposed to hate me, but there's something about the way he looks at me. I'm not completely convinced. We are standing much too close, but neither one of us takes a step back.

"What if the Devil doesn't know he's the Devil?" I

ask.

Phoenix shakes his head, confused. "What?"

"Why? Why does the bad I've done have to define me?"

"Because you're a murdering sadist," he snaps back at me.

"No, I am not." I clench my teeth, standing my ground. I am tired of these labels I am suddenly wearing. "I never, I mean never knew what happened to those girls I led to the Lettings. I am so very sorry I played any role in this vile enterprise in which we exist, but I was clueless. Maybe I'm ignorant, or downright stupid, but I would rather have been dead than be responsible for hurting anyone. And before you go throwing malicious names around, maybe it's time you consider maybe you're wrong...? What if you kidnapped and tortured me in the name of a revolution that is wrong?"

"It's not," he argues.

"But I didn't think I was wrong, either." I am exasperated. "Don't you get it?" He takes a step back away from me, but I go on. "We are completely turned around. The only information we're fed is from a corrupt enterprise. What makes you think your information is any more accurate than mine?"

For the first time ever, he looks terrified. I let a moment go by before I gesture for Raven to come over and she hurries to my side.

"This is Raven," I say, slowly, talking to Phoenix. "She's your sister."

The color in Phoenix's face drains completely, and he looks like he has just taken a bullet to the heart. He steps back, away from the two of us, but his eyes do not divert from Raven. He never looks away from her.

"It's true," she assures him, quietly.

Phoenix just stares at her, his intense eyes soften as his brain tries to fathom what his eyes see: long black hair, tanned skin, eyes the color of the brightest summer sky. The two of them are exactly the same, and they are both strikingly beautiful.

"I couldn't have…" he starts to say, but her smile drowns out his words.

"You do. Our mother was pulled from her trip to the New World and called to the Coupling soon after you left the city. She served for quite some time, but I was her only offspring. Despite her low number of offspring, she was still honored for doing her job because she produced an O. I was brought to camp as soon as possible. They let me stay with her until I was nine because O's hadn't become extinct yet."

Phoenix just nods. "Is she in the New World now?" he asks, his voice low and unsteady.

"I don't know," Raven answers. They speak in a way I imagine could only occur between siblings. They seem to anticipate each other's words, and watching their eyes glaze over at the thought of their mother, I can tell they feel each other's pain.

"So, I'm going to ask this one time," I say, looking directly into his eyes. He looks so intense and so incredibly smart, for a moment I am lost. "Are you certain you are right about all of this?"

"Yes," he replies, his focus returning to me.

"Okay. Then I'm fighting with you." He laughs for a few moments, then composes himself and stares at me. Neither Raven nor I have moved.

"So, you're telling me these past twenty-four hours

have turned you into a rebel against the very government that honors you for your…work?" He very nearly spits the last word.

"I'm tired of being a pigeon," I yell. "And I'm tired of behaving. And I'm tired of working for the wrong cause. You said yourself, the moment you thought you lost your mother to the New World, you decided to fight. Well, I had my moment of clarity, too. I want to do something to make up for all of the wrong I've done. I want to fight with you." I keep my voice as calm as I can. I look deep into his eyes when I speak. He returns my stare, hesitating for a moment, then the anger returns.

"You can't just decide to do that." He begins to pace, back and forth, just feet away from us.

"Why not?" I ask with my eyes locked on his.

"Yeah, why not?" Raven asks, in her tiny but forceful way.

"Because you're my prisoner." Like everything we're discussing is black and white. "And you're the enemy." His voice is softer, his words filled with anguish.

"Why?" I ask.

"Why? Why? Because you're Veronica Billings. That's why."

"So what?" I ask, my voice rising. I feel the humidity of the day sneak up on us. I am drenched in sweat, standing there, staring at him, ready for my words to strike deeply somewhere inside him. And as I speak, I realize I want nothing more than to be on this boy's side. I just pray it's for the right reason.

"So what?" he asks. "So what? You're the reason I started this revolution." He takes a step back and runs his hand through his hair.

"So change your reason. Do it to change the New World, do it for revenge for your mother, do it to depose Farnsworth. I don't care. But don't do it because of me. I am incredibly unimportant."

As I speak, I notice he is staring at my mouth, watching it move.

"What?" I ask, reaching up and wiping the sweat that's accumulated on my upper lip. "Why are you looking at me like that?"

"Like what?" he barks.

Despite it all, I can tell his anger is just a defense.

"I don't know. It was just…weird. Anyway," I shake my head. "I can be your ally. No one knows the Letting process better than I do. Let me help you."

"What kind of a fool would I be if I let that happen?" he asks. "Why should I believe the great Veronica Billings is just going to jump ship and fight for the good guys? Why should I believe you?" He will not back down. "You are my sworn enemy."

"I never said I was your enemy."

"But you are. All that you stand for. Everything you believe in."

"I've never known anything else. Can't you see that?" I feel the words beginning to tighten in my throat. My voice is cracking now as I try to explain. "I was ten when I was called to the camp. I was told who I was to become and what I was to do. I never challenged anyone because I thought what they told me was right. Why wouldn't I? There was never any reason for me to doubt what happened. But once you came"—I feel heat rush to my cheeks—"you showed me I was wrong. And I want to change."

"This has to be some game you're playing—"

"It's not."

"Gunnar warned me. He said I should never be alone with you because…" His words trail off.

"Because why?"

"Because Gunnar thought my feelings for you were too violent. He kept telling me hate is too close to…" His voice thickens. "He said I was infatuated with you." He tries to laugh off the statement, but he's unsuccessful. Instead, he looks down, avoiding my eyes.

"With me?" I ask, stunned at this revelation. "Infatuated with me? But why?"

"Because you're so beautiful," offers a tiny voice. I turn, startled to see Raven still standing there.

"What?" I ask, shocked by the turn this conversation has taken.

"Because you're so beautiful," Phoenix whispers, repeating Raven's words.

My cheeks burn, and my breathing grows shallow. I look down at my feet and dig a tiny hole with my boot. I shake my head. When I look up, he is still there staring at me. His eyes are as intense as always but he looks incredibly confused. My heart aches to think I'm the one who made him like this. He looks at me quietly and with resolve. Then he steps forward and raises his hand alongside my head. Despite the bruising and the beating I took at the hands of Gunnar and Buzzcut, I don't even flinch. I draw in a breath that is longer and more deliberate. I am perfectly still as Phoenix places his hand on my cheek. He strokes it gently, letting his finger cascade softly over the bruising. He stands there, touching me for what feels like whole minutes. Then he leans in, close to me. "I'm sorry," he whispers into my ear.

"What the hell?" I hear behind me, and I whip around just in time to see Buzzcut standing there with a loaded shotgun pointed straight at me.

Chapter Nine

I can feel the electricity running through my body. It comes from an odd combination of excitement from being near Phoenix, and fear from being in the site of Buzzcut and his loaded gun. As Buzzcut bounces on his toes, I become increasingly concerned he might fire accidently.

Phoenix has stepped in front of me now, shielding both Raven and me from Buzzcut. I can see the fury in Buzzcut's eyes, but despite the intensity of the situation, my mind keeps pondering what Phoenix meant by that "sorry." Is he sorry I was beaten? Is he sorry he was wrong about me? Is he sorry he can't believe me? Or is he sorry he and I could never happen? I close my eyes and silently pray that it's not the last. Then I reprimand myself for thinking even that. When did I become a rule-breaker? Could one handsome, taboo boy change me? Should I let him? But…maybe it's another change for the better…? It is very possible this law could be wrong, too. I've always believed people should be allowed to choose who they want to be with. Just one thought of his intense blue eyes and his strong hand brushing against my cheek ever-so-softly, and I believe in freedom of choice now more than ever. I drop my eyes to the ground and will myself to stay quiet and not look at Buzzcut.

"What are you doing, man?" Buzzcut asks

Phoenix.

"I'm getting everyone to the Letting alive."

"Looks to me like you were getting chummy with the prisoner."

"Well then, you'd better reconsider what you saw."

"I saw what I saw, man," Buzzcut's bouncing grows more intense, and I fear for Phoenix's safety. "What? Were you going to kiss her?"

My head snaps up and my eyes dart to the back of Phoenix's head, looking for an answer. Was he going to kiss me? I look down at Raven. She looks calm and unshaken.

"I'm not even going to answer that," Phoenix replies.

I listen for the note of disgust in his voice, but I don't hear it. My heart lifts slightly with hope, and I know this will be my fatal flaw. Hope.

I have survived all of these years by being a machine, by doing exactly as I was told, and trying desperately not to hope for something more. And yet for the first time in seven years I feel alive, and I like the feeling. Maybe to be alive, you must have hope. Maybe it's time to stop being a good follower and to jump in with both feet. Maybe I have to take a chance and fight for something. The government has lied to me and to all of us. And this boy—this rebel leader who hates me, all that I stand for, and my very soul—this boy is giving me something to hope for once again. It's time to take a chance. Because even if there is nothing for me, even if I don't survive, maybe my sacrifice can help offer Lulu, Raven, Lilly, and Violet a better world. I know it can't make up for all the bad I've done, but at least I can do one positive act before I die. I brace myself and step out from behind Phoenix.

"I want to fight with you," I tell Buzzcut, as calmly as I can.

"What?" he asks, his face turning red.

"Veronica," Phoenix cautions, his voice trailing off sternly at the end of my name.

He tries to step in front of me again, but I move away.

"I was ignorant, yes, but I swear I didn't know what was happening to those girls I brought to the New World." I speak as plainly as I can. I look at Buzzcut to see if anything I say registers with him. He shakes his head.

"You really are a rat," he hisses, icily. "The ship's going down, and you're trying to jump on any lifeboat you can."

"That's not true," I yell.

Buzzcut lifts his shotgun and aims it directly at me.

"All right," Phoenix chides. "That's enough. Put the gun down, Eric."

Buzzcut points his gun down, but still holds it tightly. Facing countless opportunities for my death is so surreal it offers me a sense of calm. Hmm. Buzzcut's real name is Eric. Doesn't matter. I'll never think of him as anything but Buzzcut. That is, if I get away from this waterfront alive.

"So, what?" Buzzcut asks, staring at Phoenix. "You're on her side now?"

"I'm on our side." Phoenix speaks as if he's consoling a troubled child. "Just as I've always been. I am here to topple the corrupt government and end the Lettings. I want to bring equality to our world, same as I always have."

"But now your plan includes trusting the enemy?" Buzzcut asks. "This is unbelievable, Phoenix, man! Come on. After all this time, you expect us to just invite Veronica Billings into our revolution? What are you thinking, man?"

"I'm thinking we need to get to the Letting tomorrow. She will be our foot in the door."

He is interrupted by the sound of footsteps at the base of the path. We all turn to see Gunnar, Gretchen, and Lulu.

"And then what?" Gunnar asks. "Then you run off with your girlfriend?"

"I'm not answering any more of that crap," Phoenix snaps.

"You'd better start talking," Gunnar warns, lifting his gun and pointing it at Phoenix. My breathing comes faster and faster, and I turn to face Phoenix. There is something about him standing there, his dark hair disheveled and his unshaven chin dark as night. Something tells me to trust him. And every instinct I have is to protect him. Without even thinking, my body moves toward Phoenix.

"Really?" Phoenix asks Gunnar. "You're going to shoot me?"

"Why the hell not?" Gunnar asks. "Have you turned on me, Phoenix?"

"No," Phoenix bellows. "But what about you, Gunnar? Huh? We got into this to make the world a better place. All you want to do is to overpower people on your way to take over from Farnsworth."

"At least I have a plan," Gunnar growls.

"And your plan makes you as corrupt as Farnsworth." Phoenix stares down Gunnar. "I've known it for a while now. I've seen it in the way you treated Veronica. You're not after peace or making this a better world. You're after power."

"And you're not?"

"No," Phoenix responds, shrugging his shoulders.

"Then if our plans don't match," Gunnar lifts the gun higher, "I see no reason to keep you around."

"He's the leader of your revolution," I blurt, suddenly terrified.

"Shut up," Gunnar barks. "I'm not going to listen to the vile words you spew." He moves so he can point his gun at me.

At that, Phoenix draws his gun and points it at Gunnar.

"So here we are." Phoenix's voice remains relaxed as he speaks, but his muscles are taught. "You shoot her, I'll shoot you. You shoot me, she'll shoot you."

I look at Phoenix. He knows I don't have a gun, but Gunnar doesn't. I may very well have a small pistol hidden in my boot. And considering what Gunnar thinks of me, he would absolutely believe I would kill him. We stand for what feels like minutes, no one daring to move. My breath is labored and sweat pours off me like running water. Finally, I can take no more.

"Enough," I yell, stepping in between them. "Enough." And suddenly I hear the sound of another gun cock. I turn to face Buzzcut, also holding his gun. He is pointing the gun back and forth, between Gunnar, Phoenix, and me.

"So is this what you want?" I ask, turning in a circle and addressing each of them. "You want to turn on one another? You have so few people already, what would you do if you separated now?" I look directly at

Phoenix. "Even if I got you to Farnsworth's door, then what? You kill him, his army kills you, and that's the end of it. They replace him with some equally brutal, uncaring leader." I turn to Gunnar. "And you?" I look at him with disgust. "You kill Phoenix and who do you have? Her?" I ask, pointing at Gretchen. "Well, you'd better think twice about that. Every inch of that girl is a traitor. And a liar. She'll tell you whatever it is you need to hear. But don't kid yourself, Gunnar, she is as power hungry as you are."

Gunnar looks at Gretchen uneasily as I turn to Buzzcut. "That leaves you. What are you going to do alone?" Sweat continues to pour off my body. "Huh? When everyone's dead? Best you can hope for is a hyper shooting spree some distance away from Farnsworth, where you'll inevitably hit civilians, because you'll never get to Farnsworth alone. You're just not smart enough."

Buzzcut gasps and points his gun at me. In that instant, I realize what I can do. I'm sorry to break my promise and leave my girls alone, but I have no choice.

"How about you, Gunnar?" I ask with my heart racing. "You going to let Buzzcut here beat you to the prize? You've wanted to kill me from the moment you laid eyes on me. Well?" I goad him. Gunnar cocks his gun. "Good," I shout, terrified. "Good. Kill me and go back to your mission." The tears blind me as they stream down my face. "All of you need to focus on what matters here. These girls."

I point at Raven. She runs to my side, and I smile at her before pushing her behind me for safety. "Kill me, but get yourselves together and finish this revolution you started."

I push Raven toward Phoenix. She hides behind him. At that Gunnar and Buzzcut walk closer to me pointing their weapons—one at my head, and one at my heart. I turn back and smile at Raven and then at Phoenix. The prospect of impending death makes one very bold.

"That's enough." Phoenix steps forward. "No one is killing her. And we are not killing each other." He turns to face Gunnar. "Go. Take Gretchen and go."

"I won't fight for you anymore." Gunnar is resolute.

"I know," Phoenix answers him, sadly.

"What about me?" Buzzcut asks.

"You've got to make your own choice," Phoenix tells him. "You can stay with me and the revolution, but that revolution will involve Veronica, in one way or another."

"That's bogus, man."

"I'm sorry," Phoenix states, "but that's the way it's going to be."

"This is bull—" Buzzcut lifts his gun and points it directly at me. Before I realize what is happening I'm startled by the sound of a gunshot.

"Raven?" I yell out names. "Lulu? Phoenix?" I take a roll call to see if everyone I care about is okay.

Raven and Phoenix are standing there, perfectly still. But across from me, I see Lulu, her arm dangling at her side, holding a small pistol.

"Lulu?" I ask, walking toward her. "Lulu? Did you shoot him?" I point to Buzzcut who is lying on the ground.

Phoenix and Gunnar are hovering over him, attending to him. She stares past me for a long while, and then slowly, she raises her eyes up to meet mine.

"Yes," she replies quietly. "I shot him."

"Are you okay?" I ask, and she nods.

"Was it an accident?" I'm looking for any feasible explanation. How could this tiny girl possibly shoot someone?

"No," she retorts, shaking her head and finding her voice.

"But how could you want to…" My words trail off. "And how were you able to?"

"I aimed high, right between his eyes." Her words are steely, like a cold-blooded killer.

"Why, Lulu?" I search those eyes I have looked into so many times before. There has to be an answer in there.

"Because he was going to kill you," she explains. Warmth begins to battle the cold panic coursing through my veins. She is just a child, and she is protecting the one person who has taken care of her for all of these months. Me. If only Phoenix realized love is more powerful than any revolution.

"Thank you for taking care of me, Lulu, honey," I reach out my hand to stroke the side of her face. "And I love you too. But—"

Lulu's head whips away from me, and she stares up at me with disdain.

"I didn't do it because I love you." She wrinkles her nose as she speaks, as if the sight of me repulses her. "I did it because I owed you. And now we're even."

With that, she marches off to stand next to Gretchen. Gunnar and Phoenix carry Buzzcut's body deep into the woods and cover it with a pile of pine needles while I stare at Lulu. What has happened to her? Why has she turned so violently against me? Can she, as young as she is, really understand what I've done? My heart aches watching her, but I can't deny my past.

"We'll leave him in a shallow grave for now," Phoenix decides, walking toward me. He reaches up and wipes the sweat from his brow with the back of his wrist. Every muscle in his forearm flexes with this action, and I sigh despite myself. "I'll come back after dark and bury him properly." Raven nods, understanding him and everything he does, completely.

Gunnar walks over to us. "I really hope you've made the right decision by taking off with your little family there." He sneers at Raven and me.

"Ditto," Phoenix quips, nodding toward Gretchen and Lulu.

Gunnar turns in their direction and then back to Phoenix. His face is red and his breath is hurried. He looks like he is about to say something but instead he turns and storms off toward the woods. He takes just two or three steps and then turns back. He walks up to Phoenix and they stand, toe to toe.

"Just remember..." Gunnar glares at Phoenix. "She's the enemy. Be careful who you trust," he warns, then spins on his heels and makes for the woods, quickly.

Gretchen looks at me, turns, and runs after him. Lulu follows. The three of them may be moving in the same direction, but they are in no way together.

I realize Phoenix is staring at me, and I meet his gaze. "What do we need to do to get you to the Letting?" he asks. His words surprise me. I had momentarily forgotten about the Letting tomorrow.

"Uh," I blurt, caught off guard. "I need to go back to camp. With Raven." I look down at her. "I need to get to my two girls whom Gretchen abandoned. And I'll have to come up with an excuse for Gretchen and Lulu." Phoenix nods.

"What happens in the morning?" he asks.

"We'll be woken before reveille and brought immediately to a waiting vehicle. Inside the truck, they'll give us tons of fluids and protein bars. We'll do calisthenics to get the blood pumping. The ride feels endless."

"Any idea how long?"

"I guess five, maybe six hours?"

He nods, thinking.

"We take a pit stop somewhere along the way, about halfway through the trip. We go to a deserted building on the side of the road. The bathrooms are still in working order."

"What happens when you arrive? Do you know where you go?"

"We drive straight up to a large white building with a vast covered entrance, and we're greeted by people in white suits. No one talks much. They just walk us over to the Prep Station where they do a quick finger prick to check for type and toxicity. I'll never pass that."

Phoenix nods again.

"Then they'll take us into the building that has sliding front doors. There will be a lot of hustle and bustle, and people rushing in every direction. Some of the people wear masks on their faces. Most of the girls are terrified when they get there. Coming from the peacefulness of camp, it seems like chaos."

He is watching me now, hanging on my every word.

"After that," I shrug, "I'm afraid I'm no help."

"Why not?"

"They never let me into the building. I just go as far as drop off."

Phoenix nods once again, and then he squats down, his gun slung casually over his shoulder. He picks up a small twig that was lying on the beach and begins to make marks in the sand. The twig is too delicate for his needs, but he is patient and gentle with it, and he is able to coax the twig to go in the direction he wants. Silently I watch him, staring at his markings, trying to decipher the map or plan he is creating. It is not until he makes the long flowing strokes I see the outline of the hair.

I step back to get the full perspective, and that's when I realize the picture he has drawn on the sand is of me. And it is stunning. Without ever looking up at me, he has created an amazing likeness. All from memory. How could he know my face so well? Raven squats down next to him and reaches into the sand with her finger. She adds the hollows I have under my cheekbones. Then she dusts her hands off and looks over at Phoenix. The two of them smile at each other before they stand up.

Phoenix stares down at the ground, looking at the picture. "Here is the face that started a revolution," he says, solemnly. He looks over at me then back down to his drawing. "I sincerely hope it is the face that can finish it, too."

Chapter Ten

I hate being alone in my cabin tonight, the night before a Letting. My Letting. Tomorrow is my first Letting, and I have no one to count on. No one to trust. If Gretchen is right, and they decide they can clean my blood, and they actually Let me, who will help me recuperate? Sometimes the girls are given a few days to recoup in the Infirmary at the Letting site, other times they are shipped back to me the next day or even that night.

I have spent many days and nights hand-feeding exhausted little girls who were too tired to lift their heads from their pillows. What if that happens to me? I steel myself against the thought. If they drain me and leave me for dead, I will have to rally. There is no choice. Because even if I've decided my life is unimportant, I am now fighting for something much greater: the revolution and the safety of Lulu, Raven, Violet, Lilly, and any of the little girls who come along after them.

I roll over in my bed and stare at Gretchen's empty cot. The silence in our room makes me miss her terribly. My minds reels with all of the times she and I had stayed awake well past taps, giggling, and talking about our plans once we were free to go to the New World. She never seemed to have as many desires as I did. I wanted to walk up and down streets in bustling towns, peering into shop windows, saying "hello" to complete strangers as we pass. Most of all, I wanted to be with my mother. To be held by her while she told me stories of her wonderful life in the New World and all the exciting things she's planned for us to do together.

When we were little Gretchen would giggle along with me. She talked about the candy that grew on trees, and she talked about these small, maybe mythical, creatures people would keep in their houses as pets. Some minute fluffy versions of the wolves that patrol these woods or the wild dogs the rebels capture and train to kill. But as we grew older, my desires never varied, although Gretchen culled hers down to one single word: freedom. She wanted the freedom to live her life as she wanted. I guess, lying here now, I see how obvious it should have been. How she had left me all those years ago, but I never bothered to notice.

The thought sickens me, and I stand, fighting to keep down my dinner of liver and spinach. I peer out the window of my cabin, although there's no reason to believe Margaret will come in here to check up on Gretchen and Lulu. She's terrified that the illness I've claimed they have is contagious.

Standing here, in the thick silence of the hot summer night, I see something. I can't quite make out what it is, but there are lights, far in the distance. I watch, transfixed, and see that the lights bounce in time with the rhythm of the road. Closer and closer, they come at an unprecedented speed, and there is no mistaking what I see are four sets of headlights, making their way directly toward me.

My heart races as I walk in circles around my cabin, wondering what to do. My breathing is hurried and forced. Have they found out what I've done? Are they coming for me because I've released Lulu? Have they discovered I'm a traitor? Did Gunnar tell them? Gretchen? Or worse…was it him?

It couldn't be him.

I think of his tall, muscled body standing next to mine. I think of his bright blue eyes and his tousled hair. I think of how my eyes drink him in whenever he is near, and how my body is willingly engulfed by his scent. I think of how protected I feel around him. It couldn't be Pheonix who sold me out. And that thought matters way more than it should. Somehow, while I watch the trucks gaining on me, I feel inexplicably and inappropriately relaxed.

I think, maybe I should run. But where would I go?

I know nothing but this camp. It's all I've ever known. And what would that do to my girls? Just the thought of them makes my stomach ache. I need to get to the girls before these trucks get to me. But I'm too late.

I peer out the window again and I see four army green, covered vehicles parked crisscrossed in the middle of the camp grounds. Suddenly, I hear the screech of a siren and the echo of a bullhorn.

"Veronica Billings," the voice bellows through the bullhorn. "Veronica Billings, please report to the camp office immediately."

There is no point in prolonging the inevitable. Despite the heat, I pull on a sweater, thinking there may be a time I'll need it. I walk to my cabin door and push it open with one hand. My other hand remains clenched in a fist, tightly by my side.

Steadily, I walk out into light that is brighter than

high noon. The vehicles headlights are shining directly into the cabins. Most of the girls are awake and have wandered out to see what the commotion is.

I walk forward, my arms raised, my hands shielding my eyes from the light and the situation.

"There she is," someone yells, pointing at me. There are people dressed in plain cotton brown pants and shirts all around me. I recognize them immediately, and judging from the way the girls are huddled together, they do as well. The brown suits can only mean one thing: Harvesters. But why would the Harvesters want me?

"I'm Veronica Billings," I announce, stepping forward. People begin to surround me. There are words and phrases said in random order, and I find it difficult to follow them.

"At least she's tall," one says. "A lot to give."

"Isn't her blood toxic?" asks another.

"We should warn the Lettors when they administer the test," adds yet another, and they go on and on with this incessant random talking. Best I can make out, they haven't come because they've found out I'm a traitor to my government, they have come to Let me early.

I find myself being led toward the back of an opened vehicle. Someone stands to the side and opens a canvas flap on the back of the truck. I think someone motions for me to step up into the vehicle but I can't be sure. Another someone uses too much force to nudge me on the shoulder, and I stumble forward.

Several of the girls gasp.

"Stop that," commands a voice I recognize. My head snaps in his direction, and I see Phoenix dressed in the same brown uniform as the others. He looks at me briefly and then away immediately, as if he has no idea who I am. As if we have no history. As if he never stroked my cheek so very gently.

My thoughts get away from me. Is this boy I fell for not a revolutionary at all, but rather a Harvester? Does he work for the corrupt government he claims he's fighting against? Have I delivered not one, but two little girls, directly into his care only for them to be destroyed prematurely? It can't be. Not him. My knees buckle beneath me.

"Be careful with her," Phoenix tells the others. "This is Veronica Billings. One of the only remaining O's, and the personal donor for Principal Leader Farnsworth."

Some mumbling ensues.

"And if that's not enough..." Phoenix adds. The other Harvesters' attention is rapt, hinging on his every word. "And if that's not enough," he repeats for emphasis, "this is the girl who has delivered more young girls to the Lettings than any other person in history. She is a highly decorated government employee."

His words work their magic because suddenly everyone is much more respectful and courteous.

"That's better." Phoenix puts out his hand to lead me into the back of the waiting vehicle. He makes eye contact only for a moment but instead of sending a thrill through me, his look breaks my heart. Because those words he has just spoken to force the others to give me respect, are the exact same words that cause him to hate me.

I step inside. It's hot and musty, and I'm somewhat glad we're making the trip at night. It would be unbearable during the heat of the day.

The truck is mostly empty. I see only some bench seating, a couple of closed storage boxes, and an impenetrable steel wall separating me and the driver. My eyes dart to the canvas flap at the back of the truck, and I can't help but wonder if Phoenix will be riding with me. Of course, he won't. What a ridiculous thing to imagine. Why would he? And much more importantly, why is he here? I sit down on one of the hard benches lining the wall and wait. I wait for my girls and for some guidance, but the waiting is brutal.

Finally, the back flap opens again and Phoenix climbs in. He sits on one of the hard benches opposite me. The breeze he makes as he walks by feels magical against my burning skin. I feel my eyes widen with anticipation, and I can't help but stare at him. Even in the ugly brown uniform of the Harvesters, he still looks enticing.

Phoenix leans forward until he rests his forearms on his legs. His fingers intertwine, and he places his head against them. He looks exhausted. Whole minutes go by like this, until I can take no more.

"Where are the girls?" I ask.

He shakes his head. "Coming now, I think."

I nod, suddenly feeling pressed for time.

"Are you a Harvester?" I ask. There is no time for tact.

"What?" He looks up at me.

"Your uniform." I nod to his clothing.

"Well they weren't going to let me on board in camouflage, carrying a shotgun." For a moment, he smiles, and I feel myself smile too. "Really?" he asks, after a few seconds. He stares at me. "You could believe I'm a Harvester?"

"You fit in. No one questioned you. You're here even though this is a surprise pick-up." He nods.

"They change the Harvesters often. And I know when the pick-ups happen because of my spies on the inside."

"Spies?" I ask, amazed.

"Well, spy." He looks down and shuffles his feet. "One of my team infiltrated the compound and reports back to me. It's the best I've got."

"It's something." I try to sound encouraging despite the odds stacked against him. "So why did they send Harvesters tonight?"

"Don't know. Maybe because the Harvesters are used to working round the clock," he's thinking out loud. "And there's something so cold about them..."

"Yes," I agree. The slightest chill runs through my body at the thought of the Harvesters. I am suddenly ten years old again, watching crying girls being pulled from their mothers' arms. "They are cold enough not to be swayed from doing their jobs, and trusted to deliver the last batches of O's."

"Probably." Phoenix looks up at me.

"And I guess I'm being harvested again." I shudder, and he gives me a small smile.

"What's the plan?" I ask, changing the subject. "I mean our plan."

Phoenix just looks away. "Phoenix?" I ask again, much more softly. But his lack of response tells me all I need to know.

He's not going forward with me, and he never planned to. Not even when he told Gunnar and Buzzcut the revolution would include me. All he needs from me is a way in. That's as far as my contribution goes. This last act of chivalry he showed outside the truck was not because he cared about me. It was a peace-offering. It was the most he could do. He is making sure I am shown some respect before I am disposed of. Despite the heat, chills begin to run through my body, and I can't stop shaking.

"When was the last time you slept?" he asks me.

"I have no idea." He walks to a small chest in the back of the truck and pulls out a blanket. I recognize the plain brown blanket. It's the same as the blankets that are often wrapped around the girls when they are returned to me. He tosses the blanket to me. It lands in my lap, heavily. The material scratches my hands as I wrap it around me. I am itchy and uncomfortable, but I'd put up with anything to get rid of these chills.

"You should sleep," he urges, and I agree.

"The girls. I'll sleep when they come." He nods and looks away, and then he looks back at me, intensely.

"You really do love them, don't you?"

"Yes." I could go into an explanation about how they are my family. And how we share a bond. And how I love to watch them learn and grow. But I don't need to say any of that. He already understands it all. So instead, I return his stare. I feel my cheeks flush but I refuse to turn away.

He stands and walks over to me. He sits next to me, and between us he leaves barely enough room to breathe. It doesn't matter anyway, because I'm unable to draw a breath, and I wouldn't want to break the purity of the moment by breathing. I sit, my body tense, my chills replaced with warmth that radiates throughout my body. I toss the blanket off, and he reaches behind me to help me pull the blanket back, away from me. He leaves his arm there, behind me. It feels so good I close my eyes, trying to remember this feeling, this moment, forever. His arm draws nearer to my waist, and he raises his hand to my back. He lets it slide gracefully up to my shoulder. His hand lingers on my shoulder, and he caresses it gently. He leans into me, and I feel his warmth surrounding me. I feel the energy emitting from his body and mine, simultaneously. I am certain there is an electrical current running back and forth between us, charging both of our bodies. He turns to me and places his free hand under my chin, gently guiding it upward. I look up at him, his eyes staring deeply into mine.

"What am I doing?" he asks, tucking a piece of hair behind my ear.

"Whatever it is," I say, quietly, "please don't stop."

He smiles at me, and softly, he touches his lips to mine. His kiss is so gentle I have to wonder if it even happened. But it did happen. The pull my body feels toward him proves that to me. His lips linger as my breath rushes in and out of my mouth. My body aches to press up against his, to feel his arms wrap around me, his mouth lock tightly against mine. Instead, he pulls back. Suddenly, his eyes grow dark, and he looks away. He sits up, straight.

"I'm sorry." He stands, running his hands through his hair.

"Don't be—"

I am interrupted by the sounds of three little bodies climbing into the back of the truck. Raven pops her head in first and rushes straight for me. She wraps her arms around me and hugs me, tightly. I look up at

Phoenix who is watching us, and I feel the situation careening out of control. I feel our moment slip away, only to be replaced by infinite, dark sadness.

"Why is Phoenix here?" Raven asks. Violet and Lilly push themselves up against me as well. We are all huddled together.

"He is here to make sure you three are taken care of," I explain, never really knowing the reason myself. "But Raven, it's really important you don't let anyone know you know him, okay?" She nods. "Please don't even tell anyone his name."

"Okay."

And I know, like her brother, she understands the gravity of the situation. She won't make a mistake. My concern is he thinks he did.

Phoenix leaves out the back of the truck, and there is nothing I can do to stop him. My only focus needs to be on these girls and getting them to survive this Letting. I must pull myself together and do exactly that. Immediately, I go to work hunting down bottles of water to keep them cool and hydrated. The water bottles are tucked in a cooler hidden beneath a seat. This truck is so much smaller than the vehicles I'm used to being conveyed in, I know the ride will seem endless. The best I can hope for is that we can all sleep.

The truck engine starts with a rumble, and my body shakes from fear and vibration. So here we go. I don't know what I expected to happen with Phoenix, but it will be me alone caring for these girls, as it always is.

I get the girls all settled in, and the truck starts to shimmy and then move forward in a slow roll. I sit back, my head pressed against the canvas side, and close my eyes. Suddenly, the back flap of the truck bursts open and Phoenix barges through. He stumbles in, panting and out of breath from chasing a moving vehicle.

I smile at him beside myself. He smiles back.

"Let's go start a revolution," he says to me, holding his hand out for me.

"All right." I place my hand in his. Gently he pulls me to my feet and my body falls forward. He catches me with his body and wraps his arm around me. Together, we move along with the truck, shakily and bumpily, into the unknown.

Chapter Eleven

An hour into the ride, I have all the girls as comfortable as possible, asleep on the floor of the truck. I know I need to sleep, but there is no way I am giving up one second of my time with Phoenix. It is just us now, quietly sitting side by side on the hard bench of the moving truck. He holds my hand, protectively. There are so many things we should discuss, so many things we should ask each other, but instead, we sit, both of us pretending we are not who we are. Both of us wishing tomorrow would never come.

I hear something buzz by and lift my free hand to wave it away. Then I feel a sharp quick pain on my thigh. I reach down and smack my leg, hard. "Ow," I complain, itching the spot where I was just pricked.

"What is it?" Phoenix asks, leaning over to see.

"Can't imagine. Feels like a little piece of glass pricked me." I look at my thigh and see a small round red spot swelling up. It gets itchier as it grows.

"Looks like a mosquito bite to me," he says. I scratch at the spot furiously. "Don't scratch." He grabs my hand. "Scratching it makes it worse. Didn't you ever learn that?"

"I've never been bitten before."

"Never?" he asks, looking at me with disbelief. "You've lived in a camp in the deep woods for seven years, and you've never had a mosquito bite?"

"Never. They've never been interested in me. Until now." Reluctantly, I break free of his grasp to scratch.

"That's enough." He takes both of my hands again. "The itching will stop soon. Until then..." He forms his fingers into the shape of an okay sign and quickly flicks his forefinger against the bite.

"Ow! That hurt."

"Yeah? How's the itching?"

"Better," I admit, hardly believing it.

He smiles at me, still holding both of my hands.

"I won't scratch again. You can let go. I mean...if you want to."

"Don't want to." His smile grows wider.

"Good." He has both of my hands in his one hand, and he reaches over to intertwine all of his fingers around mine. Suddenly, he drops my hands and stands.

"The truck's slowing. I thought you said they stop at the halfway point?" He is confused.

"Always." Panic begins to rise within me. Phoenix walks to the back of the truck and pulls the flap to one side. He peers out the back.

"Pretend you're asleep," he whispers, turning back to me. Immediately, I drop to the ground and lay next to Raven. If I wake her, I can trust her to stay calm. I fight to quiet my breathing. Phoenix huddles to the side of the canvas flap and watches everything that's happening.

The truck rolls to a stop, and I squeeze my eyes shut tighter. Through my closed lids, I see light flash, and I know another truck has joined us. I feel myself go limp, as if I have just encountered an angry bear. Outside, I hear hurried voices.

"Let's go," one voice shouts. "Now. Now. Now."

Suddenly I hear a deafening sound, like a huge machine hovering over us. I can't help myself. I sit up like a bolt. Phoenix looks at me, and I can see the distress on his face. Bright lights seem to envelop our truck, and all three girls wake up, scared and crying. I do my best to comfort them as we try to make out the situation. The noise grows louder, and it sounds like a giant fan, whirling above us. Through the opened flap, I catch a glimpse of a machine that seems to fall from the sky, yet touch the ground gracefully. I have a sinking feeling in my stomach that tells me the machine is for me.

"Get up and do exactly as I say." Phoenix's voice is hurried. I nod. "Pick up the girls like I've had you up and prepped for a while. They're taking you to Farnsworth in a helicopter. Must be an emergency." He faces out the back of the truck again.

He turns back and must see the look of confusion on my face. "A helicopter? No?" he asks.

I shake my head. Until this moment, I had no idea what a helicopter was.

"That sound you hear is its rotor. Like a propeller." He speaks to me like I'm a child, and I feel my face flush. I hate being uneducated. "Now get the girls ready and wait for my instructions."

I try to shake off my embarrassment. Quickly, I grab the girls' packs and throw them over my shoulder. I lift Lilly and Violet and carry one on each hip. Raven stays tightly against me, her small hand laced around my forearm. My muscles strain from lifting both girls. We stand at the back of the truck, ready to follow whatever direction Phoenix gives us.

I hear arguing outside. "I was told only the one girl," someone hollers.

"It's the pilot of the helicopter," Phoenix whispers loudly to me. The voices outside are shouting to be heard above the sound of the helicopter's rotor.

"I've got a truck full, and I'm not going back," another man yells. He must be the driver of the truck.

"Set 'em free," the pilot snaps. I watch Phoenix's breathing grow faster and shallower.

"They're O's," the driver of the truck argues. "No way. I was told to deliver the O's, and that's what I'm going to do." Phoenix hops out of the back of the truck, and we make our way to where Phoenix was standing only seconds before. I peer out the back flap and can see everything.

"I'm Veronica Billing's escort," Phoenix yells. "Assigned by Farnsworth."

"Bull," the pilot yells back. "I ain't heard nuthin' 'bout no escort—"

"Call him and ask him," Phoenix bluffs. He sounds remarkably like me when I was trying to escape Margaret. It seems we are both natural born liars. I sigh. That thought makes me very uncomfortable. The sweat rolls down my back, but I pull the girls closer to me. Phoenix continues. "I was told to deliver Veronica Billings and three little girls. They are the last remaining O's."

"I was never told nuthin' 'bout little girls," the pilot claims. "But I was looking forward to meetin' the big one. Heard she's quite somethin'. Like a wild goddess of the woods. Spend a little time alone wit' her. Gettin' to know her."

Before I can even gasp, Phoenix grabs the helicopter pilot by the throat and lifts him off the ground. Every muscle in Phoenix's body strains, yet he seems to carry the man effortlessly. Phoenix walks the man backward, dangerously close to the whirling tail rotor.

"What did you just say?" Phoenix shouts. "Say it again."

"Sorry, man. Sorry."

I can see the man gasping for air, and I wonder how far Phoenix will go. Phoenix backs him a tiny bit closer to the rotor.

"Shut your eyes," I whisper to the girls.

"All right. Sorry," the pilot screams. Phoenix lets him go and the pilot drops to the ground, clutching his throat. He fights to breathe.

"Fine." The pilot acquiesces. "What do I care?"

Phoenix backs away and motions to me. I walk out with all three girls in tow.

"Watch your heads, but get in the helicopter, please," Phoenix directs without making eye contact.

I keep my head down and tuck the girls' faces low against my shoulders. I squeeze the muscles in my forearm so Raven knows I have her. I rush the girls past the watchful eyes of the pilot and the other men, into the opened door of the helicopter. Once we are seated, Phoenix climbs in after us. He hands us each a headset to put over our ears. Once the girls have theirs on safely, I look at Phoenix. He is staring at me, unhappily.

"What?" I ask. It is a stupid question, but it's all I have.

"That is the reason I never wanted to meet you. Ever." He turns and looks out the window. I can't help it. I feel my eyes flood with tears. Phoenix turns back to me, his eyes wide with wonder. I blink the tears away and stare out the window myself.

We take off moments later, and if it wasn't for the fact the boy I care so deeply about hates me again, and for the fact I could be heading to certain death, I might actually enjoy the ride—especially because it's a beautifully clear night, without the threat of even one single raindrop.

The moment we lift off from the ground Raven reaches over and squeezes my hand. Phoenix looks at us quizzically, and I don't know if his confusion is because of the relationship I have with Raven, or because he is unused to girls and how we can care so very deeply about each other. Well, most of us anyway. Lilly and Violet are glued to the window, and together we all watch the only world we have ever known grow smaller and smaller beneath us. It is definitely a direct metaphor of our immediate life. Everything we knew before will seem miniscule compared to what we are up against now.

Lilly and Violet turn back to me, unsure of how they should feel about the ride. It is dark out, but every now and again, they can catch a shadow of something or a light coming from somewhere else. I smile at them. Why not let them enjoy something in their small, hard lives. For all three of the girls, it is the first time any of them has ever experienced flying. For me, it's my second time. The first was in the truck with Phoenix at my side. Just the thought of the ride in the truck brings a smile to my face, and Phoenix, who's been staring at me, smiles back.

Even though I don't know what a flight in a helicopter is supposed to feel like, I think we're having an unusually bumpy ride. I assume it's because of the altercation between Phoenix and the pilot. I keep a watchful eye on the girls, but they all seem to be enjoying themselves and even the bumps give them a thrill. Despite it all, the ride relaxes us enough so we're all smiling at one another. Whenever he sees a light or makes out a shape, Phoenix points to it out the window for the girls. It feels like we are one big, happy family. I know he feels it too, because he reaches across and takes my hand. My hand almost hurts from the spark his touch causes. I smile at him, relieved and thrilled, but he just seems more intense than ever. In my heart, I hope his intensity is not only because of the revolution, but also because he's now fighting for people he cares about.

Phoenix notices our descent first, and I only know it's happening because I read it on his face. He sits up straight and wears a grim expression. I can feel our drop now, and the girls also seem to understand what's happening. They begin to get nervous but try to calm themselves.

The cab of the helicopter grows very quiet as we all strain to see what we can make out on the ground below. I fight to see something, anything familiar, but of course, I won't recognize anything from up here. Closer and closer, we draw toward the ground, and then I see the familiar white building. It sickens me. I feel light-headed, and a cold sweat breaks out across my forehead as I stare at the building.

What have I done? How many girls have I delivered to this very building? Girls who were simply exterminated when they were no longer useful? I feel the bile churn in my stomach and cramps form on the sides of my abdomen. I look at Phoenix. What am I doing? Why should I deserve to be happy after what

I've done? What I've been responsible for?

Luckily Phoenix reads my expression, and he hands me a bag just before I vomit. He gives me a small bottle of water to rinse my mouth. He looks at me, and this time it's a look of sympathy.

I don't deserve it. No more. I cannot stand back and let Phoenix take the lead any longer. I am responsible for so many atrocious acts. I must be held accountable…if only to myself.

The way Phoenix looks at me, attentive and curious, I know he can tell I have gone somewhere without him. He shakes his head, but it's no use. We touch ground, and I know I must do this alone.

They cut the engine.

"Whatever happens," I say hurriedly. "Take care of the girls."

"We're in this together." His voice is strong and powerful.

"No." I shake my head. "As much as I wish that were true. I know I can never make amends for what I've done, but I have to try."

"By killing yourself?" He raises his voice and the vibration feels like the helicopter engine.

Lilly looks up at me with frightened eyes. I stroke her hair and speak in a calming voice. "I don't know how. But I have to try."

"We can change the world by stopping Farnsworth."

"Maybe."

"Were you planning this all along?" His eyes are sharp and intense. "Did you outsmart me? Did you only get me here to watch the girls? Were you planning to give yourself up from the start?"

"No." I search his eyes. "At least, I don't think so. I can't imagine me ever being able to outsmart you."

"Don't fool yourself, Ronnie. You are a very bright young woman."

I smile at him. There's no way he could know how much that compliment means to me.

"So what's the plan?" he asks me, only half-joking.

"Like you said, we came by helicopter because it's an urgent situation. To stay alive I have to get past the testing station. If, by some miracle I've been cleared, they'll prep me and Let me immediately."

The girls snuggle up tightly against me, and I remember I have to be careful of what I say. "After that, they'll either keep me around for another Letting, or they won't." I allow the reality to sink in. "If they don't, that's how it's meant to be, and you do whatever it takes to get these girls to a safe place."

He looks away and then at me, fervently. He nods.

"And if they do Let me and decide to keep me around, I will find my girls." Emotion overwhelms me.

"And I will find you," he promises, his eyes locked on me. I shake my head no, yet his words make me feel safe and protected.

"What's the next step for you?" I ask. My throat aches from the tears I'm fighting.

"You've already gotten me farther than I ever imagined."

"Assassinating Farnsworth won't do anything. You'll be arrested and killed. And that won't accomplish anything." I say these words deliberately, making sure he understands he cannot sacrifice himself like this. "Farnsworth needs to disappear quietly."

"But you know that can't happen," Phoenix argues.

"He's too well guarded. And loved."

I nod.

"Then you'll need to go public. You'll need to tell people in the Inferno what you're doing. And you'll need to get them to believe you."

"I know." He looks out the window, thoughtfully, and then back at me. "That's the part I haven't quite worked out."

We exchange a small smile, both of us knowing this may very well be the last time we ever see each other.

Harvesters and people in white coats begin running toward the helicopter, and my heart sinks.

Phoenix reaches out and grabs my hand. "For what it's worth, I don't know I would have done anything differently if I were in your place."

I gasp, tears of relief bursting into my eyes. Spontaneously, I lean forward and kiss him. He reaches up and grabs the back of my head. He pulls me toward him, and kisses me, long and hard. It is such a taboo move, we could only risk it because we're skirting death.

When we finally pull apart, I speak, hurriedly. "They'll take us to type us and authenticate our blood first thing. If I'm cleared, they'll walk me through that double front door. More than likely, I won't, and they'll bring me to a waiting truck, over there." I point to a field behind him. "If you see me head to that truck, you know it's over for me. Please get the girls to safety before you do anything else—"

"No. I'll follow the truck."

"And then you'll be shot, and we'll both be dead. And who's going to look after the girls?" My heart pounds.

He knows I'm right because he can't look at me.

"Can you promise me?" I ask. "Can you promise me you'll just let me go?"

"No." He looks straight at me. "But I will promise not to follow the truck."

I understand him completely, and I smile at him. He smiles back just as the helicopter door is flung open.

Chapter Twelve

I wish they would just leave me alone. Ever since my blood has been cleared at the check point, I have had a bevy of attendants doing nothing but working on me and my veins. As I lie here with them massaging my neck and pushing against my veins, I wonder how it is even possible my blood cleared. I was checked before I blossomed, and my blood registered toxic and unusable. Can blood change after a blossoming?

I'm wearing a white paper gown that is much too short on me, and I shiver in the cold, sterile room. Camp isn't exactly one of the palaces people tell me exist in the Inferno, but at least most everything at camp is green, and it's blooming with nature and life. This room has white walls, a white ceiling, and a hard, gray floor. It's empty except for the table I'm lying on, several small collection bins lined up on a steel cart with rolling wheels, and a large machine, that is the focus of the room. The machine has a confusing number of buttons and knobs, and several tubes extending out from its front. I know what those tubes are for, and I can barely look at them. Then I remember Gretchen's warnings of multiple draw sites, and I cringe. I squeeze the rubber balls they've placed in my hands harder, and I wonder how many tubes will be attached to me and how much blood they'll decide to take. It doesn't matter. They should take it all. My heart falls when I think of how many tiny girls I sent to this fate, and how terrified they must have been to have any one of those tubes sucking the blood out of their tiny bodies, let alone several tubes at once. I think of Lilly, Violet, and Raven somewhere in another room, and I wonder if they are going through the same thing right now. If they are, I pray at least they are together. My primary concern is Lilly, who is not physically big enough to Let, yet in my gut, I believe they'll do it anyway.

Someone pushes hard against a vein above my collarbone and I gasp. It's not that anything is really painful right now. It's the anticipation of what's to come that is terrifying. This would be so much easier if I still believed this was my patriotic duty, and I was performing an act that could help my country. I sigh, disgusted with myself and my gullibility. How could I have believed their lies for so long? My mind wanders to Phoenix. Why didn't he stop me sooner? And what did he mean there was a reason he never wanted to meet me? What was it?

The Lettors must have made their decision because they remove the balls from my hands and stop prodding me. For a moment, they leave me alone and become very busy with the knobs and buttons on the machine. One of them places tiny, sticky pads with long thin wire tails onto various parts of my body: my heart, my collarbone, my stomach, my arms, my inner thighs, and the tops of my feet. Those long tails are attached to a small machine next to the head of my bed. They flip a switch on the machine, and I brace myself, expecting to feel an electric current. Or worse. But I feel nothing. I turn my head slightly and see a screen flashing with what looks like spikes on a graph. I realize the spikes are in time with my heartbeat. I take a deep breath and relax slightly. If they are concerned with my heartbeat, they must be planning to keep me alive. My survival instinct is happy, but my guilty conscience prefers this would just end.

Next, I feel something cold and wet on the inside of both my arms and the top of my right foot. I recognize the smell, and I realize they must be cleaning the draw sites with alcohol. The coward in me relaxes with the thought of only three spots. They are going to draw from only three spots. This is okay. I can handle three. It could be so much worse. With every movement they make, I realize my survival instinct is much stronger than I ever imagined. Of course, I want to live, but do I deserve to?

I overhear one Lettor telling another my veins are good and strong. There is some general murmuring among them, but most seem completely disinterested in me. Then, for some reason, I hear a voice that grabs my attention, and I turn my head to see one of the Lettors speaking into a box on the wall. He holds up his hand to silence the other Lettors, and the room grows very still.

"Are you sure?" the speaking Lettor asks. He turns away from the wall and addresses the other Lettors. "He's coming," he proclaims with complete disbelief in his voice. "Farnsworth. Here. Now. He wants to meet her."

The Lettors are suddenly frozen. Something in what this one speaking Lettor has said paralyzes the rest of them. Only one moves. A young female Lettor turns to me with a look that is a combination of awe and respect.

"Well don't just stand there," the speaking Lettor snaps. "Let's look alive."

I cringe at his words.

Suddenly, there is an unexpected buzzing in the room. Lettors begin moving machines and polishing metal. Some open cabinets. One of the Lettors runs to me and places a small, soft pillow beneath my head. I never even knew they had pillows in these rooms. Why wouldn't they have used one before? I am still shivering in the cold, so someone tosses a soft white blanket over me. Immediately, I grow warmer. Someone else places a silver reflecting blanket on top of that and my chills disappear. Within minutes, I begin to perspire under the blankets, but I don't dare move. Then it all stops as quickly as it started, and the Lettors line up along the far wall opposite the door. They stand, their stiff bodies held straight from head to foot. Moments later, the door to my room is pushed open and three people enter, each dressed in black. One is a woman carrying a clipboard, and the two others are very tall men, both wearing dark glasses.

The men take a sweep around the room and one says only: "All clear."

My breath is hurried. I cannot believe I am actually meeting Farnsworth. I've never even seen a picture of him. Many of us outside the Inferno have no idea what he looks like. He is known for using a large voice but a small presence. The woman walks out of my room and comes back in, pushing a young man in a wheelchair. I gasp, startled, finding it hard to believe this is Farnsworth. Similarly, he seems to do a double take when he sees me.

"You must be the great Veronica Billings," he

muses, smiling at me. "May I say the picture I have of you does not do you justice."

I wonder how he is able to overlook my facial bruising, that is still so obvious. His smile catches me off-guard, but I offer a small smile back. I can't seem to force my eyes away from him. I have never before seen teeth so white. I am incredibly awkward lying on the cold steel bed, but I am wearing a short, flimsy gown and I don't want to risk standing. Besides, I'm still attached to the sticky pads and wires. I'm not sure of what to do, and I think he can sense it.

"You needn't get up." He speaks softly. "What you are doing for me now is more than generous. It would be impossible to show me any greater respect than by what you're doing here."

I nod, completely confused. He speaks as if this, any of this, was a choice. One of the Lettors coughs, and I believe it's a prompt for me.

"It's my honor, sir," I eke out, forcing down a nauseating feeling gnawing at my stomach. I am eternally grateful Phoenix is not here to witness this interaction. Farnsworth smiles generously at me then he turns to the woman behind him and says something I cannot hear. She wheels him forward, closer to my bedside. I turn my head in his direction and there is an immediate intimacy between us I detest. He sits for whole moments, staring at me. I steal a look at him as well, and I am so very surprised by what I see. For one, he is so much younger than I imagined. He's older than me or Phoenix, but he's certainly not past his mid-twenties. For another, he doesn't look like the slimy lizard I expected. In fact, I wouldn't say he's handsome, but he's very "pretty." His hair is blond and fairly long with light highlights, and it frames his face just right. His cheekbones are slight but well-shaped, his eyes are small and hazel, and his chin is nearly as smooth as mine. It's hard to believe he is the same gender as Phoenix; Phoenix with his twelve-hour-old scruff that scratches my chin when he kisses me. Ah, Phoenix. Just the thought of him makes my cheeks flush and I'm certain Farnsworth thinks my blush is for him. Farnsworth smiles again and lifts his arm to scratch a spot on his hairless chin. I am fascinated by Farnsworth's femininity. I know he could never shave; it would be much too dangerous for him. So he must be naturally hairless. Looking him over again, I believe it. Yes, I was right. He is definitely more pretty than he is handsome.

"Veronica." He speaks in a voice made more for whispering into a lover's ear than it was to bark commands. "How can I ever thank you?" I stare at him long and hard.

How about you stop killing children? is all I can think. But I can't bring myself to say it. He smiles again and it turns my stomach. How can someone so innocent looking be responsible for such atrocities? This man, a man confined to a wheelchair, so soft spoken and polite, this is the cold-blooded killer Phoenix has warned me about? Is Phoenix certain? Of course he is. I shake my head to stay focused. I may not know a lot of things, but I am sure in the case of Farnsworth, looks can be deceiving.

"It is my patriotic duty, sir," I whisper. "And I am grateful to assist in any way possible."

"Ah yes." He sits back. "The unshakable Veronica Billings. Even facing a fate that would scare most young women, you are forever gracious and proper."

"Thank you, sir." I choke back my hatred. "But I have sent hundreds of young women, many several years younger than me, all to this Letting facility. What kind of a hypocrite would I be if I was scared? After all of the reassurance I've given them?" He looks at me out of the corner of his eye and then focuses on the floor for a moment. He nods.

"But still." He looks back at me, his smile plastic, his voice flowing like honey. "Confined to a camp as you've been for these past seven years, you must have heard some rumors, fairytales even, about our facility here?" It is obvious he wants to know what I know. I am also painfully aware that the machine tracking the rhythm of my heartbeat is right at Farnsworth's side. One lie or case of the nerves will be obviously detected. I take a deep breath and calm my breathing. I close my eyes and consciously slow my heart rate.

"No sir," I lie. "I can't say I've ever heard anything that would make me scared of this facility."

"Good." He sits back, obviously happy with the result of my heart rate monitor. "Now one day I hope you won't be nervous around me either."

"Yes sir, thank you." Nervous? That doesn't even begin to cover it. A nurse in a white uniform walks into our room and over to Farnsworth.

"Sir?" she interrupts. "It's really time. We need the transfusion now."

"Yes, yes, of course." Farnsworth's eyes find their way to her. The woman who accompanies him starts to push his chair away. "Stop, please," Farnsworth commands and she does. He cranes his head to look at me. "I thank you, Ms. Billings, for what you are about to do. When you are through and recovered, I would like to thank you personally."

"There's no need—" I begin to say, but he stops me.

"There is every need." He smiles a wide, unnerving smile. "You'll come to dinner at my house as my guest."

"Thank you, sir…" I begin but again I cannot finish a sentence.

"I'm not asking, Ms. Billings." He is still smiling but something in the way he speaks sends a shiver down my spine. "I need to at least attempt to thank you for your years of service to the government and now your service to me." He pauses for a moment then he speaks very slowly and clearly. "Ms. Billings, no matter what else, from this moment on, you and I are more than connected. You and I are one."

"How's that sir?" I ask, my voice weak and hoarse.

"Your life, the very essence of you, Veronica, will be running inside of me. I will know what you think, what you feel and whom you love because I will be you. Now and forever more." He smiles and this time his smile is distorted and snakelike. My body begins to shake violently.

"Yes sir," I manage to squeak out, the bile turning in my stomach. Farnsworth and I are connected? Forever? How could that be possible? I look at the door to see if I can escape, but I know the answer. There is no way possible. Within the matter of an hour or less, my blood will be poured into a man made of pure evil. I feel my heart rate get away from me, and at once, all of the Lettors turn to face the heart rate monitor.

"Ah," Farnsworth exclaims with a smug expression

on his face. "We finally found something that makes the great Veronica Billings react. Now the question is, why?" He smiles again. "I'll leave you to your business." He is pushed toward the door, but he reaches down to stop his wheelchair abruptly. He looks at me. "Oh, and Veronica…I look forward to feeling you all over me." He is wheeled out the door.

Chapter Thirteen

No matter what I do, I cannot calm myself. I find myself shaking, lying on the table, gasping for air. I feel like someone is choking me and I yank at my throat to get them off. Of course, no one is there. It is just the memory of Farnsworth holding me hostage. How could he say those things to me? How could he pay me those sickening compliments, treating me like I'm a Giver? Acting like he's not a murderer? Speaking with Farnsworth has eradicated any doubts I may have had. Now I am certain what Phoenix says about him is not only possible, it's probable. I don't want to be Farnsworth's personal donor. I don't want to be anything for him, or to him. Finally, after another bout of violent shaking, I feel the sharp shooting pain of a needle in the side of my neck. I hear someone counting backwards from ten and by the number seven, I hear no more.

Now I am in a garden. A big, lush garden filled with the dandelions my mother once told me about. I look down at the picture of a dandelion she drew for me and hold it tightly in my hand. The picture begins to quiver and I watch as a dandelion springs to life and falls from the paper onto the ground. Then another dandelion falls, and another, until the already filled field is now deep with dandelions, making a warm, comforting, yellow blanket. A soft breeze blows by and then begins to grow more and more violent. A strong gust grabs the paper from my hand and whisks it away. I run after it, wading nearly waist deep in dandelions. I run until I can run no more. And there, in the distance, is my mother. Her long black hair is flecked with gray and her full hips are covered by an apron also covered with dandelions. When she stands still, it is hard to tell her from the ground. I wade out to her, and she opens her arms for me. She pulls me close and I feel warm and protected. Then, without warning, she holds me out at arm's length. I feel so very, very tired. All I want to do is lie in the bed of dandelions and sleep. "No sleep," she whispers. "No sleep, my angel. Mushrooms."

"What?" I murmur.

"Mushrooms," she repeats. I smile, desperately wishing I was still a child and she was still right here, with me. I would do anything to be back in a mushroom patch with her, foraging for the mushrooms that make me strong.

She squeezes my hand and backs away. "Wait," I say, calling after her, but she doesn't stop. "Wait," I yell, tears choking my words. "Mom. Please. Mom!" But she continues to move slowly away, until she blends completely into the field of dandelions, and is gone. I look around my field filled with flowers but now, without my mother there, it looks cold and lonely. I close my eyes and open them when I feel wetness at my feet. I am ankle deep in the lake at my waterfront. Dandelions are floating on the water all around me. I can sense he's here even before I feel his strong hands on my shoulders. I turn to face Phoenix. His look is serious, but still, he smiles at me. He leans down and kisses me softly on the lips. I feel him linger and I breathe him in.

"You are a very smart young woman," he whispers, pulling away from me. "Remember that."

"I'm not," I start to say. "I've never been educated past the fifth grade." But as I protest, he has also turned away. My body aches, wanting him near me again, but he slowly walks out into the lake until he is completely submerged.

"Wait," I yell. "Don't leave me." But he is gone. And I am all alone. I feel a sharp prick on my arm and I slap away another mosquito.

"She's coming around," someone announces. It's a voice I don't recognize. My throat is scratchy and I try to turn in the direction of the voice. Now I feel something cold and clammy touching my hand.

"Are you sure, sir?" It is another voice.

"I can walk, thank you." It is Farnsworth. He's here. So I was dreaming. My mother and Phoenix; neither are here. But Farnsworth is. I hear the beat of my empty heart and wonder why it bothers.

"Is it over?" I whisper, certain no one will understand me.

"Yes, my dear," Farnsworth coos, patting my hand. "You were magnificent. I knew you wouldn't let me down." I attempt to turn my head, trying to face the monster, Farnsworth. I am sick to think that now my blood runs through him. "Now you must rest. And eat. And when you are better, in a day or two, you will be my guest for dinner." I narrow my eyes, wishing they were weapons. But they're not. And I need to keep up appearances if I want to stay alive.

"Thank you," I whisper. I turn my head back and close my eyes, hoping he'll think I've simply passed out from exhaustion.

"Come," Farnsworth orders. "She is still very tired. Let her rest."

"Yes, sir." Someone answers him as I feel a sharp pain in the back of my hand. I wince. "It's your fluids and vitamins," the voice explains softly. "It won't hurt so much once you're stronger."

"Thank you," I whisper and whoever was speaking pats my leg very gently. I hear the door close after Farnsworth and his entourage, and I am overcome with sadness. Images of my dream flash before me and I grow more and more devastated, thinking I may never see Phoenix again. Simultaneously, my brain is alive with the idea of an escape for me, and especially for my girls. But this, I know, may never happen.

Alone in my room I ponder my dream. The images grow more and more vivid before me, and I can't shake the idea the dream was telling me something. But what? Despite my situation, despite it all, that dream gave me hope. Hope for redemption and hope for a future. There it is again, my nemesis, hope. But why would I have hope now? What did any of it mean? The mushrooms weren't unexpected. Mushrooms are the only remaining connection I have with my mother, and I've missed eating them these past few days. I probably should have eaten them. They would have made me stronger. Mushrooms make sense. The mushrooms keep my mother near, so of course they would be in my dream. The dandelions? What do the dandelions mean? Why was Phoenix there? And why did he tell me I'm "smart?" I know it's not true…He knows it's not true. He knows about my lack of education and frankly, if I were smart, I would figure out this dream. This dream, this dream...I close my eyes and try to take myself back. What does any of it mean? I go over it again and again until the words play through my mind like a freight train, chugging up a hill. The dandelions, the mushrooms, my mother, Phoenix...why does he tell me I'm smart? Why does she need to remind me of the mushrooms? Simply because I haven't eaten them for several nights? I won't forget her. And when I get back, if I ever get back, I will eat our mushrooms again. Ugh. Mushrooms, mushrooms, mushrooms. Those mushrooms. Those damned mushrooms. They taste horrible...so they made me tall...so what? Why is being tall and strong such a gift? Both of those traits make me the perfect pigeon for Farnsworth. I'm sorry, but why won't she just shut up about those damned mushrooms? Why does she have to bother me with them even in my dream? It's not like they're the answer to anything.

I gasp. Suddenly my eyes widen with excitement and I try to sit up but I am still too weak. The room begins to spin. I lay my head back on the pillow and squeeze my eyes shut, trying to sort it all out. What if those mushrooms didn't make me tall after all? What was it my mother said to me all those years ago? She said, "These will save your life." All these years I've thought it meant they would offer me extra nutrition, but no. The mushrooms make my blood toxic.

"That's it," I blurt out to no one. My eyes fly open and I am still all alone in my room. The heart rate monitor is working overtime to keep up with me. "That's the answer," I whisper, barely able to believe it myself. Now all I have to do is to get to Phoenix.

Chapter Fourteen

For two whole days, I lie here like an animal being prepped for the slaughter. I am fed and massaged and monitored, and generally fussed-over. And I am really done with it. For two entire days, I have had the answer. I know how to assassinate Farnsworth without anyone knowing. But I can't do it alone. I need Phoenix and I need my mushrooms. But how will I get to either one?

"Knock, knock." I can tell by the gentle yet definitive tap on the door that it is Farnsworth. He has visited me several times a day these past two days. I get that he's grateful, but he's becoming a bit obsessive. I'll never be his friend, no matter how many bouquets of exotic flowers he sends me. And if he's here only because he's worried about his blood, well, he should be.

"Hello, sir," I mumble, purposely lowering my eyes. He'll undoubtedly think of it as a sign of respect and subservience. The truth is I can feel myself getting stronger, my time to heal is ending, and I just want to break free of him. I have to be sure he can't tell what I'm thinking.

"Veronica," he murmurs, softly. There is a long, awkward silence.

"Um, how are you feeling, sir?" I don't know what else to say.

"Well, thank you. And thanks to you. And you,

Veronica?"

"Uh, much better, thank you." My words are nearly a whisper. I am so very uncomfortable with him so near.

"I wish you would look at me," he purrs. I am reluctant to do so. I don't want him to see me and I don't want to see him. But I force myself to raise my eyes. "Ah that's better. Except you look sad. Oh Veronica, I wonder what is happening behind those exotic, beautiful, dark eyes?" He's asked, so I'm going to tell him.

"I'm worried about my girls." I look at him steadily. "The ones I brought in. To this Letting. I'm their caretaker, and I'm really worried they're somewhere, alone, scared to be without me."

"I see." He looks away for just a moment.

"Can I see them?" I ask, my heart pounding.

"I don't think that's possible." Farnsworth walks away from the edge of my bed. My pounding heart stops cold. No. He couldn't have. He could not have sent them to the New World already.

"Have you..." I ask, my voice faltering. "Have you sent them on to the New World?"

"What?" He turns to me, sharply. He looks amused by my question. "You ask it like it's a bad thing, Veronica. Why is that?"

"No," I respond, covering. "It's just, I never got to say goodbye. And I had grown very fond of them."

"Ah, I see. Well they're not in the New World. Yet." He punctuates the "yet" watching me, waiting for me to slip up. I brace myself and continue.

"Then why can't I see them?"

"Because they're back at camp."

"They are?" I ask, flabbergasted. "Already?"

"Yes." He leans over to smell one of the flowers he's sent me. "Do you know what this flower is called?" he asks, obviously wanting to change the subject. I shake my head, but my mind is racing, trying to imagine who is looking out for my girls. "An orchid. Have you ever seen an orchid before, Veronica?" I shake my head again. "Well you can see more orchids, and other riches, things you could not even begin to fathom, if…" His words trail off.

"If what?"

"If you decide to stay here with me."

"What?" I snap. I stare at his face, trying to understand what he wants.

"You don't have to decide now. But I'll leave the choice to you. If you stay in my world, with me, you'll have your own private quarters with everything you have ever desired. Your sparse life at camp with protein bars and powdered milk will be a thing of your past."

"Sir, I…"

"Shh…" He places his hand on mine. The feel of his touch makes my skin crawl. "You will come to dinner tonight, and you will see where I…and hopefully you…live. After that, you can make your decision. Either you will live a life of riches with me, or you will go back to your camp and I will summon you once a month when I need a transfusion." I nod. "And understand Veronica, if you choose camp, your days of freedom are over. You will have a guard on you twenty-four, seven." I feel my heart drop, but I nod my response again. "You will be brought to me tonight at six. Some of my staff will help you dress and prepare." He turns to leave. "Veronica, I do truly hope we can be friends," he adds, before he walks out the door.

I sit on the edge of the bed with my feet dangling off the side. They are tingling and still fairly numb, but I need them to work. I am feeling an unending exhaustion I wish would just go away, but only time will help that. Now, I need to focus. I look at the clock on the wall and it reads four o'clock. That means I have two hours to guess what Farnsworth is up to.

Farnsworth tells me my girls are back at camp. In my heart, I don't believe it, but if by some miracle they are, I know Phoenix delivered them, which means he is also at camp, waiting for me. Somehow, I have to get Farnsworth to allow me to go back to camp unaccompanied, or, at all. In my gut, I know darn well Farnsworth's option of living with him or living at camp is a flat-out lie. He would never let me, one of the last remaining O's, leave his sight, especially since my blood has been cleared. But why would he bother to lie? Why wouldn't he just force me to stay? Why would he want me to choose to stay with him? What does he care? These are all questions I need to answer, but in the meantime, I need to find a way back to camp.

Soon a woman from Farnsworth's entourage appears and helps me out of bed. I recognize her as the woman who was so nice to me on the day of the Letting, the one who patted my leg. I smile at her and she returns it with a terse, tense smile of her own. "Come now," she coaxes, helping me to my feet. She holds my hand to help me up, but once I stand I tower so far over her it is rather comical. She looks up at me, smiling, and wraps an arm around my waist. It takes every ounce of her strength to help me down and into a wheelchair. Once I am seated, I hear her exhale.

Helping me move was a huge effort for her. I know I am so much taller than she is, but it seems to me everyone in the Inferno is very weak.

She pushes my wheelchair out of the white building and into the blazing sun. Although I know Phoenix is probably at camp, I keep a watchful eye, just in case. She escorts me to a waiting vehicle that is longer than any truck I have ever seen. "It's a limousine." She speaks reassuringly. "He wants to be sure you see all of your options here." I try to smile at her as she helps me into the backseat. A driver folds up my wheelchair and places it into the trunk of the car. She climbs in with me. "I'm Grace," she offers, smiling as the vehicle pulls away.

We drive for at least an hour, and although I am exhausted, I cannot help staring out the window. I have never before seen anything like this. All types of vehicles pass us on many-lane roads. Stores line the streets and people are busy walking in and out, always carrying bags. My fascination turns to revulsion when I think of how any one of these people could have the blood of any of my girls, running through them. A family stands outside a toy store. A father and mother are holding their child's hands, swinging her between them as she giggles along. I smile at them briefly; then I grow very, very sad, realizing this was never an option for any of my girls. All of them were taken from their mothers, and none of them has ever known their fathers. How ridiculously unfair this is. I sit back, brooding, sickened by the excesses of these ridiculous people. Then we turn a corner off the main road and the limousine finds a dirt path. Ironically, the path reminds me of camp. The dirt path continues for miles, and I am amazed at how the ride feels completely smooth. There are no potholes or craters here like there are at camp. The path opens up into a wide entrance and there, before me, is perhaps the largest house ever made. There are an unfathomable number of white columns along a massive front porch, and a red front door that is so shiny I'm certain I would be able to see my own reflection in it. The house looks like it's made for a family of giants. My eyes gaze lazily across a sprawling great lawn, overlooking…something. "Is that?" I ask, pointing out the window.

"The ocean." Grace smiles.

"The ocean," I repeat.

I knew our world was made up of land masses and bodies of water, but I had never before seen the ocean. I barely wait for the car to stop before I push my door open and pull myself to standing. Carefully I walk forward, ignoring the light-headed feeling and the dizziness. I hear Grace call out behind me, telling me I must be in my wheelchair, but I just ignore her. The lure of the sea is pulling me forward. Slowly I hobble forth until my feet touch sand. I bend down to run my hands across it. I scoop some sand into my hand, and it glides through my fingers. This is nothing like the dirt beach we have at the waterfront at camp. This is…glorious. I stand. I'm a little wobbly, but I don't let that stop me. Carefully, I put one foot in front of the other until I make it to the water's edge. The noise coming off the ocean is deafening. The waves roll in and out and crash against the beach with such force, it looks like they're trying to wash away the Inferno and once again make things right in the world.

Without thinking, I lean down and pull off my

boots. I dig my toes into the sand and it feels warm and gritty. I take a step forward, then another, until I touch water. The cold shock of the ocean water sends a chill up my spine. It is painful and wonderful all at the same time, just like being with Phoenix. Then I reach up and pull my sweater over my head, exposing my tank top. I throw the sweater back onto the sand. The sun revitalizes my tired shoulders. I take another step and think about taking another and another. I wonder if I were to keep going would the ocean be my friend or would it swallow me whole? I step forward again, still contemplating, but I never have the chance to find out.

"Veronica." It is Grace, standing behind me, holding my sweater. I turn back to the ocean, watching its beautiful, serene violence, wondering if I should just dive in. If I did go forward, and the ocean swallowed me whole, would that be the answer? Farnsworth would be out his personal donor, but then I'm certain he'd turn to the girls. He'd keep them locked up in a dungeon somewhere, waiting to Let them whenever he felt weak. My stomach aches with the thought, and I know this would be too easy an out for the likes of me. I need to spend more time on this earth, righting my wrongs. I can't let the ocean swallow me up, and I can't let Farnsworth, either. Deep down I'm relieved to have a reason to stay and fight. I don't know if Phoenix and I can ever happen; I don't know if he can forget what I've done, or if I can ever forgive myself, but the truth is, I want to be here to find out.

"Veronica?" Grace's voice is soft and I can barely hear her over the roar of the ocean. I turn back to face her. "Let's get you ready for dinner," she says, smiling.

****

The room Farnsworth has assigned me is larger than the entire camp base. It's decorated in red flowers and carved wood. There is a massive bed on one end of the room, with ornately carved bedposts and billowy netting cascading over the top, falling gracefully into a canopy. To me it looks like mosquito netting and I'm surprised they have that problem here, in paradise. In another corner, there is a tall dresser with large doors instead of drawers. That too, is made of carved wood. Everything is made from carved tree trunks and has bold red accents. There is so much excess that even at my height I feel overwhelmed. Grace walks to the large dresser and opens the doors to reveal several evening dresses. "This armoire has been filled for you," she explains. I make a mental note of the word "armoire." "See if there is something in here you would like to wear to dinner."

"Can't I wear my shorts and sweater?" I ask, surprised.

"No, dear." She pulls open heavy red velvet window curtains, so I can see the ocean from my room. "You need to wear a dress. You're in his palace in the New World. You need to dress appropriately."

"Oh, okay." I look back into the armoire. There is nothing in here I would ever want to wear. And there's certainly nothing appropriate. What does a secret assassin dress like anyway? I pull out an emerald green gown. "This?" I ask Grace.

"I think it's a lovely choice." She nods her approval. Truthfully, I don't care. I simply grabbed the green gown because it was the closest thing I could find to my army green fatigues. "Now why don't you take a bath and we'll get you to dinner?"

The bathroom alone is larger than any of the cabins at camp. It is long, with opulent fixtures and mirrors lining the walls. I step in and see two delicately crafted sinks with luxurious towels folded next to them. I walk a few feet farther in, sincerely hoping I can navigate my way to the bathtub. First, I see the shower, a giant stall framed in gold with two seats and a fresh array of soaps and shampoos. But, it's what is next to the shower that grabs my attention: the bathtub. The bathtub that appears to be as large as my lake. I'm grateful I'm a strong swimmer. The tub is held up by golden claw feet and has already been drawn and filled with luxurious bubbles that look like they're made of silk.

"I thought you may need to relax," Grace offers. I jump, startled. I had no idea she was in the bathroom with me. She takes me on a mini-tour to show me a towel warmer and the separate room for the toilet. "And here is a dressing area." She takes me to a separate wing of the bathroom. "Enjoy," she adds before scurrying away. I waste no time stripping and jumping into the bath. I have no idea what's in the water, but it smells heavenly. I lean back and I'm amazed to find I am able to stretch myself out in the tub. I sink down, submerging as much of me as I can, and feel the bubbles tickle my nose. It all feels way too good. Although I know I should feel guilty, I take a few minutes just to enjoy.

Five minutes into my bath, I am ready to go. I can't lie here all night and I want to get to dinner so I can face Farnsworth's ultimatum and get back to my girls and Phoenix. And right now, for some reason, I cannot get Lulu off my mind. I keep wondering how she is and where she is. I wonder if she's scared, and if Gretchen is taking care of her. The longer I lie here, the more determined I am that I will make that trek back to camp tonight. One way or another. I pull myself out of the soapy water and towel off. I go to the dressing area and find my gown and shoes waiting for me. I slip into my dress that fits me perfectly, but as well as it fits, it is equally uncomfortable. The material cuts right across the top of my breasts and dips low in the back. It is fitted through my waist and hips, and hangs loosely near the ground. It flows when I walk. It is absolutely beautiful, but it's so not me. Then I see a rectangular box about twelve inches long and open it to reveal a pair of matching green satin heels. This makes me smile. Not because of the thrill of wearing a pair of shoes like this, but because Farnsworth thinks I need heels. I slip the shoes on and stand tall. I wobble slightly; I have to be at least six-foot-four in these heels. With these on, I'm probably even taller than Phoenix. Grace walks in and smiles at me. "You look beautiful," she declares.

"Really?" I ask, looking down at myself. It never occurred to me to look in a mirror.

"See for yourself." She turns me to face a full length mirror in my dressing room. One look at myself and I burst out laughing. "What is it?" Grace is genuinely confused. I laugh until I can calm myself. Then I speak slowly, in between gulps of air.

"I look ridiculous." I snort as the laughter comes back. I have to flop myself down in a chair to keep from falling over.

"Actually, Veronica, you look quite stunning," Grace assures me.

"Well, thank you, Grace." I am suddenly aware she

may have picked out the gowns in my armoire. "It's just that I'm not used to looking like this. I'm used to old ripped jeans and stained tank tops."

"I understand." She looks up at me, suddenly serious. For the first time I see her eyes are a beautiful shade of gray. Her lashes are long, and she blinks several times before she speaks. "But do you think you could get used to this?" she asks.

"Probably not." I know she's asking about so much more than the dress I am wearing.

"That's what I thought." She sighs and walks over to me. She places a hand on my arm and pats me. "He's not well, you know. He pretends to be healthier than he is. He plans to Let you again. Soon. Maybe as soon as the day after tomorrow. Maybe even tomorrow. But you have an advantage. He's in awe of you. He thinks you're a superwoman who possesses super blood and he wants it. I just don't know how fast even Superwoman can recuperate." Her eyes water, and it looks as though this conversation is truly bothering her. "Please," she whispers. "For all of our sakes, don't tell him you know."

"I won't." This time I take her hand and squeeze it. "Thank you, Grace." She just nods. She is certainly the embodiment of her name.

"Could you sit please, Veronica?" Grace asks, and I do. Slowly she brushes through my long black hair. "So lovely," she murmurs, and she begins to hum a song I have never heard before. As she brushes I close my eyes and suddenly I am seven years old, sitting in our kitchen with my mother brushing my hair. The feeling is so intense I lose myself.

"They're not at camp, are they?" I ask. She keeps

brushing but her humming has stopped abruptly. "My girls. If he's that desperate, he has them here somewhere, doesn't he?" Her humming starts up again as quickly as it stopped. She finishes brushing my hair and turns me to face her.

"Have you ever worn makeup?" she asks and I shake my head. "That's what I thought." She slicks something greasy on my lips. "There." She takes a step back. "You look magnificent."

"Thank you," I mumble, frustrated that she won't tell me what I desperately need to know.

She leans over me and looks me straight in the eyes. She places her hand gently on my chin and tilts my head upward. "Veronica, things may not be as complicated as you think they are. Above all, just remember who you are." And then she is gone.

I look back into the mirror and stare at myself long and hard. "Remember who I am," I repeat, closing my eyes. Just remember who I am. It would be so easy if I had a clue. There is a knock on my door and an escort with a wheelchair waits to take me to dinner. My first impulse is to refuse the chair, but then I remember Farnsworth may want to Let me tomorrow and think better of it. This way, if I go to dinner in the chair, he may decide I'm not ready to Let, yet.

****

My escort pushes me down a hallway lined with portraits and filled with more opulence. Surprisingly, there is what looks like sports memorabilia—things like a set of black leather thick gloves and a baseball bat— placed on pedestals, sporadically lining the hall. And everywhere, in complete juxtaposition, there are soft chairs and couches waiting to absorb one's exhaustion and ease the endless journey to dinner. Finally, I am wheeled into the dining room and greeted by a staff of four. One helps me into my dark wooden carved chair and glides me up to the thick solid wood table. I am struck by the fact that my wheelchair is immediately removed from the room. Another of the staff lays a red lace napkin on my lap. A third pours water into a gold rimmed glass. All stand by, waiting for Farnsworth to enter. I look around the room, hoping something in this overstuffed room will spark an idea, a plan. There's nothing. Nothing except proof that Farnsworth lives in pure luxury.

Moments later, Farnsworth enters. He's wearing a dark suit that is perfectly tailored to his thin body. His shirt collar lies casually under his suit, and a loosened tie dangles from it. His shoes are shiny and angular, jutting out from the tight hem of his pants. His face is glowing and he looks happy. He reaches up and pushes a stray piece of very blonde hair into place. "Veronica," he nearly giggles, holding out his hands for me to join him. It just now occurs to me I should be standing. I struggle to push my chair back and rise onto my heels. I wobble when I stand and he looks at me, perplexed. "I was hoping you were feeling better." A frown clouds his otherwise chipper demeanor. So he thinks it is still blood loss, and not these ridiculous heels, that is making me unsteady.

"Much better, thank you sir." He walks to me and I have to suppress a laugh when I realize in these heels, he comes up to my chin. He squeezes both of my hands.

"Maybe those shoes are a bit much for you, huh?" He looks up at me and smiles in his shifty way.

"What shoes?" I ask, suddenly remembering he has

only ever seen me lying in bed, or when he was confined to his wheelchair. We have never before stood toe to toe. His eyes widen with shock. There. I have the upper hand, if only for a minute. His look turns dark, and I can tell he doesn't like to be made a fool of. Wrong approach. Quickly, I slip out of my shoes and stand flatfooted. Now he is only an inch or so shorter than me. It's barely even perceptible. I smile at him and he softens slightly. He checks his anger and smiles back.

"You are everything I had hoped you would be, Ms. Veronica Billings." He holds out his hand. "Shall we?" Once again, I am helped into my chair and within minutes the food begins arriving. Our first two courses are a bean soup, and artichokes dipped in drawn butter. They are served on thin porcelain dishes with a flower pattern. I have no idea what the flower is, but it's large and purple. He sees me staring at it. "It's a giant allium. Pretty, aren't they?"

"Very," I agree, savoring the taste of real butter. At camp, we eat grease from a can that is supposed to taste like butter. Because none of us has ever tried butter before, we never knew the difference. I do now.

Then our steaks are served, each one overflowing its plate. I cut into the steak and eat away, and slowly, the plate becomes visible. This plate has a long white flower that is shaped like a folded sleeping bag, atop a long thick stem. "Calla lily," he informs me. "One of my favorites." After a few more bites, I push my plate away, feeling uncomfortable by both the food and him. "Saving room for dessert?"

"Dessert?" I am unable to imagine stuffing in anything else. But no sooner do I ask, and the servers bring forth small, delicate plates with tall brown towers on top. I gasp when I see mine, not because of the confection, but because of the plate it is balanced on. This time the flower needs no explanation. These tiny yellow flowers are the flowers of my dreams. They are unmistakably dandelions. I can feel Farnsworth eyeing me.

"Something interesting?" he asks. I look at him, trying to remain calm.

"I've never seen anything like it."

"Really?" He raises an eyebrow. I don't know if it's paranoia or if he is truly skeptical. But how could he know about my connection to dandelions?

"Do you eat it?" I ask, looking up at him, my eyes wide. I am praying he buys this.

"Ah, the chocolate tower." He sounds relieved.

"Yes." I do my best to sound innocent. "How do you eat it? Where do you begin?" He smiles at me in a way he never has before. He looks almost...loving. The thought of his love threatens my ability to keep food down. He picks up his fork and taps into the side of his dessert.

"Like this." He cracks into the tower with his fork.

"It's too pretty to break," I say. And he just smiles at me.

"Believe me," he baits, "it's worth it."

I pick up my fork and stab straight down, into the tower. It crumbles at my touch. I shove a large piece of the thick, gooey, earthy chocolate into my mouth. After Phoenix's kiss, this is the best thing I have ever experienced. I am just sorry it has to be in the company of Farnsworth.

Farnsworth looks at me, his eyebrows raised.

"When will you ever stop surprising me, Veronica?" he asks. I wish I had a clever response but instead I find myself scraping the bottom of the empty plate with the back of my fork. The dandelions are lying there, looking up at me, waiting for me to find the answer. I push them aside.

"Let's go for a walk," he decides and he holds out his hand to me. Reluctantly, I place my hand in his and he pulls me to my feet. I leave the silly shoes under the table, and we walk out of the dining room. I slip out of his grasp as soon as possible. We walk down another long hallway, and I notice a very definite trend in the decor. Everything is opulent, and there are even more pieces of sports equipment hanging in this hallway. There's a bow and arrow, several guns, and more balls than there are sports I know of. All are hanging or placed on pedestals with dates underneath them.

"Do you play all these sports?" I ask him.

"When I can," he mumbles, and we walk out double doors that lead to a large flower garden.

"Oh," I hear myself exclaim as I look around. Lights are placed all around the garden, and the flowers are shining like it's midday. I can feel him beaming at me.

"Beautiful, isn't it?"

"Yes," I whisper, thinking of the grass at camp that is often more brown than green. I look around at a white picket fence with large flowering bushes and I am awed by its beauty. "Why do you love flowers so much?" I ask him.

"Because they are so very capable, yet so very fragile." He stops for a moment, looking lost. "They stand tall, reaching for the sun, shining in all their glory, providing food, pollination, and profound pleasure…" He draws in a labored breath. "But they have no defenses. No strength, really. Something as unimportant as a strong wind can decimate my entire garden. The flowers bend and try to rally against the storm, but they have no inherent strength at all. They have nothing to fight with." If I didn't know he was a tyrannical murderer who pities himself and analogizes himself to a flower, I might almost feel bad for him. But as it is he just sounds weak. And he is all of those horrible things and more. And what's worse, he made me a horrible thing too. And for that, I will never forgive him.

We walk through the garden and out onto the beach. I keep a comfortable distance so I'm certain he cannot hold my hand. The bottom of my gown drags as I walk, and little clouds of sand burst up over the hem of my dress. He stumbles on the sand but I feel remarkably strong after the dinner of iron, iron and chocolate. He watches me move, my body returning to its normal state, growing stronger and stronger by the second. I can't help but run a little ahead of him, and the next thing I know I am splashing in the ocean, laughing. I wait for him to join me but he stays back.

"The water's surprisingly warm." I don't know why I've extended the invitation.

"Thanks," he replies. "I'll pass."

"Guess when you see it every day it's not such a big deal." I slow my splashing.

"It's not that," he explains. "I can't swim."

"Really?" I stop and stare at him. "You live here. Why not?"

"Well, you are straightforward, aren't you?"

"Sorry," I mumble, hoping I didn't just send myself to a premature Letting. "I just mean with the ocean here…"

"My mother was always afraid I would hurt myself," he shares. "She sheltered me from…well, everything." Even in the darkness, I can tell his face has grown very, very sad.

"So learn now."

"It's not that easy."

"Why not?"

"Because everyone is afraid and no one will teach me."

"I'll teach you," I offer before I realize I've said it.

"Really?" he asks, sounding genuinely interested. Then I remember Gretchen telling me Farnsworth wants nothing more than to be strong and to partake in all of the activities his constituents play. And then I realize there could never be a battle of strength with Farnsworth because he will not play it. There will only be a battle of the minds. Unfortunately for me, I am deficient in that area. But it can't matter, because I'm all any of us has. No one else, not Phoenix, Gretchen, Gunnar or any of the girls can get as close to Farnsworth as I can. If I'm going to fight with Phoenix in his revolution, I need to be brave and face my biggest fear: the fact I may not be smart enough. The truth is I'm just going to have to be. Starting now.

"Yes," I say. "I'll teach you. But you can't learn here. The water's too violent."

"I have a pool," he offers. "Actually several."

"You have several pools, and you don't swim?"

"I know." He shrugs.

"Pools are no good either. We need to make you

169

strong if you want to swim, and frankly, giving you my blood's not enough." He looks at me, genuinely interested. "And to give you my blood regularly, we need to make me even stronger."

"How do we do all of this?" he asks.

"The same way I've prepped every girl I've sent to you." I stare him dead in the eyes. "We go to camp."

Chapter Fifteen

Getting Farnsworth to agree to go to camp is so much easier than I ever imagined. "You want me to go camp?" he asks me, utterly shocked.

"Yes," I answer. The ocean water laps at my feet and the moon hangs lazily on the horizon. "I can help you get stronger there. Teach you to swim."

"Like my own personal trainer." I see he is lost in his thoughts. "Are you joking?" I hear the vulnerability in his voice. "I run a country," he explains, talking himself out of it. "I couldn't just go…"

"Okay." I turn my face toward the sky and feel the warmth of the purple twilight surround me. "It's up to you. Stay here if you want. I'm sure you'll have plenty of opportunities to grow strong and learn new sports." I pull my gown up over my calves and wade deeper into the water. "The ocean is beautiful." He is standing near enough to me to hear without having to yell. "But it's nothing like my lake. At night, my lake is so quiet it's peaceful. Many sleepless nights I have paddled out in a canoe and lay back, letting the sounds of nature and the gentle rocking of the canoe lull me to sleep. During the day, the girls and I fish right off our dock, catching lots of small sunfish and sometimes even a large bass. And of course, there's the swimming. The lake water temperature is always perfect. On the hot summer days it cools you off completely, but on the chillier spring and fall days, it feels as warm as a bathtub." I glance at Farnsworth and see I have his rapt attention. "I've also built a diving board," I add, splashing my feet in the water.

"By yourself?" he asks, flabbergasted.

"It wasn't difficult. I love that board. I run up to it and jump and feel my whole being, body and soul, spring up into the air. It feels like I am stretching up into infinite space. Then I glide in the air for what feels like a beautiful eternity, the wind I've created blowing gently against my face. Then splash!" I slap my hands together for emphasis. "Suddenly I break into the water, my arms, then my head, my entire body, and finally my feet. The water caresses me gently and welcomes me in. After long moments of slithering through the water feeling more fish than human, I come up for air. When my head bursts through, I hear nothing but the sound of my own heartbeat, racing from the thrill of it all."

"Let's go to camp," he declares.

"Okay."

"We'll leave tonight." I nod, wondering how I will ever be able to build and set-up a diving board before Farnsworth makes his way down to the waterfront.

****

It is only Farnsworth and me in his helicopter traveling back to camp. He has refused any help, assuring everyone my blood has made him somewhat invincible. He is so invested in this trip I have to be sure I am absolutely ready, mentally and physically. If I waver, if I'm weak in any way, it will instill doubt in him and I will be sent back to his mansion for sure. I am also sure the girls will be waiting for me at camp, because he already told me they were there. I take a deep cleansing breath as the helicopter takes off. Just like Farnsworth, I have to do everything exactly right so I'm not caught in my web of lies.

The flight feels endless with Farnsworth sitting across from me, watching my every move. From time to time, I close my eyes and think about Phoenix, and how different our helicopter ride was. I smile as I think of him, how he would point to things through the window, explaining what they were to the girls; or how he told me, in no uncertain terms, that he would never forget me. The thought of him warms me and I snuggle into myself, imagining his arms around me. I open my eyes and Farnsworth is smiling at me, with that same unnerving look of love. I give him a quick smile back and immediately look out the window.

We land as close to the cabins as we can and I am home. I try to push open my door before the rotor stops, but I'm stuck. Glued to my seat. I feel trapped and claustrophobic in the small cabin of the helicopter with Farnsworth so near, and I look out at the brown-green grass and tiny cabins longingly. The first thing I have to do is get Farnsworth settled and then, I have to get word to Phoenix. Somehow. Naturally, Farnsworth's entourage is coming, but they won't arrive for another three or four hours. Our helicopter moves so much faster than the vehicles. Finally, the rotor stops and my door is released. I stumble out of the helicopter, very nearly tripping on my gown. Farnsworth sees me. Damn. I have to be more careful. A superwoman would not stumble. I steady myself and look back at Farnsworth who is still waiting in the cab. He looks nervous about his decision so I motion for him to join me. He walks down the steps warily, so I hold my hand out to him. He slips his hand in mine and my arm turns to stone. I try anyway possible to free myself. "Here it is," I say. In the darkness of the night, the helicopter spotlight lights the camp. Inside the cabins I see silhouettes of terrified girls, frozen, staring out of the windows. I step forward so I can drop his hand, pretending to show him around. "These are our cabins." I point to the various buildings around camp. "Over there's the mess hall, and over here is Margaret's office." Just like the girls, she could not have missed our entrance. "I'm certain she'll be out to join us momentarily."

"Ah yes, Margaret," Farnsworth recollects, like the name means something to him.

"The woman who runs the camp."

"Oh, I know. Believe me, I keep a very close watch on the camp that supplies the New World, and me, with the blood we so desperately need. That's why I know so much about you, Veronica." His voice sends a chill through my body.

"So uh, this cabin's empty." I point to a cabin on the outskirts. "We used to use it when we were busier." He nods. "I thought that could be your quarters."

"Nonsense." It's Margaret's voice. I turn and see her there, she is dressed in her regulation green, but she has obviously just woken up. Margaret is seething as she looks at me. Surprises of this kind are not Margaret's thing.

"Hello Margaret." I smooth my hand down the side of my dress and her eyes follow. It's so wrong but I can't help but enjoy her jealousy. I turn to Farnsworth. "This is Margaret. As you know, she runs the camp." Then I turn to her. "And this is Principal Leader

Farnsworth."

"Hello, Principal Leader Farnsworth, sir," Margaret says, curtsying.

"Hello," he answers.

"As I was saying, Veronica, Principal Leader Farnsworth can't sleep in just any cabin. He can have my quarters," she offers.

"That's very nice," he replies, "but I wouldn't dream of putting you out. That cabin will be perfect."

"But sir," Margaret protests, "you must understand…If I knew you were coming…" Again, she shoots me a look of death.

"Oh, don't blame Veronica," Farnsworth chuckles, turning to me and squeezing my hand for just a second. "The trip to camp was entirely my idea. She told me you would be a gracious host, even with no notice. Obviously she was right." Even in the darkness I can see Margaret's face blush bright red. I turn to Farnsworth.

"I'll help you make up your cabin, but then we should turn in. It's probably best to get some sleep tonight. Tomorrow's going to be an exciting day." I speak with as much manufactured excitement as I can muster.

"Of course." Farnsworth looks as if he would agree to anything to get away from Margaret.

"I will help you, naturally," Margaret insists.

"Oh thank you, Margaret." Farnsworth flashes a very charming smile. "But Veronica is more than capable of helping me set up my cabin for the night."

"Of course sir, but—"

"But I do look forward to seeing you first thing in the morning for breakfast," Farnsworth interjects, smoothly dismissing Margaret. "It's in a place called the 'mess hall,' correct?"

"That's correct, sir." Margaret is not at all her usual vibrant self.

"The 'mess hall.' " Farnsworth tosses his head and laughs. "How wonderful. Well Margaret, I will see you in the mess hall first thing tomorrow. Have a good night."

"Yes sir, you too, sir." Margaret curtsies once more then walks to her cabin slowly, looking back to scowl at me every now and again. Farnsworth seems to have forgotten her already. He turns to me.

"Tell me, Veronica, if that is my cabin, where will you be staying?"

"In my cabin, of course." I'm surprised he could ask such a thing. "Over there." I point in the direction of my cabin.

"So far from me." His words sound like a combination of disappointment and fear.

"You'll be perfectly fine there, sir."

"Of course I will," he snaps, squaring off his shoulders. Obviously, I have insulted his masculinity. Damn.

"I just mean the quarters are nice even though they're old."

"I see." He is obviously trying to let the perceived insult wash past him. "So tell me, Veronica, are you alone in your cabin?" His eyes travel up and down my gown.

"No. Never," I lie, backing away. "Sometimes there is another Leader, sometimes the girls stay with me." I avoid going into detail about Gretchen, and how she is trying to lead a revolution against Farnsworth.

"Of course." He sounds somewhat disappointed. Could he have truly believed we would share a cabin? The thought makes my dinner threaten to make a reappearance.

"Come on," I say. "You start walking to the cabin and I'll grab your sheets from the laundry over there."

"As long as you don't leave my sight, Veronica." The words make my stomach cramp. Does he really think we'll be together, constantly? How will I ever get to the waterfront and Phoenix?

"Uh, just a sec." I pull up the hem of my dress, amazed I am still in this stupid thing, and make my way to and from the laundry room as quickly as possible. "Okay." I am carrying an armful of white sheets. "Let's get you set up."

Before Farnsworth can even take off his tie and unbutton his shirt I have his bed made, complete with military corners. "The bathroom is there"—I point out the window—"and reveille is at o-seven-hundred hours. You won't miss it. I'll collect you then, and we'll head to the mess hall. After that, we'll begin our day of training."

"Got it." He salutes me. I try to smile. "But just one thing, Veronica." He is deliberately slowing his pace. "Why are you in such a rush tonight?" I freeze. I thought I had been so cool, but obviously, I nearly tipped my hand.

"Honestly sir," I say, careful to look him straight in the eye. "I'm really incredibly eager to see my girls."

"Oh, your girls, yes, of course. Well, don't let me keep you."

"Thank you, sir." I rush to the door and stop, then turn back to face him. My throat tightens, but I manage to choke out the words. "Sleep well, sir. Tomorrow will be a lot of fun."

"Thank you, Veronica. You, too." I push open the door to his cabin and walk out into the night air. For the first time in days, I feel like I can breathe again. The warm summer air is heavy in my lungs but it feels so incredibly right. I walk faster and faster until I break into a jog. I throw open the door to cabin O and immediately hear the squeals.

"Veronica," they shout in unison. Then all three of them, Lilly, Violet, and Raven throw themselves into my arms.

"Oh my girls," I say, snuggling up to them.

"You look beautiful." Lilly is stroking my hair as she speaks. I pull them off me and hold them at arm's length.

"Thank you," I laugh softly. "Are you all okay?" Lilly is still wearing a bandage on her arm.

"We're okay," Violet promises. "We knew what to expect so it wasn't as awful as it could have been."

"They couldn't get much from me." Lilly points to her arm. Looking at her tiny cherub face, so innocent and sweet, I just want to kill Farnsworth. Luckily for me, I can.

"You are very brave, all of you." I hold them near.

"You too," Raven adds, her hand on my shoulder. She is so mature it is heartbreaking.

"Yeah," Violet continues. "We heard you had the biggest Let in history. They never expected you to survive it." I can see she has been crying. They all have.

"Way to stick it to them," Raven declares. When she speaks, she looks just like her brother. It makes me smile, but my brain trips up on Violet's words.

"Really?" I ask. "The biggest Let in history?" Violet nods. So that's why I felt so incredibly weak for so long. It is amazing I'm as alive as I am. This is why Farnsworth thinks I'm superhuman, because my body is stronger than most. "Well, you don't have to worry anymore." I smooth Lilly's hair. "Because I'm here now and we're all together." They snuggle against me again. "But you need to know something." I hold them out from me and look at each of them. "He is here. At camp."

"Farnsworth?" Violet asks. I see the fear in her eyes.

"Yes," I say quietly, and she and Lilly shrink back. Raven, however, remains still and unaffected. "So it is extremely important you do not say a word about anything you may have heard. If he asks you, you tell Principal Leader Farnsworth all you think about is prepping for the next Letting. That goes for you too, Raven. We will all act together when the time is right. Do you understand?" Raven stares at me and nods reluctantly.

"Good. Thank you." I turn back to all of them. "My friend who watched out for you—" I smile at the thought of him. "You must never mention him or he could be in real danger. Do you understand?" They each nod.

"Okay." I peer out the window and over toward Farnsworth's cabin. I'm certain I can speak freely. There is no way he could walk here fast enough to overhear what I'm saying. "Now tell me, when did you get here?" I ask. "Back to camp?"

"Just a little while ago," Raven answers. "But our chaperone tried to convince us today was yesterday."

"Yeah," Violet adds. "They gave us some song and dance about losing track of time because we had just gone through a Letting."

"What did you say?" I ask the girls.

"We said *okay*." Raven shrugs. "We figured if it was important enough that they were lying to us about what day it is, we had better just play along."

I pull the girls to me and hold them close. "I am so proud of you girls. You know that?"

They look up at me with their little angel faces smiling. So I was right. He only returned the girls to camp because I asked to see them. Otherwise, he would have held them as prisoners.

"Okay," I say. "Now I have to go out for a run. I'll check in on you in a bit, but right now, snuggle down and try to rest." The girls obey without a fight. They must be exhausted. Only Raven eyes me and gives me a coy smile.

"Nice dress to wear for a run." I smile at her before I tuck them all in. Looking at them lying on the floor under their netting, my heart aches at the empty spot Lulu has left behind.

"Good night, my angels," I whisper, just as my mother said to me every night. They yawn and snore in response.

****

As soon as I am clear of their cabin, I inch my way to the path that leads to the waterfront. I am eternally grateful I have chosen a dark colored gown, and not one that would glow in the moonlight. I continually look over my shoulder, but I see no sign of Margaret or Farnsworth behind me. Farnsworth is too far away to see me from his cabin, and Margaret has undoubtedly woken poor Willy to have him start prepping breakfast for Farnsworth. She'll be too busy to care about me right now. I have very little time until Farnsworth's entourage arrives and someone looks for me in my cabin.

I trudge along across camp, and with every step, I'm closer to the gravel path. I breathe in the night air that is alive with the sound of cicadas. My body wants to go, go, go. I am aching to get to Phoenix and am running out of time. When I am clear of the sightlines of camp, I break into a run, straight toward the waterfront. As I run, I swat a mosquito. How I wish my blood was toxic once more. Soon, I tell myself. Soon. I wince when my feet hit the gravel and stones, but I don't slow down. I lift up my gown and run full speed to the waterfront. Before I even hit the beach, I see Phoenix standing there, waiting for me. I slow my pace and run my hand through my hair. For the first time ever, I wonder if I look all right. But I don't have time to care. I stop a few feet in front of Phoenix and want nothing more than to rush into his arms. I smile at him.

"Is that the proper way to dress for a Letting?" he asks. My smile fades quickly as I realize there is no humor in his voice.

"I was at dinner..." I mumble, confused.

"Did your boyfriend give you the gown?"

"What?"

"Your boyfriend. Farnsworth. Heard you two are pretty chummy."

"Then you heard wrong." I am on the verge of tears.

"Really? I hear he wants you to move in."

"I said no." My eyes search his, trying to

understand what is happening. "And no one's allowed to have a boyfriend or girlfriend. You know it's illegal."

"Not for him it's not. Not for anyone in the Inferno. So if he's not your boyfriend, then tell me, why did he offer to take you to dinner? And why did you say yes? Are you that hungry?" He has a look of disgust on his face.

"I went to dinner because I'm trying to stay alive. Okay?" I nearly yell. "Is that okay by you? Or do you hate me so much you wish Farnsworth would have bled me to death?"

"How can you even ask me that?" Phoenix asks.

"Me?" I scoff at his question. "How can you treat me like this? I was summoned. I went. He thinks I'm some kind of superwoman, and he wants more of my blood. The only reason I am alive is because my toxic blood passed inspection, and now I know why. I think the reason God saw fit to make me survive is to stop Farnsworth. And I know how to do it."

"Tell me." I notice his beautiful eyes are rimmed with red. I wonder if he's been crying and if I'm the reason why.

"Mushrooms," I say, and he looks at me, confused. "I have eaten mushrooms every day of my life except for the few days before the Letting. My mother told me they would keep me alive. Only now, I understand why. They made my blood toxic. It never hurt me, I grew immune to the poison, but the poison will kill someone who gets a transfusion from me. Someone like—"

"Farnsworth," he says, finishing my thought. "It's brilliant."

I see the excitement come back to his eyes.

Painfully, I wonder if his revolution is the only thing Phoenix will ever love.

"He's here," I tell Phoenix and he nods. "I convinced him to come back here so I could see you…" My words hang out there, making me feel so incredibly vulnerable. "…and tell you my plan."

"It's a good plan. A great start. And I know Farnsworth's here. I saw you two get out of the helicopter. I saw you hold his hand."

"It was the only way to get him out. Otherwise, I was going to be kept in his mansion like a prisoner to be Let whenever he needed it. At least here, we're on my turf. And I thought here…never mind…" My words trailing off, I look down at my feet.

"What?" he asks. "Ronnie? Tell me."

My heart warms with the familiarity of the name, "Ronnie."

"I thought here I could see you." Tears stream down my cheeks. "And we could work together. You said…" I trip on my words. "You made it seem like—"

"Like what?" he asks.

"Like you liked me." I feel the heat rise in my cheeks. "Like we could be a team. You said I would help you with this revolution. You said you would never forget me." My voice is soft and shaky.

"All of that is true. And I want all of that with you, Ronnie." He takes a step closer. I watch as he lifts his hand and places it gently on my cheek. I close my eyes for only a moment.

"You say you do." I pull away. "But it really comes down to trust." My chest tightens as I speak to him. "Look at the way you reacted when I held Farnsworth's hand."

"I was jealous." His eyes mirror mine. Despite how exciting it seems—that Phoenix likes me so much the sight of me with another boy makes him jealous—I know there's so much more to it than that.

"It's not just jealousy," I say, softly. "It's trust. If you trusted me, you would have known I was obligated to hold Farnsworth's hand, for one reason or another. You would have felt sorry for me, not angry with me. For God's sake, Phoenix, you asked me if he was my boyfriend. After all this time, you still think it's possible I could be lured in by Farnsworth? I don't know if Phoenix the Revolutionary can ever really trust Veronica Billings. And without trust, Phoenix, we have nothing." It breaks my heart, but I begin to back away from him. I wince when my foot hits a stone. I feel a trickle of blood squirt up from between my toes.

"You're hurt." He points to my foot.

"Yes." My chest feels like it's caving in on itself. I look at him and wonder if deep inside he understands the hurt I'm feeling is not from my foot. It's from my heart.

Chapter Sixteen

I can't stand here, staring at him anymore. It's too painful, and I'm just running out of time. Whatever Phoenix has planned for his revolution, he had planned long before me. And I'm sure he'll complete it successfully without me. But I'm not the same as I was before I met Phoenix. Not in any way imaginable. Now I understand about the atrocities of the world we live in, and I need to do whatever I can to change them. At the very least, I need to save Lilly, Violet, and Raven even if they are the only three I ever save. My heart grows heavy when I realize Lulu was not on my short list.

I turn away from Phoenix and walk to the old shed that stands not far from the waterfront. I push open the door and fight my way in through the cobwebs. In the darkness it is nearly impossible to see, but I manage to find a piece of wood that may be wide enough to serve as a board; one hinge, though I probably need two or three; a short, old, rusty, but very strong pipe; and two old horse reins with bridles attached. This is just going to have to do. I also find screws and a screwdriver. That's just lucky. It takes me two trips to lug everything to the dock, and Phoenix is still standing on the beach, staring at me.

"Do you need help?" he asks.

"No thank you," I respond, immediately getting to work. Quickly I pull the board so the majority of it overhangs the dock. The board is heavy and the weight pulls me forward, toward the lake. I curse under my breath, knowing I'm about to fall in. Suddenly the weight of the board lessens tremendously, and I see Phoenix has come to help me. In the interest of time, I don't protest. It is difficult to work in this silly dress, but I don't have an option. I squat down to better position the board and the side of my gown rips up to mid-thigh. My eyes dart up to Phoenix who has most certainly noticed. My cheeks grow warm and my body longs for him. Just having him so close may be more than I can bear. With every breath, I wonder how he can smell so good, even though he is a rebel, living in the woods. Then I realize I have no idea where he lives. "Do you have a cabin?" I ask, as I place the pipe under the board. He holds the board steady for me.

"Yes, a ways from here." The pipe slips and the edge of the board smashes against his finger. "Damn it," he curses beneath his breath, shaking his hand.

"Oh, I'm sorry." Grabbing his hand, I examine his finger. "Do you think it's broken?"

"No." He flexes his hand. "No." He lifts his hand and strokes my hair. It is too much.

"Phoenix," I whisper, feeling my body respond to his touch in ways I've never felt before. "Being near you, it just—"

"I know. It's the same for me, too."

"But I meant what I said." I look up at him.

"I know you did." His hand lingers behind my head.

"Phoenix," I whisper, "I want nothing more than to fall against you, right here on this dock. To feel your arms around me. To have you kiss me again. But I can't and I won't do anything until I know you trust me."

"I do."

"I know you think you do. Your brain says you do. But your heart needs to lead on this one. If and when you can ever really trust me, then let's make a date to meet again, right here, exactly as we are tonight."

"Okay," he agrees, resolutely letting his hand drop to my shoulder. "Can I just ask one thing?"

"What?"

"Will you wear that dress?" He smiles at me and I smile back, both of us sharing a carefree moment in the middle of hell.

"It's a deal."

"Want to seal it with a—"

"Phoenix." I put my hand up. It takes all of my willpower to block his kiss. But I simply will not kiss him if he doesn't think enough of me to trust me. "We need to get to work."

He nods and scratches his head. "But Ronnie?" he asks.

"Yeah?"

"What the hell are you building anyway?"

"A diving board, of course." I refit the rusty pipe and use the reins and bridles to tether the board to the dock.

"Of course. Everyone builds a diving board in the middle of the night while they're waiting for the Principal Leader and his entourage."

"They would if they promised that Principal Leader a diving lesson."

"Ah," Phoenix laughs, tossing his head back. "So that's how you convinced him."

"Yup."

"And all this time I thought it was the dress."

"That didn't hurt," I say, smiling. He smiles back at me. "Come on, we've got to screw this hinge on and pray for the best. The rusty pipe is good. Makes it look like it's been up against the elements for a long time."

"Thoughtful touch." We adjust the board and test the tethers a few times.

"Well, I guess the only thing left to do is to try it."

"Want me to do the honors?" he asks. "In case it breaks? If it holds my weight, it'll certainly hold Farnsworth."

"No, thanks, I've got this. Believe me, he's pretty slight. There's no way he weighs as much as me."

I stand up and walk over to the board. Tentatively, I put one foot on then the other. I stand in the middle, but still I feel myself spring against the wood. Then the pipe rolls and I lose my balance. Phoenix grabs me by the arm and helps steady me.

"Thanks," I whisper. Slowly he removes his hand from my arm. The pipe finds its way into a groove on the dock, and the board feels much sturdier. "Here goes." I inch my way out to the end of the board where it is overhanging the dock.

"Wait," Phoenix hollers. I turn back to him. "Are you jumping in, in that dress?"

"I don't really see much of an option, do you?" I ask.

"Not one you'll approve of." He flashes the largest smile I have ever seen from Phoenix.

"Hm. Thought so. Now stand back or you'll get splashed."

"No way."

"Fair warning." I back up on the board. I let myself

run the two or three steps and then I put my arms into the air. I spring up and suddenly I am flying. I crash into the water and swim a few long, deep strokes before I pull myself up for a breath. My head pops through, and I grin at Phoenix. It feels every bit as good as I told Farnsworth it would. "It's incredible," I exclaim, while treading water.

"See? Completely dry," he teases, pointing to his clothes.

"I didn't mean my dive would get you wet." I splash Phoenix.

"Hey." He backs away from the dock. I splash him again and his fatigues get soaked. "Hey. Watch out for my gun." He holds it out from his body.

"I take no prisoners." I splash him again.

"You asked for it," he warns, laughing. Before I realize what is happening, Phoenix pulls off his gun and jumps in after me. He swims steadily and quickly. "You want to get splashed?" He pushes me under. I come up seconds later, laughing.

"You're soaked," I giggle.

"You too."

We tread water, side by side.

"Yes," I agree. "But I have a change of clothes back in my cabin. Do you? Do you still have those jeans you wore on that first day we met? All I ever see you in now are those fatigues and that horrible brown outfit of the Harvesters. Where did you ever get that, anyway?"

"I had it."

"What? So one of your revolutionaries was a Harvester and you took his old uniform?"

"Not exactly," Phoenix discloses, the joy leaving

his face.

"Well, what then?"

"It was mine."

"Yours?" I ask, growing tired from the swim. "Yours like you took it from a Harvester during a revolutionary battle?"

"No. Mine. Like it was my uniform."

"You were a Harvester?" I ask, stunned.

"Yes." He looks at me long and hard. Beads of water drop from his hair down his face.

"Back at the helicopter pickup when you were dressed in their uniform, you asked me how I could have even thought that. And I felt so horrible for asking. But I was right? How?"

"I didn't know. Once I knew what they were, I—"

"I can't believe this," I shout, swimming to the dock.

"Ronnie?" he pleads, swimming after me. "I thought you of all people—"

"Me of all people?" I yell, trying to catch my breath while crawling up on to the dock.

He is right beside me.

"Me of all people...? You...you lying hypocrite." I drag myself to my feet.

"Ronnie, wait. Listen—"

"No, you listen to me. All this time I've thought I wasn't good enough for you. That you were some saint who fell from heaven to save us all. But the truth is, your past is no better than mine."

"That's not true," he blurts. "I harvested maybe a few dozen. You led hundreds of girls to the Lettings."

I step back, appalled. As soon as he says it, he realizes what he's said.

"Ronnie, listen." He tries to take my hand. I push him away.

"No. No," I repeat with tears streaming down my face. I turn away and begin to walk toward the path that leads to camp. After a few steps, I turn back. "Do you know the worst part?" I ask him, letting the tears fall freely. "The worst part isn't how you made me feel. The worst part is how you judge everyone else based on the hatred you have for yourself. You can't trust me, because you don't trust yourself. And after all this time worrying if I was too stupid for you, or not perfect enough for you...after all that, I realize the problem isn't with me. It's with you."

I step away and squeeze some of the water out of my dress. "Now if you'll excuse me," I snip, "I have to go hunt up some mushrooms. Then soon, I have to pretend to be awakened by Farnsworth. And in a few hours, I have to begin to train a boy I detest, so I can detain him long enough to poison my own blood."

"Then what?" Phoenix asks.

"Then he will take me away again, and he will Let me. And after a few transfusions, he will die. Slowly and painfully. And during that time you'd better come up big, Saint Phoenix, 'cause I've got nothing else."

"Ronnie!" A tortured cry from the woods interrupts us. I turn, panicked it's one of my girls.

"Ron—" he says.

"Shh," I quiet Phoenix. "What was that?"

"Ronnie," the voice calls again.

"A trap?" he asks.

"No. I know that voice. It's weaker, but I know it..." I begin to walk toward the woods. Phoenix jogs up next to me.

"You're not going alone." He grabs my forearm and holds it tightly.

"Fine," I snarl through my teeth, shaking free of him. We walk a few feet up the path, and I hear the whisper.

"Ronnie," it cries. "Over here." I turn and there is Gretchen, half-dead, lying on the ground.

"Gretchen." I squat next to her. "What happened to you?" Her teeth are chattering, and the pale blue circles under her eyes are a dark gray. Her hair is knotted, and she looks like a ghost of herself. I wrap my arms around her.

"He's out of control," she whispers.

"Gunnar?" Phoenix asks with fierce determination. She nods.

"He's been petitioning people in the city to join his revolution. He wants to be the new Principal Leader. But his motives are just as bad as Farnsworth's." She coughs as she speaks.

"Take it easy," I say.

"What is he planning?" Phoenix asks, with no regard for Gretchen's condition.

"A huge takeover. He wants everything that Farnsworth has: money, power, position. He wants to kill as many Leeches as he can and then move his followers into the Inferno." She moans softly as she speaks. "He's riled everyone up—all of those lonely men in the city—they want revenge. He wants to get even. He's going to kill every girl in the Inferno who's ripe, and any girl who's blossomed will be sent to Coupling facilities with his rebels. It's horrible, Ron. He's a sick, sick man."

"What's his strategy?" Phoenix asks. His brow is

furrowed, and I can see worry lines etched in his skin.

"He's armed his followers, and he's planning to march his masses from the city to the Inferno. All of them. He has talked every man, woman, and child into it."

"Why wouldn't he?" Phoenix asks. "They are tired of living in squalor, the girls being summoned to the Lettings, and the young women to the Couplings. It's a disgrace. Any idea when he's planning his move?"

"Yes." She tries to breathe through a hacking cough. "He said he will march on the Inferno before the next full moon."

"That's no more than five days away." Phoenix clenches his teeth.

"What do we do?" I ask them.

"That's why I came to you." Gretchen wheezes. "He'll have me killed for treason, no doubt. And I wouldn't blame you if you killed me first, after what I did to you. But I had to risk it to tell you."

"Lulu?" I ask.

"She's right there with him, of course." It's painful to listen to Gretchen speak. Her voice sounds exhausted. "She is his biggest selling point. Every mother will listen to a girl who's escaped the Lettings, and every man will listen to Gunnar and his stories of the Inferno. The city's like a festering boil, ready to explode."

I can see the fear in her eyes.

"We know how to stop Farnsworth, secretly," Phoenix tells her. "Ronnie figured it out. But then the Inferno will be without leadership. And it will be the perfect time for Gunnar to make his way to power." Phoenix looks devastated. "So we will be replacing one tyrannical dictator with—"

"A psychopath," I interject, finishing his sentence.

"Yes." Gretchen nods along.

"What was your original plan?" I ask Phoenix.

"It seems so useless now, but...we were also going to rally the people of the city, but not in anger, in a peaceful demonstration. Together we would say, 'no more.' My contact would get Gunnar and me in, and Gunnar would stop Farnsworth in hand to hand combat—not to kill him, just detain him—while I reasoned with the masses. Back then, we didn't even think about killing Farnsworth. But now, that's changed," he says, quietly, looking down. "Just like so many other things." His eyes dart up at me for a moment.

"Anyway, the people of the city would be assembled in a peaceful, non-violent way, not allowing the men and women of the Inferno to escape until I had convinced them of what Farnsworth had done." His words are running together, quickly. "I had heard about protests like this in an ancient history book I found buried deep in a cellar of an abandoned building when I lived in the city. Somehow, those leaders of long ago changed their worlds in completely non-violent ways by just having people band together for the greater good. Then, Gunnar and I would serve as interim Principal Leaders, with a kind of system of 'checks and balances' I heard existed so very long ago. It sounded like a good way to govern. While we served, the people from the city and the Inferno would elect their new Principal Leader together. Now I realize what a load of crap that whole plan was."

"It wasn't crap," I say. "It was just idealistic. And

there's nothing wrong with that."

"Yeah, except it doesn't work."

"Well, the first thing we have to do is get Gretchen to base. Can you help me with her?" Phoenix leans down, picks up Gretchen, and throws her over his shoulder. Even though Gretchen is tiny and frail, I am still amazed by his strength. "You can only walk us to where the gravel path morphs into base camp. Otherwise you'll be spotted for sure."

"Okay," Phoenix agrees. We walk up the hill carefully, and in silence. Even though Gretchen is tiny, I can see the exertion in Phoenix. Once we make it to the top, he sets Gretchen down, carefully.

I turn to him. "I'll take her from here. I'll take care of her. You'd better get moving on your plan, because we're officially out of time."

He nods, solemnly. Out of the corner of my eye, I see a mushroom patch. I run over to see if they're my mushrooms. "These aren't mine," I mutter, disappointed. "I need to look for mine if we want to get this plan started."

"There's more over here." Gretchen points to another patch. I eye her skeptically, grateful I am the one who knows what the mushrooms look like. For all I know, this is an elaborate ruse and Gretchen is here to kill me. But I figure I have cheated death so many times, what's the sense of being afraid now. I look at the mushroom patch and surprisingly, she was right. These are my mushrooms. I bend down and pick four.

"Are you sure those are yours?" Phoenix asks.

"Very." I dust the dirt off one. "See?" I turn the mushroom over. "This is how you tell." I show him exactly what my mother showed me, how the large round, circular spores hang onto the bottom of the cap.

"You eat all four at once?" he asks.

"Un-uh." I wipe the mushroom off the best I can. "Only one. Eating more than one at once...wouldn't be good. The other three are for the next nights, in case I can't break free of Farnsworth again."

"Can I try one?" Phoenix asks, curious.

"No." I pull them away from him. "If you're not used to them, even one can make you black out for hours. I've built up a tolerance." I chew and swallow the mushroom, quickly. "Okay," I say to Phoenix, dropping the mushrooms to the ground. "Let me have your shirt."

"What?" he asks. "Why do you want my shirt?"

"Because there is a very good chance someone, namely Farnsworth, would have noticed I was missing. I am putting the soaking wet shirt on Gretchen to make it look like she had been sleepwalking and she fell into the lake. I woke up, saw she was gone, and ran to the waterfront. Naturally, I jumped in after her." I shrug and sigh. "It's the best I've got."

"It's good," Phoenix responds. He takes his gun off from around his neck and lays it on the ground by his foot. I keep a watchful eye to make sure Gretchen doesn't go for the gun. Honestly, she looks too weak even to try. Then, forgetting the buttons, Phoenix yanks his shirt up over his head with one hand. He stands there, bare-chested in the moonlight, and I have to steady myself. He looks so incredibly strong, powerful and handsome...I can barely move. I feel my jaw go slack, but I can't seem to close my mouth. Only now do I realize I've never before seen a boy without his shirt. But still, I know there's no way they could all look like this. He is so perfectly chiseled I can see every muscle of his abdomen. My eyes wander up across his bare chest to his broad, toned shoulders. Then I watch the muscles in his biceps flex as he hands me the shirt.

"Ron?" He holds the shirt out to me. "Ronnie?"

"Oh. Thanks," I mumble, shaking my head from embarrassment. I know he saw me staring at him. I look over at Gretchen who is grinning through her pain. He slings the gun back across his bare chest as I slip his shirt over Gretchen's head and help her to her feet. His shirt hangs down to her knees and, standing there, she looks no bigger than my three sleeping girls. I smile at her, wondering if I can ever forgive her for setting me up to take the fall for our entire corrupt government.

"Come on." I bend down to scoop up my mushrooms, wrap my arm around her shoulder, and she wraps hers around my hips. Slowly, we make our way up the few remaining steps of the path toward camp.

No sooner do we hit the grass, I see a flashlight being waved just yards ahead of me. "Damn," I say. "It's Farnsworth. He's incredibly needy. Do you remember our story?"

"Yes," she whispers, barely able to speak.

"Veronica!" It's Farnsworth, all right. His voice is stern, but relieved. "I have been looking everywhere for you." I hide the mushrooms in my palm and tuck my hand carefully under Gretchen's arm.

"Why?" I can tell that is not the response he expected.

"Why?" he asks, gathering his thoughts. "Because you're supposed to be in bed and you're not."

"How did you know?" I ask, standing my ground. There is something about being on my own turf that makes me very bold. Maybe too bold.

"Because I knocked on your door, and you didn't answer." His eyes are steady on mine.

"At this hour? What if I had been asleep? Would you have barged into my private quarters?"

"Well," he takes a step closer. "Technically, it is my camp. So technically, I do own everything in it. Including the cabins—"

"Maybe you do own everything in it," I say. "But you don't own every*one* in it. That includes me. Your personal donor. But now that I know how you feel… I'll be just fine sleeping outside of camp, so I can have my privacy and not crowd any of your possessions." The lack of sleep and my fight with Phoenix is making me too brazen.

"That won't be necessary," Farnsworth declares, eyeing me coolly. "So tell me, Veronica, who is your friend?"

"Gretchen, sir. She is a fellow Leader. Surely you know of her."

"Gretchen, Gretchen…" He repeats the name over and over. I'm certain his mind is reeling with thoughts. Does he know her? And what were we doing?

"Well, maybe it will spark your memory, sir, when I tell you Gretchen is in poor health. She is also prone to sleepwalking. When I woke tonight, and I realized she was gone, I knew exactly where to look. Thank goodness I arrived in time."

"Yes," Farnsworth agrees. "Thank goodness. But tell me, Gretchen, why do you think you go to the waterfront when you sleepwalk?"

"She doesn't know where—"

"That's okay, Veronica." Farnsworth holds up his

hand to silence me. "Let her speak."

"She's very weak, sir."

"I have time." He looks at Gretchen. I see her tremble.

"I think I go to the waterfront because...well, because I can't swim." Gretchen looks directly at Farnsworth, and he raises his eyebrows, intrigued. I see she has sparked his interest.

"So you're trying to do away with yourself?"

"No, sir," she mutters, her eyes staring at the ground. "I think my subconscious wants me to be stronger. It pushes me to do those things I am most afraid of so I can grow healthier and more resilient."

"I understand," he murmurs, and I know he actually does understand. Probably better than I ever could.

"Maybe I should park myself at the waterfront round the clock, just to keep an eye on you." While he speaks to Gretchen, he eyes me.

I don't flinch. Then I think, maybe I'm too still, so I allow myself a small smile. "That would certainly help with our training, sir."

"Yes, wouldn't it?" He smiles along with me, as if he knows so much more.

"Luckily," Gretchen says, trying to rescue me, "Veronica is always there to save me."

"Yes," he agrees, his eyes darting to mine. "Luckily Veronica is there to be our savior." For a moment, I almost feel bad for him. Then I remember my girls, asleep, after having nearly been bled to death.

"Well, I'm not going to be able to do anything for anyone if we don't get some sleep," I announce. My arm is still under Gretchen's shoulders, keeping her upright, and I feel the mushrooms growing sweaty in my grasp.

"Just one more thing," Farnsworth asks. "Why are you wearing a man's camouflage jacket?" Gretchen tries to remain cool but her eyes dart up to me. Farnsworth may very well think Gretchen had gone to the waterfront to meet her boyfriend, and I am covering for her. If that were true, we could both be convicted for breaking the law, but she would be punished much more severely than me. I could just let her take the blame and walk away virtually unscathed…but no.

"I told you," I tease Gretchen, good-naturedly.

"You did," she banters back, obviously unsure of where I'm going with this. I speak to Farnsworth.

"I have told her, I don't know how many times, the camouflage jackets belong to boys. But we don't get a lot of choices of clothing here, and she is always hiding herself in those oversized jackets."

"I'm always cold," she explains, visibly shaking.

"That's true," I add. "We really don't have much need for proper fashions here."

Farnsworth nods, and he may even believe us. Thankfully our conversation is interrupted by the sounds of Farnsworth's entourage arriving. He looks sadly in the direction of the trucks that have just pulled up.

"Well, I guess the party's over," he whispers. He looks profoundly depressed. His nurse is one of the first people out of the truck. He sighs.

"Well, since this is for you, if you don't mind, I'm going to take Gretchen back to bed, and I'm going to get some sleep too. We have a busy day ahead."

"Fine, fine, of course." Farnsworth dismisses us,

but I feel him watching us as I walk past. "Veronica." He speaks just as we've taken a few steps toward the cabins. "I'll have some proper clothes sent to you and the girls, so why don't you leave that horrible shirt outside your cabin tomorrow and I'll have it disposed of for you." My blood runs cold. He knows something. I turn slowly, suddenly wishing I could eat all four of my mushrooms at once.

"That's very kind of you, sir." Despite the sweat pooling on my lower back, I remain calm, my eyes locked on his. "But we have very little use here for dresses of this type." I motion to the gown I'm wearing.

"Well I would have thought that dress works just fine, since you were either sleeping in it, or it was the thing you threw on to run to the waterfront."

Damn, I forgot to justify my wardrobe.

"I fell asleep in it, sir. And we don't mind keeping the boyish clothes. What we could use, if you would care to be so generous, is better food." Both Farnsworth and Gretchen look at me like I've gone insane. No one ever speaks to Farnsworth like that.

"Really?" he asks. "The cuisine's not to your liking?"

"No sir, it's not." My voice is level and even. "You know we live on protein bars and powdered milk."

"And what would you like, Veronica?"

"Fresh milk, for the girls. And solid food."

"And what do I get in return?" He sounds snakelike.

"Stronger, healthier girls with stronger, healthier blood."

"Ah ha!" he exclaims. "Well, I'm sure something can be done."

"Thank you, sir. And I'll be sure to leave the offensive shirt outside our door to be disposed of."

"Very good, Veronica." We walk past him and into our cabin as voices and shouts are heard from the trucks belonging to Farnsworth's entourage.

****

I drop Gretchen onto her bed and collapse on the floor next to her. "What were you thinking?" she asks.

"I don't know. The truth is I just don't care anymore. Over the past week I've found out I'm a monster, my mother is probably dead, my best friend's betrayed me, and the boy that I like has turned out to be someone I don't know at all. The only thing I'm living for is to save those little girls."

"I thought Gunnar and I would be together forever," Gretchen confesses quietly. She flips onto her side and snuggles against her pillow. "Like in those secret stories people used to tell about the Old World and how people fell in love and had babies, and nothing had to do with arrangements or blood types."

"So what happened?"

"He only used me to get to you. Then when he realized you were being protected by Phoenix, he threw me away."

"I'm sorry," I say. She nods.

"I'm sorry, too." She looks at me, her large eyes soft and sincere. "Here." She slips out of Phoenix's now dried shirt. "He'd want you to wear it, not me."

"I can't," I whisper, fighting back tears. "I can't do anything with him. He isn't who I thought he was."

"No?" Gretchen asks. "Well, you weren't who he thought you were either." Before I can even process her words, she has fallen asleep.

Chapter Seventeen

I wake up on the floor of my cabin with Phoenix's shirt wrapped around me. "Phoenix?" I whisper, but then I realize I'm alone. It's only the scent, lingering in the air from his shirt, that makes me think he's here. I bury my nose deeply into the warm camouflage pattern and breathe him in. Just the scent of him sends a thrill through my body and brings a smile to my face. Then my smile turns to tears when I realize Phoenix and I could never and will never happen. When I finish crying, I wipe away my tears and pull myself together. How did anyone ever survive a relationship that wasn't prearranged? How impossible it is to do anything when you are led by nothing but emotions. I throw Phoenix's shirt outside the cabin and strip out of my dinner dress. I change into my black swimsuit, black shorts, and tank top. I tug on my boots and pull my hair back into a ponytail. I catch my reflection in the glass. I look...determined. I am ready.

Moments later, I hear reveille. "Gretchen?" She doesn't stir. "Gretchen?" I repeat, and she moves slightly. "It's breakfast." Then I turn and walk out of the cabin into the hot summer day, knowing Gretchen may not be able to drag herself out of bed in time to make it to breakfast. But since she's been gone for days, surely Margaret won't be surprised to see Gretchen miss another meal. Truthfully, I think

Margaret doesn't care. She is still willing to believe Lulu is confined to an old cabin, quarantined because of her illness. And considering what Gretchen's done to me, I did more than enough to help her.

I take a deep breath and walk to Farnsworth's cabin. I knock on the door, hastily, before I change my mind.

"Good morning, sir," I offer in the most upbeat voice I can muster. Farnsworth pulls open the door looking better than usual. His normally pale cheeks have a slight blush to them. He is wearing a pair of red silk pajamas. "Sir? Good morning."

"Veronica," he exclaims, looking happy to see me. "You came?"

"Of course I did, sir." I shift my weight from one foot to the other. "Breakfast is in fifteen. If you want to shower, it's over there." I point to the latrine. "And please wear a swimsuit. We'll be heading to the waterfront as soon as breakfast is over." I turn to go.

"Veronica," he calls, just as I've walked a few feet away. His voice makes my skin crawl, but I turn back to face him. "I just wanted to say thank you." This I was not expecting.

"You're welcome, sir." I feel just the slightest twinge of guilt. I turn and rush away as quickly as possible.

****

The feeling of guilt I have toward Farnsworth is immediately eradicated when I step foot in the mess hall and see Lilly, Violet, and Raven all hunched over bowls of oatmeal, cramming the food in as fast as they can swallow. "Ronnie." Lilly smiles at me.

"Come try this," Violet squeals. "It's called

oatmeal. It's delicious." She speaks between mouthfuls, and Raven nods along. All three girls dive back into their bowls of oatmeal.

"You've never had oatmeal before?" I ask the girls. When I was young my mother would often make me oatmeal for breakfast. It was by no means considered a luxury food. She called it "stick-to-your-ribs" food. Sometimes, it was all we had to eat all day, but at least we had a good start. Come to think of it, I don't think I have seen oatmeal at all during my time at camp.

"Ronnie." It's Willy, behind the counter, waving me over.

"Hi, Willy," I exclaim, rushing up to him and throwing my arms around his neck. It feels good to have a friend. He gives me a big bear hug and spins me around.

"You have no idea how glad I am to see you." Willy plops me back on the ground. "I was worried there," he says, his voice low and hurried.

"You don't have to worry, Willy. I can take care of myself."

"Oh I know that, Ronnie. I know. But when they start talking biggest Let in history…" He looks away and shakes his head. "All for what? To keep that little weasel of a Principal Leader we have alive? I say good riddance to him. Everything's gone from bad to worse since he came into power." Willy busies himself, pouring milk into glasses. I take another gallon and pour along with him.

"At least we have fresh milk this morning," I offer, trying to lighten the mood.

"For today," Willy grumbles. "For today."

"Just please be careful of what you say. You know

Farnsworth and his entourage are here, on campus."

"Oh, I know." Willy takes the filled glasses and lines them up on the counter for pickup. "Tell you the truth"—Willy leans in close—"crossed my mind to poison him while he was here." I start for a second, wondering if I should tell him. No, of course not. This has to be my secret.

"I get it," I say. "But don't do it. Poisoning's not your thing." He nods, acquiescing. I give him a big kiss on the cheek and start passing out glasses of milk to all the girls at breakfast. I smile at each one as I hand out the milk, wondering how many will be changed by this revolution, and how many will simply die. It's a harrowing thought, and I fight a chill as I pass out cup after cup.

"Look at this now," Willy complains. I can hear the disgust in his voice. Slowly he waddles to the fridge and back. This time he carries a few dozen eggs, huge packages of some kind of meat and a bunch of green spears. "Eggs, bacon, and asparagus for their breakfast." He shakes his head. "And wait, that's not all." He waddles away again and comes back with a large bowl filled with small round fruit on a vine. "Grapes," he announces. "Go ahead, try one." Willy nods to the bowl.

"No, thanks, Willy. That's Farnsworth's breakfast."

"Just try one," Willy dares.

"Uh-un."

"Oh, go ahead, Veronica, why don't you try one?" I freeze when I hear the voice. It's Farnsworth. In the commotion of breakfast, I didn't hear him slither in.

"Principal Leader Farnsworth." I stand up straight,

trying to hide the grapes behind my back. I feel like a child who just got caught sneaking an extra piece of candy. "I didn't hear you come in."

Willy has taken the grapes and moved away. I turn to the mess hall that is loud and chaotic. "Girls?" I call. Only a few quiet down. "Girls," I repeat, raising my voice.

Willy picks up two pans from the kitchen and bangs them together. He startles Farnsworth with the noise and smiles a small secret smile at me. A hush falls over the mess hall.

"Thank you, ladies," I begin. "Now, as most of you know, Principal Leader Farnsworth will be joining us for the next few days, and he is here right now. I would like you all to show him the utmost respect. Principal Leader Farnsworth?" I move to the side. He takes my place at the center of the floor and everyone in the mess hall stands.

"Thank you, ladies." He walks down the center aisle. "I am honored to be here at your camp. Thank you for inviting me."

Inviting? The girls are doing a wonderful job of welcoming him. Well, all except Raven. Her arms are crossed in front of her body, and her jaw is set tight. I raise my eyebrows at her, and she understands. Immediately she drops her crossed arms but refuses to smile.

"Well, I hope you all have a wonderful training period here with Veronica." Farnsworth smiles directly at me. "I know I plan to. Carry on," he finishes, dismissing everyone.

The girls stand still, unsure of what to do.

"Finish your breakfasts, please, girls," I say. "And

then report to your first period activities."

A general murmur is heard, but the girls are speaking quietly. I overhear one of them saying she thinks Farnsworth is "cute." Maybe he is handsome, but to me he is as attractive as a venomous moccasin snake that's slithered out of the lake and made his home in my boot. Behind me, I hear the clatter of pots and pans being thrown about as Willy cooks Farnsworth's breakfast. Margaret waltzes into the mess hall to survey the situation. She salutes Farnsworth and glares at me. Raven is standing next to Violet and Lilly, telling them something meant for their ears alone. And I am about to take a non-swimming, uncontrollable bleeder to the waterfront to jump off a barely tethered piece of old wood, held in position by a rusty pipe, all while I secretly poison myself. Today is going to be interesting.

****

It takes Farnsworth a very long time to make it down to the waterfront. "Are you sure we're going the right way?" he asks more than once.

"Positive." I want to tell him I've only made this trek six times a day, every day, for the past umpteen years. But I don't. I just keep offering encouraging smiles. Finally, I see water before us. "Just there." I point ahead. I wish I had my girls with me as a sort of buffer between me and Farnsworth, but I decided to send them to train with the AB's today, keeping them a safe distance from Farnsworth.

Suddenly he stops.

"Principal Leader Farnsworth, sir? The water's just there. Are you okay?" I watch him stare blankly ahead. He doesn't answer. "Sir?" I repeat. "Would you like me to go get some help?" I knew it was a terrible idea when

Farnsworth refused to allow anyone to accompany us to the waterfront. He shakes his head, slowly.

"No, thank you Veronica," he whispers. "I just need a moment."

"Okay." I stand there awkwardly next to him. We stand for full minutes and the sun beats down on us, hard. The glare is giving me a headache, so I reach down to a patch of muddy dirt and run my finger through it. I smear the dirt on my cheekbones under both eyes and immediately I am relieved. I stand up and Farnsworth is staring at me.

"What?" I ask. "The sun's too bright. Want some?"

He nods.

"Okay." I scoop down to retrieve more mud. "We're lucky, I didn't know it rained. Gives us a little mud." I reach up and smear the mud under one of his eyes. I am very gentle when I smear it, like I am touching one of my girls. I gather more mud and begin to smear it under his other eye when he reaches up and grabs my hand. "Oh!" I say, with a start. "I'm sorry sir, did I hurt you?"

"No," he snaps, "not at all. I'm a man, Veronica." He still has a grasp on my arm. "Why would you think you would hurt me by smearing some dirt on my face?"

"Sorry sir." I am painfully aware he is still holding on tightly to my wrist. "It's a habit I have from taking care of little girls for so long."

"I understand."

"Um, sir?" I look at him directly. "You are still holding on to my wrist. Um…could you please let me go?"

"Reluctantly," he sighs, smiling at me. I feel my eyes open wide in response to Farnsworth's creepy smile. He drops my hand, and I desperately feel the need to get clean. My glorious lake is only yards away.

"Uh, let's swim." I turn away from him and walk toward the lake. As soon as I hit the beach, I yank off my boots, tank top, and shorts. Without looking back or waiting for him, I run out and dive into the water. The lake feels welcoming and forgiving, and cleansing. I never want to get out. I feel like staying immersed here forever, away from all my problems, but eventually I need air. When I pop my head up, there is Farnsworth, on the side of the lake, waiting for me. I am suddenly, and for the first time ever, extremely uncomfortable in my swimsuit. But I am stuck in the water, and my clothes are lying haphazardly on the beach next to Farnsworth.

I swim toward the shore and stand. I walk to him, aware that he is watching me too closely. But I don't care. I refuse to let Farnsworth take away the freedom I feel at my waterfront. And for goodness sake, I'm in my swimsuit. I'm not naked.

"Your turn," I say, standing in front of him on the beach. I feel the water drops make their way from my hair down my face and body. The mud I smeared on my cheeks is long gone, but his is beginning to dry in the sun. I know in a few minutes it'll become very itchy. "We should get the mud off your face or it'll itch soon. It's only a temporary fix."

"Okay." He stares at the water like it's his enemy, and I can tell his confidence is waning.

"Uh, did you wear your swimsuit?" I ask. Slowly he slips out of his athletic pants to reveal a swimsuit underneath. He unzips a sweatshirt and he is wearing some sort of long sleeve swim top under the sweatshirt.

I've never seen anything like it, but I know better than to question it. "That must be better." I dig little holes in the sand with my toe. "Were you incredibly hot?"

"No, not at all," he tells me.

"Oh, okay." Like Gretchen, he must be cold all the time. "So let's get started. Why don't you wash that mud off now?"

He looks as if he's unable to figure out how. Does this man truly run our government?

"Just squat down and rinse it off." He does, and when he stands up again, I see he has bruises on both of his cheeks, exactly where I had placed the mud. "What is that?" I ask before I realize what I'm doing. I reach up and touch his cheek but he shies away.

"Nothing." He moves away from me, embarrassed. "I fell off my horse the other day. Probably some leftover bruising you didn't notice before."

"Oh, sure." I'm shocked by how my light touch could have caused him to bruise like that. "Well then, let's start by getting your feet wet." I am painfully aware that for the next three hours, I am going to have to teach a porcelain doll how to swim.

****

Later, Farnsworth sits next to me, exhausted. We are on the beach, staring out at the lake. His breathing is labored, but he looks happy. He should. He was much braver in the water than I ever anticipated he would be, and he has made real progress toward becoming a proficient swimmer.

"Thank you, Veronica."

"You're welcome." I pick up a stick and start to trace shapes in the sand, absentmindedly.

"You know," he continues, still looking out at the

water. "I knew I could trust you."

"Why's that, sir?" I am actually curious.

"Because of your loyalty to the government, for one thing. You know the impressive record of Veronica Billings has not gone by me unnoticed."

I flinch when he says these words.

"Thank you, sir," I manage to eke out.

"I also know someone who's been as successful as you would have to be smarter than the rest."

"Well, that's very nice of you to say." I'm still looking at the dirt by my feet. "But I promise I am no smarter than most. As a matter of fact, I am probably one of the least intelligent people you'll ever meet." I feel sad as I say these words.

"Why would you say that?" he asks.

"Well, for one thing, I am incredibly naïve."

"Really? Elaborate, please."

"Well, I believe just about anything. And I've made some bad decisions. And I trust when I shouldn't." I wonder if he knows I'm talking about him.

"I don't believe that," he debates. "Look at us." He's turned, facing me now. "You have been at this camp for what, seven years now?" I nod. "And in that time you must have heard countless stories about me and what a horrible dictator I am."

"No…" I mumble.

"Of course you did." He flashes his overly white teeth. "But you're still here, helping me. You didn't believe any of the nonsense people told you about me. I know that because you've had ample opportunity to let me die out here today, and you haven't. It's hard to know whom to trust." Farnsworth lets his shoulder nudge mine, like we're old friends. "And I'm glad to know I can trust you." He interlaces his hand in mine. I pull my hand from his and look him dead in the eyes.

"You can trust me, sir. But you can't push me to do anything I'm not ready to do. Friends don't do that to one another."

"Friends?" he asks. "I'll take that, Veronica. I would very much like to be your friend." He puts out his hand, and we shake on it. "That's the toughest part, you know." He leans back. He lifts one long, elegant arm in the air and points to an eagle flying overhead.

"What's that?" I ask.

"The trust. Finding someone, anyone, who wants to be my friend because I'm me, not because of what I can do for them."

"I can understand that." I dig a hole with my stick.

"But you flat-out said no to my offer to live in my mansion. You'll take the cramped quarters and the horrible food and the damned mosquitoes—by the way, why aren't they biting you?"

"Built up a tolerance." I shrug. "Believe me, in a couple more days they won't want to bite you either."

"Oh, I hope you're right," he retorts, swatting. "My nurse would never allow me more than a couple of bites." He looks away. "Anyway," he looks back at me, "you'll take all of it to stay at your beloved camp, rather than living in paradise with me."

"Everyone has their own version of paradise I guess," I whisper, thinking of Phoenix and me in this very same lake, just last night.

"I guess. But that's one of the ways I know you're for real," he expounds. "You turned down the luxury and the money. You asked for food for the girls, and nothing for you."

I shrug again.

"Not many people would, Veronica. And about you not being smart, well I think that's nonsense. Even if you weren't one of the last remaining O's, you'd still be a very special person." My heart warms slightly.

"Thank you," I mumble.

"Just promise one thing."

"What's that?"

"Don't let anyone convince you of horrible things about me. Form your own opinions. People who don't have, so often attack those who do. I appreciate all the hard work you've done over the years." As he speaks, my stomach flips over. "I appreciate you exactly as you are. Not despite the choices you've made, but because of them."

I turn to him, stunned.

"I'm not saying I'm perfect or without fault," he continues, looking away. "But I am doing my best in an imperfect world. My father died when I was fourteen," he admits suddenly. "And I took over for him. Many people love me, and what I've done for them. Many others do not." He tosses his head and laughs, almost as if it's a private joke between us. He smiles at me, and then his face grows much more serious. "Just remember when you're in a leadership position, like you and like me, it's hard to find someone who truly cares about you without having their own motivation."

"I've never thought of that," I say, quietly.

"Because you haven't dealt with that many rebels," he explains, arching his back to stretch his spine. "One day someone will try to convince you that I'm the Devil and you are therefore guilty by association. And one day they'll try to get you to turn on me. I just hope you remember today, and that we're friends, real friends, because of who we are. Not despite it."

My head grows dizzy, and I'm clouded by confusion. Is it possible this boy cares about me because of who I've been, and the other, despite it? We hear a noise from the woods and Farnsworth is on his feet, before me. It is a soft noise, almost a flutter, like someone very light on his or her feet.

Not Phoenix, I pray silently. Not now. It's too soon. But when I open my eyes to see what is happening, Farnsworth is walking toward me with a small, injured bird in his hand.

"It must have fallen from its nest," he concludes, looking up through the trees for the bird's possible home.

"Is he hurt badly?" I ask, walking to Farnsworth.

"It's hard to tell. Might be his wing." He opens the bird's wing with one hand while he holds its body in the other. When he tests the second wing, the bird squawks. "That's it. I don't think it's broken, but it might be sprained. If it's okay by you, maybe we should head back to camp and see what we can do for him."

"Okay," I mumble, utterly confused. "I'll uh, call for the cart to drive back up that hill."

"I can walk up a hill, Veronica." There is a note of sharpness in his voice.

"I'm certain you can, sir. But I thought it would be better for the bird if we hurried."

"Of course," he mumbles, letting me radio for help. Truthfully, I know he could never make it up that path, but I won't tell him that right now. Not now, when he is doing such a remarkably selfless thing. The three of us sit together on a large rock as we wait for the cart to come to take us up the hill. Out of the corner of my eye, I watch him petting the bird so gently it moves me. He catches me looking at him, and his eyes meet mine. I sit there, my eyes searching his, looking for an answer. Looking for proof he is the killer I think he is, and not the kind, confident, misunderstood leader he is being right now.

Chapter Eighteen

I am lying on my cot with three mushrooms resting on my belly. They rise up and down in time with my breath, and I debate, over and over again, eating them. What happened this afternoon? Who was that man at the lake with me? Is he a ruthless, selfish dictator? Or is he a soft, gentle man who is doing the best he can to handle a world that is out of control? And more importantly, why am I having these doubts?

I look over at Gretchen who is sleeping soundly in her cot. I wonder if she ever even woke up today. I look at her for a long time, questioning who she really is. What happened to the best friend I shared everything with? Is she still in there, somewhere? Did disgust over our perceived world make her change into this new person, this rebel, or is it all because of love for a boy? And what about Phoenix? Gunnar and Buzzcut made no secret of the fact they were hunting me, so how do I fit into this picture? Has Phoenix really fallen for me? Or am I simply a valuable commodity? And is he certain Farnsworth is behind all of these atrocities?

I lift the mushroom up and stare at it, long and hard. How can something so small be capable of causing so much damage? Then I think of tiny Lulu, rallying troops to help Gunnar in his planned overthrow of our government. I close my eyes and concentrate. What do I know for sure? What are the facts? I have strong feelings for Phoenix, yes, but in truth, I don't know him at all. I thought I knew Gretchen inside and out, yet for years, she kept the ultimate secret from me. People tell me Farnsworth is, in no uncertain terms, a child-killer, but today I saw a very kind man who saved an injured bird's life. What is real? And how do you ever know? Underneath it all, there is only one thing I can be certain of. My mother. My mother would be in contact with me if she were alive. So the only plausible explanation is that Farnsworth has taken her life, directly or indirectly. I pop the mushroom in and chew quickly. I swallow hard before I can change my mind. I just hope I have the right reasons for sending a man to his death.

I doze off for awhile, but I'm awakened by a light scratching on my screen window. *Phoenix?* I wonder as I spring up out of bed. I rush outside careful not to let the door slam shut behind me. I run to the side of the cabin and my heart drops when I realize it's only a June bug, bouncing against the screen. I turn, heartbroken, and begin to walk back to the door, careful not to wake anyone in camp. Then I hear something.

"Ronnie?" I turn in the darkness and see Phoenix, crouching low on the ground beside a bush.

"Phoenix..." I cry, rushing into his arms. We embrace, and I let all the concerns I have fall away for the moment. I let the excuse of my sleepiness allow me to act without thought. I just want him and here he is.

"Ronnie..." His hand strokes my hair.

"It's not safe here, you have to leave. He's here, right here, in that cabin..." I point toward the once abandoned cabin at the edge of camp. "He has guards. Anyone can spot you. Please," I beg.

"I know. But I couldn't stand how we parted. I do trust you, Ronnie, more than anyone ever in my life. And I'm sorry I never told you about me having been a Harvester. I just...I guess I just want to pretend it never happened. And there is no way I think I'm any better than you. Please," he pleads, holding me by the shoulders. "You have to believe me."

"I do." And right then and there, I know how to recognize what's real and what isn't. I listen to my heart. And my heart says I have to believe Phoenix.

"I always believed I needed to keep my friends close and my enemies closer, but Ron, I don't want to live like that anymore. I don't want to push you away. I don't want us to be apart, ever again."

"Me either," I say, my eyes tearing. "But what can we do?"

"I don't know how, but we'll find a way. None of this has gone as I've planned. None of it. But maybe that's how I know it's right."

"Veronica?" I hear, and I turn, startled. In the black cloak of night, Farnsworth has found us.

"What are you doing here?" I ask.

"I think that's the question I should be asking you," Farnsworth snaps, looking at Phoenix deliberately. "It seems to be a nasty little habit you have, sneaking off to meet your friends in these remote places in the middle of the night."

"I wasn't sneaking. I heard a noise," I claim, having no better lie prepared. "I didn't know what it was." I am stalling, trying anything. I know Phoenix must have his gun, but I know if he uses it now, the small army Farnsworth brought to camp will retaliate and shoot him for sure. We are all standing still, waiting for someone else to make a move.

"And what was it?" Farnsworth asks in his snakelike tone. "The noise you heard?"

"It was me." Phoenix steps forward. "I'm a wanderer. I stumbled into the camp and this girl came out to head me off. All I'm looking for is some food."

"Really?" Farnsworth asks, skeptically. "And you just happened to guess the nickname of this girl you just stumbled upon?" I look at Phoenix, panicked. There is no way out of this. Everything we've done is illegal, from our feelings for one another, to our plans for a revolution. Gunnar will march into the Inferno in a few days if we don't stop him, and there is no way out of any of this for us.

"It's not her, it's me," Phoenix declares, pushing me behind him and standing up tall, toe to toe with Farnsworth.

"You?" Farnsworth asks. I can see his small eyes trying to look deep into Phoenix's mind. Trying to figure him out.

"Yes."

"But I know you, from… somewhere…"

"My face is common," Phoenix shrugs and despite everything, I have to smile, knowing this is anything but the truth. "Veronica has no interest in me." He is trying to sway Farnsworth. "I've tried, but I've gotten nowhere with her. As a matter of fact, she's told me in no uncertain terms that it will never happen between us."

"Is that true, Veronica?" Farnsworth asks. He sounds honestly interested.

"Yes," I lie, closing my eyes and letting the words hiss out. "It's true."

"I see." Farnsworth looks past Phoenix, at me. "I'm sorry for you," he tells Phoenix. "Must be horribly disappointing. Veronica is..." I can see the muscles in the back of Phoenix's neck clench as he waits for Farnsworth to complete his thought. "Well, she is something, isn't she?" Even in the dim light we are standing in, I can see Farnsworth sizing up Phoenix. He must feel inferior. "Even I got farther than that, didn't I, Veronica? Those few lovely, special moments between us?"

"I'm sorry, sir," I stammer. "I-I don't know what you're talking about."

"Of course you do, Veronica. Those moments holding hands. Or when you taught me to swim. Or how about just this afternoon; that beautiful time we shared on our beach when you saw me save an injured bird and you must have wondered if you were wrong about me? Do you remember that, Ronnie?" He spits the syllables of my name. I don't say a word. "So now what," Farnsworth asks, speaking to both of us. "I suppose you think I should just let you go back out into the woods and Veronica here, just go back to bed?"

"Yes," Phoenix answers. "I don't care what you do to me, but let her go. She hasn't done anything to you except help you. Prove to her she is right to think only good things about you."

"Oh, I'd love nothing more than to do that." Farnsworth licks his lips as he speaks. "But the problem is that I heard most of your conversation here, tonight. And now you're both enemies of the Principal Leader. And that just happens to be me. GUARDS!" Farnsworth shouts.

And before I know what is happening, Phoenix

draws his gun, then we are swarmed by six or seven of Farnsworth's entourage, all pointing guns at us.

"I am really so very disappointed in you, Veronica." Farnsworth shakes his head. "I really thought you were the one."

With that, the guards grab Phoenix and me and march us to one of Farnsworth's waiting trucks. "Ronnie," Phoenix yells.

"Silence him," Farnsworth commands, and one of the guards uses the butt of his gun to hit Phoenix on the side of his head.

"NO!" I scream as they push me into the back of a truck and slam the door shut.

****

It's quiet and dark in the back of the truck. I can hear the welcoming sounds of my camp, but I know, soon I'll be leaving them forever. I wonder what's happened to Phoenix and where they're taking me. I hear the rattle and pop of the engine starting, and I know it is over. All of it. My chance to help Raven, Lilly, Violet, and my life with Phoenix. And I've only had the two mushrooms. I hope to God it's enough to poison Farnsworth after they Let me. Then something strange happens, and the truck engine stops as quickly as it was started. I walk to the back of the truck bed and push the canvas flap aside, trying to see what's happening. In the darkness, I can see only shapes, but they are running back and forth very quickly. Then I hear my name. "Ronnie?" it is a quiet voice.

"Raven?" She shimmies up the back of the truck and climbs in through the flap.

"I brought you these." She hands me my last two mushrooms. "I found them on the floor of your cabin when I went to look for you. I don't know why, but they seemed important."

"Oh Raven." I pull her tightly to me. "They are important. Very, very important. Thank you my brave, brilliant little girl." I take the mushrooms out of her hand. She tilts her face up to me and smiles.

"Sisters?" she asks, holding out her pinky for me.

I am struck by her word. I raise my pinky and lock it in hers, wondering if, without all of this, there might have been a day when Raven and I could have been sisters. My thoughts turn dark when I remember the last time I made a pinky promise it was with Lulu. Sadness overwhelms me.

"It will be okay." Raven tries to comfort me.

"I hope you're right," I confide. "I really hope you're right."

Moments later, the door on the back of the truck flies open.

"Grab her," someone orders and one of Farnsworth's guards climbs up into the truck and takes me by the arm.

"Stay safe," I whisper to Raven, who manages to sneak out the back without being seen. I pray no one knows who I'm talking to. "You need to go. Get the others and leave this place." I speak to her back as she runs away. I know Farnsworth will come after them next, the last remaining O's. "Find your brother if you can. Stay safe and stay together," I call after her as they lead me off.

I watch over my shoulder to see that Raven makes it to her cabin without being spotted. They walk me to another far cabin, one that we hardly use, the Infirmary. Once I see it, I know exactly what is going to happen.

"Is he hurt?" I ask, panic overwhelming me. This is too fast. It's all happening too fast. No one will answer me so there's only one thing I can do. Quickly, I stuff the last two mushrooms into my mouth. It's a risk, sure, but if I'm dying anyway, I may as well try to take him down with me. Then, maybe by some miracle, Phoenix can break free of this place and right our upside down world. I feel the effects of the mushrooms almost immediately. My stomach begins to cramp and I double over, groaning. Then the cramps move higher, and I am certain I'll vomit. I can't. Whatever I do, I have to keep these mushrooms down. I breathe deeply and try to relax my stomach. It knows these mushrooms. It just doesn't know them in this quantity. I can keep these down. I can do it. By the time we reach the Infirmary, my cramps have subsided some, but they've been replaced by blurry vision. Everything around me seems cloudy and thick. I see lights flashing, and there is a constant dull ache at the very back of my tongue where it meets my throat. Waves of nausea grip me, and I hold onto the guard's jacket for dear life. He doesn't flinch. I stumble up the steps to the Infirmary and fall inside. I am doubled over on the floor, my body starts trembling and then shaking, violently. Someone picks me up and lays me on a table.

I stare up at the ceiling of the Infirmary, and it seems anything but cold and sterile like the Letting room of the facility where they kept me. This is my camp. This is my home. If they're going to drain me to death, it might as well be here. I got the girls back to the camp, and Phoenix, if he can stay alive, will take care of them. I know it. I'm sorry it's the end for me, but as I force down another wave of nausea, I know

I've done my part as best I can. Even my old friend, hope, seems to be packing up, getting ready to leave me and move on. But before hope is gone entirely, there is one thing left to wish for, that is the mushrooms take effect before they Let me.

I am alone for whole minutes and glad I've overdosed on those mushrooms, because if I hadn't, my instinct would be to get up and run. But this way, I have no choice. I simply do not have the strength to move, so my blood will be pumped out of me and into Farnsworth, where it will poison him, hopefully. I hear voices outside the Infirmary door, and I stretch my neck to see who's speaking, but my vision has nearly failed. The best I can do is hear what people are saying and wait for something to happen to me. For someone who's always been in control of every situation, it's a harrowing experience to do nothing but wait, paralyzed. I hear the door slam shut, and I can tell at least two people are standing near me.

"Why is she so out of it?" one asks.

"Beat's me. But who cares," the other voice answers. "She's got the O." I can feel them touching the pressure points on me, looking for veins that are plump. There was no time to make sure I was fully hydrated, no concern for heart rate monitors, no huge machine with knobs and buttons. It is just two people and me, and I imagine, many, many vials to collect my blood. For a fleeting moment, I wonder how they'll do the transfusion of my blood back into Farnsworth, but I let it go. It's just not my concern. I hear the sounds of many jars and drawers being opened and closed, and then I feel the cold, slick wipe of the alcohol on my arms and feet. Then I feel the prick, first one, and then three more. Four draw sites. But at least this time they'll be using vials, so it will take a significant amount of time for them to drain me completely.

I begin to fade away. I hear their voices, fading in and out, and I feel the pressure of the vials being filled and replaced every so often. They talk as if I wasn't about to die. They complete their business without knowing this incredibly valuable blood they are carrying will kill their leader. I feel the corners of my mouth turn up into a small smile. If I have accomplished nothing else in my life, at least I will be responsible for stopping Farnsworth.

What happens from there is up to someone else.

I hear less and less of their idle conversation, and now I hear a siren, wailing. I know I must be dreaming because I see myself back in the city park, stepping over the animal clock that lies dormant on the street. My mother stands just a little ways from me in a bed of dandelions. I begin walking toward her, but every time I take another step, she backs away. I move more quickly and yet she seems to keep pace with me. Then she lifts her hand and points into the park, and I see Phoenix, looking so very worried, standing there with his shirt opened and his gun slung across his shoulder.

"Ronnie," he cries. "Come with me."

I keep trying to tell him I'm okay and that this is my mother, but I know he can't hear what I'm saying, and he still looks terribly concerned.

He beckons to me to go with him, but there is another force, bigger than me, making me walk toward my mother. Finally, she lifts her hand, and I think I can make it to her to take it. Instead, she reaches up and blows me a kiss. I begin to cry uncontrollably, my body convulses, and I drop to the ground. I can't lose her again. I just can't. I try to crawl along the ground after her, but she is moving much faster than I can. Suddenly, I stop and vomit all over a patch of dandelions at my knees.

"That's it," I hear Phoenix saying. "That's it."

But I can't see him, and I can't understand what he means. Again and again, I vomit until there is nothing left to wretch except bitter tasting bile. My head hangs low, and I fight to breathe.

"Take a breath," Phoenix murmurs, stroking my hair, "take a breath."

I drag in a long, labored breath, and Phoenix pulls me to my feet.

Suddenly, I am back at the Infirmary, but there is no one here except Phoenix and me. Or so I think. I can barely make out the sight of a gagged and bound Lettor, tethered to a pole on the far side of the Infirmary. He fights to break free of his binds, but he's unable.

"Did I survive?" I ask, and Phoenix holds me by the waist.

"Yes," he whispers. "I don't know how, but thank God you did."

"I did." I smile at Phoenix. His face is the last thing I remember before I slip into complete blackness.

Chapter Nineteen

When I awaken, I find myself lying on a strange, small cot in a tiny cabin. I sit up panicked, wondering where I am. The room spins, and I drop back down onto the cot.

"No," a voice cautions, a voice I know well. It's Phoenix. He rushes to my side. "Don't move so quickly. Go easy." He helps me to sit up. "You're here with me. Everything is okay." He sits next to me, and I let my entire body rest against his chest.

"The blood?" I ask, my throat raw and scratchy. Phoenix fetches me some water, and I drink it down so quickly I choke.

"Easy." He pats my back and takes the canteen from me. I pull the canteen back and slug at it again. I stop when I drain the water dry. I sit there, panting, trying to catch my breath.

"The blood?" I ask again, my voice a bit stronger. "Farnsworth? My girls?"

"I wish I had an answer for you," he tells me. "Midway through the emergency Letting, the alarms sounded through the camp..."

"The sirens, I heard them." Phoenix nods. "Rebels?" I ask.

"Worse." He looks at the ground. "Gunnar."

"Gunnar's back?" I ask, stunned.

"Yes, and he's not alone. He had a group with him

of at least sixty very angry and very hungry rebels. He came walking into the camp like it was his. The men started shooting randomly. It was chaos."

"The girls?" I ask. "What happened to all of the girls?"

"Most of them were left alone. Gunnar's beef isn't with children. It's with Farnsworth."

"We have to get back to camp!" The panic in me makes my head woozy. I develop a booming headache and force myself to sit forward, rubbing my temples fiercely.

"They're okay," Phoenix assures me. "They've left Margaret in charge, and Gretchen has stepped up to help her."

"And they've killed Farnsworth?" I ask. I am somewhat saddened I put myself through this agony for nothing.

"No. He's escaped. As soon as his entourage got wind of an organized rebel attack they packed him, and your blood, up and headed back to the Inferno."

I nod. "Gunnar's earlier than we anticipated, but not much else has changed in our plan," I say, trying hard to focus. "Farnsworth will still be getting my poisoned blood. And he will die. But now you won't have just the insurmountable task of winning over spoiled, rich people who kill our children to preserve their own beauty. Now you have to do that and battle Gunnar. Wow." I hold my head.

"Yes, wow," Phoenix agrees, his hand resting on my back. "Why did you do it, Ron?" His tone has changed noticeably. "Why did you eat all the mushrooms at once?"

"I thought for sure the Lettors were going to kill

me. I thought I'd better try my best to do anything and everything I could to stop Farnsworth."

"I understand. But they didn't kill you last time. So what if they weren't planning to this time either? Then what about me? What about us? Didn't you think of what it would be like for me if you were gone?"

I shake my head.

"There wasn't time for that luxury," I explain, saddened.

"You can't think like that." His hand rubs my back.

"How else can we think?" I ask, looking at him. I am so weak just turning my head makes me swoon. He offers me more support with his arm around my waist.

"I used to think I knew what I was doing," he confides. "I had a definite plan, with a beginning, middle, and end. I also believed there was a finite amount of room in one's heart, and once you filled it with a passion, like the revolution, there was no room for anything or anyone else. But that's all crap, because then I met you, and I realized the reason I thought I hated you so very much—" I flinch but he puts up his hand so I let him finish. "The reason I thought I hated you so very much was because you stirred these feelings in me I didn't even know existed. And it scared me, terrified me, until I realized these feelings meant I was alive, and you are the reason I want to live."

"I am?" I ask, searching his eyes.

"Yes." He moves a piece of hair from my face. "So to think there's no time for us is letting Farnsworth win completely. To be so focused on the revolution and stopping Farnsworth that we forget ourselves, is to give him ultimate control over us. His father outlawed relationships between a boy and a girl, unless they were a blood match, and developed the Couplings. Farnsworth took his ideas and ran with them. They have taken our blood and our basic human needs, and profited off them. What they can't take is what's in here." He places his hand on my heart. "Your spirit, which you have a whole hell of a lot of." He laughs, softly. "And your heart. Whatever is in there is yours to keep. He can drain your blood, but he can't drain you, Ronnie. And he can't ever change what's in there unless you let him."

"I'm so..." I begin to say, completely overwhelmed and unable to make sense of the situation. But somehow my head feels clearer and my stomach rumbles. He gets up without saying a word and comes back with an empty plate. He hands it to me and I stare at it, hoping there's more than nothing. Then he pulls a can of something from his pocket and takes it to a small table in the corner of the cabin. He picks up a large knife and in one swift motion, stabs the top of the can and manages to peel back the lid. He comes over to me and dumps the entire can out, onto my plate.

"What is it?" I ask, my eyes wide.

"Ravioli."

"Where did you get this?"

"In the kitchen at camp. Some had just come in as an answer to your demand for real food."

I don't wait for a fork or even really pay attention to what he's saying. As fast as I can, I lift one slippery, cold ravioli and stuff it into my mouth. It tastes like aluminum and spicy sauce and stale cheese and pure heaven. I stuff in another three more raviolis and hold my plate out to offer him some. He shakes his head, smiling, and I realize he's holding a fork for me. I grab the fork away and dive back into the pasta. I don't come up for a breath until the entire plate is empty.

"I really hope you didn't want any. Hope you weren't just being polite."

"No, I'm fine." He's beaming at me. He stands on the other side of the cabin, watching me as we speak.

"Well, thanks, Phoenix," I say. "Really, for all of it. For rescuing me and feeding me and helping me. Always."

"I've never thought of it like that."

"No?"

"No. I've never thought about it at all. I just did what my heart told me to do."

I smile at him, but looking at my empty plate, my brain goes elsewhere.

"What about Willy?" I ask. I'm frightened by the possibilities, but I need to know.

"Honestly, I don't know." He looks at the ground. "I'm sure they went into the kitchen for supplies, but I can't imagine they would have a problem with Willy. Maybe they are just having him cook for them. They need someone to feed them."

I nod, hoping he's right. It's a plausible explanation. It's just that it's Gunnar, and nothing that Gunnar has done has ever made sense. I look around. I am still weak but finally, I can begin to make out our surroundings.

"Your cabin is nice." I look over the tiny folding table where he opened my dinner. Next to it is a chair with a pile of books stacked beside it. He looks at the chair too but seems unable to sit down. His nerves have him frazzled.

"Thanks," he laughs. "I'm sure it's not anything

compared to his place." I look at Phoenix, confused. There is something in the way he says it.

"Are you jealous?" I ask.

"What?"

"Jealous? That I've been to his house?"

"Honestly, yes. I don't know why. But something about it irks me."

"If it makes you feel any better, I was forced to go."

"No." He looks down at the ground and then back to me. "No, that doesn't make me feel any better. I'm sorry for the irrational feelings."

"They're feelings." I shrug. "I don't think they're ever really known for being rational." He smiles at me.

"Ron..." He moves closer to me. I can tell something is on his mind. "I have to tell you—"

"What?" I fluff his makeshift pillow and lean back on his cot. I simply cannot keep my head up any more. In this position, I can see papers stuck to the wall hanging over my head. "Hey, what are these?" I ask, trying to sit up to get a better look. Maybe they are his plans for the revolution.

"Ron, wait—" But it's too late. Hanging over my head are at least a dozen, if not more, sketches of me. They are all portraits, showing my face and my hair flowing down my back.

"These are—"

"Please don't be freaked out," he begs.

"Freaked out? These are gorgeous," I exclaim, running my hand over one of the pictures. Some have been drawn in pencil, others chalk or charcoal. Each one focuses on my eyes, only half-opened compared to his, but they are bright and intelligent. "This is how you see me?" He only nods. "I-I don't know what to say. I am so incredibly flattered." It dawns on me. "So this is how you drew me so effortlessly that day at the lake. That's how you did it without ever looking up at me. You've memorized my face, down to every detail."

"Yes." He looks down at his feet, guiltily.

"What?" I ask.

"I wish I could say these were all drawn out of friendship and respect..." I hear the unhappiness in his voice. "But unfortunately, most of these were drawn when I was still hunting you."

I look at him, smiling.

"Look at them," I say. "Look at the detail. Look at the way you drew my eyes. These were drawn out of friendship." I slip my hand in his. "You just didn't know it yet."

He smiles at me, warmly, but there is still something in those gorgeous eyes.

"What is it?" I ask.

"I did tell you the truth before," he explains, his eyes steady on mine. "I just didn't tell you all of it."

"What? What are you talking about?" I whisper, fear beginning to overtake me.

"The girls. Your girls. Like I said, most of them are at camp." He runs his hand up through his hair.

"Yes," I nod. "With Margaret and Gretchen."

"Yes." Then I realize what this means.

"Most of them?" I ask, working it out. "You said most of them. Who isn't at camp?" I panic. "Phoenix? It's the O's isn't it?"

He nods.

"Why didn't you tell me immediately? Why?" I ask, raising my voice.

"Because you were in no position to do anything." He raises his voice to match mine. "Look at you. You can barely keep your head up. Between the mushroom poisoning and God knows how much blood you've lost, after just having been Let a few days ago…Ron, even you have a breaking point."

"But they're my girls," I shout. "And one of them is your sister. How can you just stand by—"

"I'm not just standing by," Phoenix yells. "Okay? I know how much you love those girls, Ron, I know it. But I also know saving them has become an obsession for you. You cannot gain absolution by saving those three girls."

"How dare you?" I try to stand up and fall back down. My head pounds, and I know I have to rest. "How dare you? You think the only reason I want to save them is so I can forgive myself?"

"Of course not." He draws in a breath and sighs it out. "But I think you can't forgive yourself unless you save them. And that's not right, Ron. You have to know you did what you did based on the information you had. As horrible as the situation was, Ron, you didn't do anything wrong. But I can't tell you that, you need to know it. In here." He points to his own heart. I sit quietly, staring at him. "And as far as helping the girls, of course I want to save them. But I also want to save you."

"They're children," I share, my voice wavering.

"You're not much older yourself," he banters.

"Nonsense." I shake my head.

"I thought of going after them. But you would have died. And Farnsworth's troops certainly would have killed me if they caught me. Which they would have.

And if, by some miracle they didn't find me, Gunnar would have. Then, I would have let you die, so I could die, and no one would be there to protect those girls. Farnsworth will Let them, yes. But Gunnar, God knows what Gunnar would do to them. Who he'd sell them off to on the black market."

"I get it," I say, holding up my hand to stop the horrible images in my brain.

"I kept you alive for selfish reasons, yes. But also for practical ones. Now we have the two of us to go find those girls and bring them to safety."

"Yes. I'm...sorry. It's just, I would do anything for them."

"I know that." He sits next to me.

"What are the selfish reasons?" I ask.

"What?"

"The selfish reasons you kept me alive."

"Not reasons, just reason."

"Which was?"

"Me. And that I don't want to be without you."

"Ever?"

"Ever." He slowly lets his arm climb up to my shoulder, and then coaxes my shoulder around so I face him, and softly he leans down and kisses me on the lips. Considering everything, his kiss should do little more than warm me and make me feel protected, instead, it fires electrical currents through my body, and I want more, more...more. I kiss him back, less gently than he kissed me, and his mouth returns my kiss, hungrily. His lips part mine, and I nearly climb up him as I experience the feeling of our two beings intertwine. We are locked now, arms around each other, devouring each other like it was our last moment on earth. And who knows, in our crazy world, it just might be.

He pulls me off him, though I can tell he doesn't want to. I feel like a hungry, wild animal, panting, desperately wanting more of my prey. We each take a moment to catch our breath.

"I uh," he says. "We…we need to be…Oh damn." He chuckles, and leans forward, resting his forearms on his thighs. He runs his hand through his gorgeous dark hair.

"I need a minute," he mumbles, dragging his hand across his face. For some reason, knocking Phoenix off his feet makes me smile. He sees me. "Think it's funny, huh?"

"Little bit."

"Brat." Then his face grows much more serious. "We need to get you better," he states. "Not tire you out."

"I'm not tired at all, anymore." I watch his mouth as he speaks. He has a slight beard growing again. "How do you keep that under control?" I ask.

"What?" He narrows his eyes at me, and tilts his head sideways. I feel myself blush five shades of red.

"Your beard," I whisper, aching from embarrassment. I may be naïve, but I know about boys and girls. I also know under law, this kiss was forbidden.

"Oh…" he laughs. "I shave with my switchblade." He reaches down into a pocket in his cargo pants and pulls out a knife. He pops it open. "If we're going to kiss like that"—he closes the knife and slides it back into his pocket—"you must have some questions. Some things you want to know about me. But do you think you can eat some more while we talk? We've got to build you up as soon as possible."

"There's more?" I ask, my eyes wide. "I don't want to eat all your food," I protest.

"You won't." He takes a can out of the cupboard and holds it out to show me. "Not nearly as good, but probably really good for you." I read the label. "Creamed Spinach."

"Okay. Thanks." He opens the can and sticks a fork into it.

"I thought you might want to use a fork for this one." He smiles.

"Yup." I feel myself blush again. He hands me the can and sits back down next to me.

"So? Shoot. What do you want to know?" I shove in a bite of creamed spinach and it tastes divine.

"This is really good," I mumble with my mouth full. "Want some?" He shakes his head.

"All yours. So? Questions?"

"Just one," I say in between bites. "How old are you?"

"Eighteen."

"Eighteen?" I repeat, utterly stunned. The can of spinach slips from my grasp, but I catch it before it hits the ground.

"Good catch."

"But how can you be eighteen?" I ask.

"The same way you're seventeen, I guess. Neither of us has really had a chance to be a kid."

"No," I agree. "We haven't." I stab the fork into the can of spinach and twirl it absentmindedly. "That's why we have to get to those girls. They need a chance to be kids, not just hostages kept by that leech, Farnsworth."

"Yes," he agrees.

"And I guess, one more question. Do you have another name? I mean your sister is Raven, so I guess your mother named you Phoenix?"

"Yes." He narrows his eyes and looks away. "She had high hopes for me. People say a Phoenix will rise from the ashes to be reborn. He is a symbol of renewal, and, unfortunately, the exceptional man."

"Why unfortunately?"

"Because I'm not an exceptional man. And it's a heavy burden to carry."

"I'm sure it is. But I believe you're exceptional."

"That's nice of you to say, but…passion can cloud one's vision."

"Maybe so, but I thought you were special long before you ever kissed me. Only an exceptional man can try to lead a peaceful revolution. Only a special person could have seen past my façade to see who I was underneath. Only someone who is truly extraordinary would care about changing the world, not just for himself, but for everyone in it."

"Thank you," he murmurs, looking deeply into my eyes.

"I can see all of this," I continue, "and I'm not very bright. Imagine what someone who—"

"Ron, why do you say that? Why do you always say you're not smart? On the contrary, I think you are one of the brightest people I know."

"Then you couldn't know too many." I look off.

"No. Enough." His words are clear and direct. "Why do you think you're not smart?" I look at him, feeling the pain in my eyes.

"Well, for one thing"—there is a dull ache in my

throat—"I never knew what I was doing for all those years. What I was doing to those little girls." The tears spring to my eyes.

"How could you know?" He takes my hand and holds it. His grasp is gentle but firm, and I relax with his touch.

"For another, I was never educated past the fifth grade."

"Really?" he asks, looking at me. "I never would have known. Your vocabulary is very good."

"Sometimes. I pick up words wherever and whenever I can."

"Only someone very intelligent would care enough to do that."

"I wish that were true," I mumble. "What I wanted more than anything, what I thought was happening, was that all of these girls I sent to the New World were going to get an education. I wanted that for them, and I wanted it for me. But now…"

"I know," he says, gently. After a moment, he speaks. "It's just Phoenix. No last name."

"None?"

"If I had one, my mother never shared it with me. I was arranged through a Coupling. Of course I was a boy, so my blood was considered no good, and I was sent off to work in a factory as soon as I was able."

"And then you became a Harvester."

"Yes." He stands and walks away from me. He turns back, his eyes rimmed with tears. "All of those girls you led to the Lettings," he shakes his head, "so many of them were my finds." I nod, understanding the anguish he feels. After a few moments, I speak.

"Day."

He looks at me. "What's 'Day'?"

"You. Your last name. If I were to give you one, it would be Day."

"Phoenix Day. I like that," he decides. "Any reason?"

"Who we were and who we've become…it's night and day."

"Yes." He smiles at me, agreeing completely.

Chapter Twenty

Phoenix and I have walked for at least fifteen miles. Somewhere, up ahead, he knows of another rebel camp where they have two-wheeled vehicles, Phoenix calls "motorbikes." He has friends at the camp, and he's certain they'll lend us a bike. I sincerely hope he's right because there is no part of me that could go on even one mile more. We have been walking for hours now, both of us knowing I don't really have the strength to do this. Phoenix begged me to wait just one day, to sleep and gain my strength.

"Do you know me at all?" I asked him. "I've rested long enough. My girls need me and every second we sit here, Gunnar is gaining on the Inferno."

Quickly, Phoenix stuffed two packs with water and rations to get us as far as we can. I know I'm not strong enough, but I'm going to attempt it anyway. My girls are somewhere locked up in Farnsworth's Letting facility, and I am not going to let them spend one minute longer there than they have to.

"You all right?" Phoenix asks me, and I nod. It's become a thing we do, every two miles or so. He asks the absurd question, and I nod to prove I'm still alive.

"You wouldn't stop even if you were dead," he mumbles, and I snicker. Something has to lighten the mood. The heat is muggy and oppressive, and we've left at that perfect time of day when the insects are all out, looking to ruin some unsuspecting human's day. At least the mosquitoes are leaving me alone, but they are having a field day on poor Phoenix's bare arms and neck.

Suddenly, I feel a drop of water on my face that is colder than normal. It's not sweat.

"Rain," I say, looking up at the sky, alarmed. The rain will help keep us cool, but it will make traveling that much more difficult. The worst part is it could also mean a storm. And that's something I don't even want to imagine right now.

"I don't think it's that much farther ahead." He tries to sound convincing, but I can tell he's not really sure where we are. I hear the uncertainty in his voice. He looks up every now and again to check our position by the placement of the sun, and each time I agree with his coordinates. That's the good news. The bad news is the sun is now covered by dark, ominous clouds, and we are walking in the deep woods without any sign of shelter. The rain starts coming down steadily, and I pull my jacket up over my head. Not too far ahead, we both see a bolt of lightning strike one of the mountains. I count silently to check how far away the storm is, and I start when I only get to four seconds. "You okay?" he asks.

"Yeah, but I think we're walking right into it." I feel my breath growing hurried and shallower. Thanks to the storm, my bravery is wavering.

"I know," he shouts to be heard above the heavy rainfall. "There's a break right up there." He points to a small lean-to that has been formed by some fallen trees. I rally everything I have to rush ahead to our shelter. We fall under the lean-to, and I know we've definitely caught a break. We slide out of our packs.

"We'll be okay here," he insists, putting his arm around me.

"Okay," I whisper. Despite everything, I've never been good in a storm. A clap of thunder sends a shiver through my body.

"You okay?" he asks and I nod, terrified to even breathe. The rain falls lightly on us through the gaps the trees have allowed at the top of the lean-to. "Are you scared?"

"No," I whisper, but the tremble in my voice gives me away.

"It's okay, you know. To be afraid of something. We all are. Want to know what I'm afraid of?" I give him a small smile. He's doing to me what I do with my girls whenever they're scared. He's redirecting my thoughts away from my fear.

"Okay."

"I've never told anyone before."

"Tell me." I turn toward him. I close my eyes as the thunderstorm settles right over our heads.

"I'm afraid of losing you," he confides.

I open my eyes to smile at him.

"And you want more?"

I nod.

"I'm afraid of failing."

"Because so many people are counting on you?"

"No." He holds me tighter with each thunder clap. "Because so many others aren't. Me and my plan, together we're so inconsequential. But for so many years, I've tried to convince people in the city and my fellow rebels that I knew the way—" The loudest clap of all booms right over our heads.

"Oh," I blurt, squeezing my eyes shut.

"I've got you." He kisses me softly on the side of the head. It feels so wonderful I almost forget both storms are raging not so far away.

"So why are you afraid?" I ask, forcing myself to think of something other than the thunder.

"Because a peaceful revolution isn't sexy. It doesn't offer enough drama, not like Gunnar and his plans for revenge. A peaceful revolution is a complete gamble. And it's one I may very well lose."

"No, you won't." There is another loud thunder clap and my stomach muscles clench. Then the storm slowly begins to move, and I relax a tiny bit. As the thunder rolls away, I can look at him and focus on his words. "Something brought us together, and something is watching out for us," I say. "Call it God or fate or whatever you believe, but there is a reason we are here. Together. Look at this shelter we found in the middle of a thunderstorm. It's not just chance. By now, my blood should be getting ready for another transfusion into Farnsworth. If we hurry, we can get there right when his entourage is trying to guess what's happened to him. If we strike during the chaos, we have a chance."

"Together."

"Together." He wraps his hand around mine. He lets go so I can slip my pack onto my back.

"Wait," he says, "here." He pulls a can of condensed milk from his bag and pokes two holes in it. "Drink as much as you can." He holds the can out to me.

"What about you?"

"I can survive on near nothing. But you need nourishment right now." He pushes the can toward me.

"So split it with me. The food you've given me is already more than my body eats in a week."

"I want you—"

"I'm not drinking unless you drink first." I cross my arms in front of me and tap my foot, impatiently.

"You are something," he mumbles, downing half the can. He holds it out to me and I finish it. "Up here." He stashes the can in his bag and tosses his head in the direction he wants us to go. We walk out into an oppressively hot, wet day.

The rain did nothing to cool it off. Actually, it's made it worse because of the humidity. We trudge along, wearily. I still can't trust my body, and my eyes are still seeing random spots and wavy lines. Once in a while, I jump from seeing a snake that doesn't exist. The hallucinations are the hardest challenge to overcome.

After another few miles, Phoenix points up ahead. "There," he exclaims, and he picks up his pace. Even with my long legs, I have to run to keep up with him. "There." Phoenix drops to his knees. I drop down next to him. For whole minutes we are silent, scoping out the small camp ahead of us. I can't be sure if my eyes are playing tricks on me, but I am certain I see a glimpse of someone in a brown uniform, mulling about.

"Are those—" I mean to ask Phoenix if there's the possibility there are Harvesters in the camp, but he is staring dead ahead, fixated. Finally, he turns to me.

"Do you trust me?" He looks at me intensely.

"Of course."

"Good. Then get to your feet." Phoenix pulls his gun on me.

"What?" I ask, confused.

"If we're going to get in and out—"

"There are Harvesters in there, Phoenix. I just saw the brown uniform."

"No way. This has always been a rebel camp I can count on." He is still pointing the gun at me. "And there are many, too many, rebels just like Gunnar. They'll never see past who you were."

"Who I was?"

"I mean who they thought you were." Phoenix is clearly frustrated. "Please, Ron."

"Sorry." We've gotten off track, and we're out of time. "If it's a rebel camp," I ask, "then why are there Harvesters? Could they be people who've left to join the revolution?"

"No. They have to burn their uniforms when they join."

"You have yours," I argue, questioning him.

"That tradition started after me."

"So if there are friends of Farnsworth in there— you will be killed for capturing me. But if you're my prisoner, they won't touch you once I tell them Farnsworth wants you delivered alive. And no one, no one, not a rebel or a government official would kill me. My blood is too valuable. If you become my prisoner"—quickly I take the gun from his hands— "then we stay alive. It's the only way." I see him staring at me, wondering what is going to happen. "This is it, Phoenix. Either you trust me or you don't."

Slowly, Phoenix turns and raises his arms in the air. He places his hands on his head and begins to walk forward. I am walking behind him, holding a gun to his back. Amazingly, as little as two weeks ago, I would have been thrilled to deliver the leader of the rebels to

Farnsworth. I would have considered it my duty and my honor. Phoenix would have been killed for sure, and I would have been given another small plaque to hang on the wall of my cabin. And everything would have gone on as usual until Farnsworth bled. But it's not two weeks ago. It's now. And now I had better put on a performance that will save both of our lives.

"Hello," Phoenix shouts, walking boldly into camp. "It's Phoenix. I need help." A few people run back and forth, confused.

"What's going on here?" a short man with greasy hair and a bulbous nose asks. He holds a shotgun he points at both of us.

"I'm Phoenix, the leader of the Peaceful Revolution. I have been captured by Veronica Billings. I need your help to get to Farnsworth." The man raises his gun to aim at my head, and I feel myself gasp.

"Wait," someone orders. It's a girl who walks out of one of the cabins and directly toward us. She is tall, not as tall as me, but much taller than Gretchen or Margaret. She has long brown wavy hair pulled back in a loose ponytail. Her face is a perfect heart shape, and her lips are remarkably rosy. She raises her large eyes to look at Phoenix, and their perfect amber color softens when she sees him. She holds up her hand for the greasy man to put down his gun, and he obeys. My eyes travel down her uniform of green fatigues to find she is incredibly curvy in all the right places. She is stunning, and by the looks of it, she knows it. I feel like an absolute child compared to her. In the midst of all of this, my heart falls slightly.

"Phoenix," she trills, nodding to him.

"Brooke," he acknowledges her.

I knew they knew each other. I feel the inexplicable urge to poke Phoenix in the back with his gun, but I resist.

"Seems you've gotten yourself into quite a pickle." Brooke smiles a soft, feminine smile. She acts as if I'm not even here, holding a gun to Phoenix's back. I have never before felt so inconsequential, and it feels awful. Out of the corner of my eye, I spot what must be the motorbikes. I wonder if I can leave Phoenix and Brooke to their reunion and sneak off to grab a bike without them ever noticing. I don't know why I hate this girl so very much, but now I understand how Phoenix felt when I was playing house with Farnsworth. It feels awful, and all they've done is say hello.

"Ms. Billings," she hisses, finally acknowledging me. "Why don't we go into my tent and see if we can come to some sort of arrangement."

"Okay," Phoenix agrees.

"Okay." My voice sounds weak and thin. I stumble forward as we walk toward Brooke's tent. I have to pull myself together, or no one will believe I'm capable of holding Phoenix hostage. I take a deep breath and push my way through the partially opened flap leading into Brooke's tent. Once we're inside, I'm dumbfounded. Brooke's decor looks more like something that belongs in a Coupling house than a rebel base camp in the middle of the woods. She's hung billowing mosquito netting from the tent poles that make it look nothing short of romantic. Large candles burn on tall tables. One of her ample-sized bras is tossed casually onto a folding chair. It looks more like a seduction scene than a camp.

"Are you kidding me?" I mumble without meaning

to.

Phoenix watches me out of the corner of his eye, and I see his lips turn up into the smallest smile.

"Make yourselves comfortable," Brooke offers. Neither Phoenix nor I move. "Come on, Phoenix," she says, pointedly. "You know your way around." She smiles when she speaks, and her words fly from her mouth into my mind, forming a bitter taste in my mouth.

"Thank you," Phoenix snips. "But it's a little hard to be comfortable with a gun pointed at my back."

"Ah yes, the gun." Brooke sits in the chair and leans back against her bra. I hope those ridiculously large cups poke her in the back. "Let's get past this little charade, shall we?" she asks, smiling at both of us. "Word on the street is that you two are working together."

"Well, I don't know where you get your information Brooke," Phoenix stays remarkably calm while he speaks. "But you're wrong."

"You've always trusted my sources before," Brooke teases, making the conversation between them incredibly intimate.

"This time they're wrong." He speaks flatly, without a hint of reciprocal flirtation. "I tried to capture Veronica Billings, but instead she captured me. We've been traveling for days now. I'm asking you, Brooke, as a friend, to lend us one of your motorbikes, so we can move on to the Inferno. Farnsworth wants her. I don't know what will happen to me, but she knows I'm more valuable alive than dead." Brooke breaks out into a high-pitched squeal. She leans forward and rests her hands on her knees, laughing. I think she does it to flash her cleavage at us.

"That's your story?" Brooke giggles, composing herself. "Really? I don't expect much better from an uneducated child-killer." She stands up and walks directly to me. Her words are hard and ugly when she speaks to me. "But you, Phoenix, you could do so much better." She looks me up and down when she says this. I feel the anger brewing in my stomach and it's all I can do not to spit in her face. "So," Brooke stands in front of Phoenix and reaches up to place her hand on the side of his face, "what do you say you and I work on that story. Together." She strokes his cheek slowly and mechanically. Then she lifts herself to her tiptoes and kisses Phoenix softly on the lips.

That's it.

"All right," I snap, aiming the gun away from Phoenix and pointing it at her. "Enough."

"So the great Veronica Billings does have a breaking point." She steps back and gives me a wide, victorious smile. "And it looks as if I just found it."

Crap. I blew it. She knows.

"You probably want to put that gun down, Veronica," Brooke warns. "All I have to do is whistle and every person in this camp will come on in here to kill you."

"No one will kill me." I stand up to her, daring her with my words. "I'm the last remaining O. You know that. Or you should, anyway. Unless you were too busy seducing every stray rebel you could find to get them to join your camp."

"Oh, let's not get ugly, shall we Veronica? Oh wait, you can't help but be ugly."

"Brooke," Phoenix snaps, reprimanding her.

"Oh, so the feeling's mutual, is it?" Brooke saunters past us. "I had always wondered who would win the heart of the great leader of the Peaceful Revolution, Phoenix." She smiles a big, beautiful smile. "It doesn't matter, you know." She talks directly to me. "Whatever he tells you, he will never love you like he loves that revolution." She tosses her hands in the air and makes a grand gesture. "There's a finite amount of love in that boy. And he sure as hell isn't going to waste it on you, you overgrown baby-killer."

"I am not, and never have been a baby—or a child—killer."

"Ron—" Phoenix interjects but I cut him off.

"I was misguided, yes," I finish my thought. "But all I want now is the same thing as you. I have three little girls who are in my care who have been taken by Farnsworth. Give us a bike and let us go get them."

"Why would I do that?" Brooke asks.

"Because it's the right thing to do." Brooke laughs again, but this time not as loud.

"I'm sorry for those three girls," she concedes. "But we're close now. Farnsworth's weak, and we have a way in. There's no way I'm going to let three little girls stop our planned revolution. There just have to be some casualties."

Something tells me to keep quiet about Gunnar and his march on the Inferno.

"So you won't let anything sway you from your job—a job you believe in?"

"Exactly," Brooke snarls.

"Well, you sound remarkably like the person you accused me of being," I say as she takes a step back from me. "Except I didn't know what was happening to the girls I led to the Lettings. You, on the other hand, are perfectly happy sending three little girls to their deaths. Brooke, despite your outward appearance, I would say that makes you the ugly one."

"And so we reach a stalemate," Brooke states flatly.

"I could just kill you and be done with it." I still have my gun pointed at her.

"Really?" Brooke asks, her large eyes widening. "But there are a couple of problems with that. First, as soon as my camp hears a gunshot, they'll come running. And when they see me dead, they'll kill you. They wouldn't care if your blood was pure gold."

"It is."

"Second," Brooke continues without missing a beat. "Second, you're not a killer. Or so you say."

"Not a child killer. I have no problem with an overinflated old woman."

"Tsk, tsk, an old woman at twenty-one, huh?" she smiles again. "Maybe so. But lastly, he won't let you kill me." She points at Phoenix. "We have too much history, don't we Phoenix?"

"What Veronica does is not up to me," Phoenix states definitively, clenching his jaw.

"Oh, I see...How incredibly weak of you. Not your best quality I must say."

"So, what's going to happen, Brooke?" Phoenix asks.

"Well, I guess that's up to you, isn't it?" She bats her eyes at Phoenix. "You two stay the night with me here at my camp, as guests, and tomorrow morning I'll give you a bike to go save your precious little girls."

"Why would you do that?" I ask.

"Because in exchange, I get what I want from Phoenix."

"And what's that?" he asks.

"You know." Brooke pats his arm.

"Not going to happen, Brooke," he responds.

"Stay with me tonight for old times' sake. I'm not asking you to do anything you don't want to do," she lets her fingers walk up his forearm. "Though if memory serves, there's nothing you don't want to do."

"Brooke, that's enough! Why would you want that?" he asks, genuinely confused.

"Because I want her to ache." Brooke looks at me.

"Why?" I ask.

"Because I had a beautiful life built on destroying you," she explains, looking directly at me. "Then one day I realized his obsession was no longer based on hatred. And he threw me aside to go find you."

"That's not what happened," Phoenix corrects.

"Your life can't be beautiful if it's built on hatred," I say. "Don't you get that?"

"What I get," she snaps, "is what I want. Or I kill him. And turn you over to Farnsworth. Simple." She is right. It is simple. This was the one scenario we didn't plan for: traitorous rebels.

"Fine," Phoenix spits.

"What?" Brooke sounds surprised.

"What?" I am appalled.

"I'll stay with you tonight," he informs Brooke. Then he turns to me. "It's the only way." He turns back to Brooke. "On one condition. I want to see the motorbike. Make sure there is a real payoff for us."

"Of course. Right this way." She walks us out of her boudoir and into the oppressive heat of her camp.

"There." She points to a field not far from the tents. "There are seven of them." Phoenix is staring hard at the bikes.

"Keys?" he asks.

"You haven't changed a bit." She smiles. "Tonight should be lots of fun."

She is toying with him, and her words make me want to vomit.

"Oh all right." She speaks in a normal tone. "The keys are in the ignitions. No need to hide them. No one steals from me and lives." Brooke looks pointedly at me then at Phoenix and smiles. "Shall we?" Brooke asks, slipping her hand in his, exactly where mine should be.

"What about Veronica?" he asks.

"She's welcome to watch." There's a lilt of optimism in her voice.

"I'll pass," I hiss. "I'm sure I won't be missing much."

"Your loss," she giggles, sounding sugary sweet. "Why doesn't Veronica sit right there then?" She points to a tree stump just outside her tent. "I'll get someone to fetch a sleeping bag for her in case she gets sleepy." I plop down on the stump, unable to comprehend the surrealism of the situation. "Oh all right, she can go in there if she wants." Brooke points to an empty tent directly across the way.

"No one touches her," Phoenix orders.

"No one does anything around here without my permission," Brooke snaps.

"Fine. Then make sure you tell them not to touch her. I'm going to check out the bikes."

"Don't trust me?" Brooke asks, batting her eyes again.

"Never have." Phoenix walks away. As soon as Phoenix reaches the bikes, Brooke turns to me, her eyes red with anger.

"You'll never completely have him you know."

"I already do," I tell her, smiling. She looks at me, confused. In my heart, I know what Phoenix had said to me is right. Farnsworth could never have what's in my heart, and Brooke could never have what's in his. Brooke looks toward Phoenix. I see the beauty in her profile, but I also see the anger. "Brooke, I know it's none of my business, but, how did you end up here?"

"At this camp?" she asks, turning to me.

"At this camp, yes, but also in this position as an angry leader. How does a woman who looks like you end up here?"

"I could ask you the same thing." Suddenly I realize her hatred for me is based on jealousy and not just dislike. She looks at Phoenix and then back to me. "I'm an AB. You know there are so many of us. Always have been a glut."

"Until now," I say sadly, and she nods, agreeing.

"But when I was young, there were plenty of AB's. There weren't plenty of girls who looked like me. So they let me stay with my mother with the understanding that as soon as I turned fourteen, I would be matched for the Couplings."

"At fourteen?" I'm disgusted. Brooke only nods.

"So, for my fourteenth birthday my mother paid someone—a Traveler—to take me as far from the city as he could. I think she had hoped my beauty would get me into the Inferno, and there I could blend with the locals until I was old enough to marry. The first Traveler she hired took me to the other side of the city and dumped me. He took her money and ran. The government officials found me and knew I'd be easy to match. But because I'd run, Farnsworth made my first match with Lucus."

"Lucus?"

"The man you met when you first came in. He's nice enough," she looks down at her feet when she says this. "But he's not the man a fourteen-year-old wants to be matched with."

"I would say not." I think of Lucus's greasy, gray hair and festering, bulbous nose.

"Farnsworth claimed together there was a chance for better than an AB."

"How did you escape?" I ask, my attention rapt.

"Lucus couldn't believe his luck. He was enamored by my beauty. I told him he could be with me that one time, and I would make him hate every moment of it, or we could escape the Coupling house together and run. I told him if he helped me break free, he could be close to me always, just not in a Coupling way."

"It worked?"

"He couldn't bear the thought of being without me." She shrugs.

Then I think of something. "Everyone I've seen at this camp is male. Is that what you do? Use your beauty to control men and make them do whatever you want?"

"Worked every time except one." She looks at Phoenix. Brooke straightens up and pulls down the waistband of her fitted shirt. We've become much too chummy. "Phoenix," she calls, and he puts up a hand to wave to her. Within moments, he has come over to us. He walks up to me.

"I will get you as soon as I can." He lets his hand

linger on my cheek before he drops it and turns away. Brooke takes Phoenix's hand and leads him into her tent, smiling at me over her shoulder.

Chapter Twenty-One

For two hours, I've been sitting on this stump staring at Brooke's tent. Something perverse is holding me here. My mind keeps telling me to hop on a bike and take off, but my heart has nailed my feet to the earth. For two hours, the boy I care about more than I ever thought possible has been in a hot, dark, romantic tent with a stunning woman who wants him. Countless times, I wanted to barge in but was afraid I would see something I could never forget. Yet, despite it all, my heart tells me to stay put.

I stare at the stars in the sky and wonder so many things. Do my girls see these stars, or are they locked up somewhere with blood-sucking machines attached to them? What about Gretchen? How is she, and what has she decided to do? Where are Gunnar and Lulu? Will Lulu ever come back to me? A shooting star passes overhead, but I don't need to wonder about that one. "Hello Mom," I whisper. Suddenly everything feels okay and the emptiness in me is filled with warmth and security. A mother's love will transcend all.

Seconds later, Phoenix rushes out of Brooke's tent. "Ronnie," he whispers, holding out his hand. "Let's go." I stand up and look at it, but I just can't take his hand. I latch my fingers around the straps of my backpack to make it seem like my hands are otherwise engaged. Together, we walk quickly but steadily to the bikes. Phoenix tilts a bike upright and pushes up the kickstand. Quietly he rolls the bike forward, and I walk beside him in silence. It's difficult moving through the darkness, but when we are finally a mile or so clear of Brooke's camp, Phoenix mounts the bike and turns the key. I see him exhale when the engine turns over.

"Hop on." He nods his head to the seat behind him and I climb on.

The bike is fairly small, and we are cramped on the seat, but I am eternally grateful for the ride.

"We should have a fighting chance. Gunnar is moving a large group on foot. We'll stay ahead of him with this. Wrap your arms around me," he shouts over the roar of the engine.

I hesitate, but then I put both arms around his abdomen just to keep from falling off. My head leans forward, and I rest it on his back for a second, allowing myself to forget what just transpired between Phoenix and Brooke. Phoenix strokes my hand, holding it for a moment, and then we are off.

Mile after mile we ride, pushing the bike to its limit. Pure adrenaline works its way through me, and I give my body over to the movement of the bike. I sway through every turn and dig my nails into Phoenix's abdomen as he pushes the bike faster and faster. I am caught up in the pure ecstasy of the machine, but still have nothing but time to think. I wonder, over and over again, what we will do once we reach the Letting facility? How will we get in? How will I find the girls? And how will we save them? Slowly the woods fall away behind us, and we are on open roads. These roads lead to more roads and then even more. I look ahead to the multilane highway with trepidation. It is proof we'll be in the Inferno soon.

"We have to cross a huge bridge," I yell, and Phoenix nods. One wrong turn and we'll end up back in the city. Before we reach the open highway, Phoenix pulls over to a tiny rest stop with a gas pump.

"We need gas," he explains. "We're on empty. We'll have to steal some somehow, or there's no way to keep going. If we abandon the bike and hitchhike, there's a real chance we'll be recognized. We are running the risk even here." He looks around warily. "You're infamous by now."

I nod. "So what do we do?"

"You'll have to distract the owner of the gas pump while I siphon gas from one of his other vehicles."

"Okay, should I distract him the same way you distracted Brooke?" I know it's incredibly petty, but I can't seem to help myself. As soon as I say it, I'm immediately regretful.

"Sorry," I mutter. Phoenix doesn't acknowledge me. We both look around at an incredibly empty lot.

"There has to be some vehicle we can siphon from in the back," Phoenix decides. "How about we worry about getting gas first, then we'll deal with our personal stuff later."

"Fine," I mumble, embarrassed. We roll the bike around to the back and find an old man sitting on a tattered lawn chair. He has a distressed hat pulled down tightly over his eyes, and his arms are crossed in front of him, cradling a shotgun. He sits under a lone lamp, attached to the building.

"Is he asleep?" I whisper.

"Even when I'm asleep, I'm awake," the old man chortles, startling us both.

"Oh, well, hello," Phoenix exclaims. "We need some gas. Can you help us out?"

"You got money?" the old man asks.

"Not exactly. But I do have opportunity."

"What's that?" The old man lifts his hat and looks at us. I take a step back into the darkness, hoping he doesn't recognize me.

"Opportunity, for a better life. Help us out here and give us enough gas to get us into the New World." I notice he is careful not to call it the *Inferno*. "We can promise you a better life."

"How's that?" the old man asks, sounding interested.

"I'm Phoenix Day." I'm touched he's used the name I gave him. "I'm the leader of the Peaceful Revolution. I am heading to the New World to free us all from their clutches."

The old man chuckles, and I look at Phoenix. He is unwavering.

"Oh, I know who you are." The old man wheezes as he speaks. "And I know your girlfriend there, too. You're the boy who started off with all that promise, but who never rallied the people like we all hoped you would."

"Yes," Phoenix replies quietly. "That's me." I slip my hand into Phoenix's and squeeze.

"And your girlfriend there," the old man points at me. "Well, she's Veronica Billings. Thing is," he raises his gun, "I just don't know whose side she's on at this moment."

"I'm on the right side." I stand tall in front of this man.

"Well, I'm glad to hear it." The old man looks up

at me. "But whose right is it? Yours or mine?"

"I'm hoping they're the same." I am painfully aware with every endless second we stand here, the girls are being Let. And then there's Brooke, who must be on her way to find us and seek revenge by now.

"You want me to give you some gas so you can go make another lame attempt to overthrow the government? Why would I do that? May not be a lot, but Principal Leader Farnsworth makes sure I have food on my table and gas in my pump. He's the reason I can make a living. For me and my three boys up there." The old man nods to the house behind us.

I look at the house and in each of three separate windows, I see a tall young man pointing a shotgun straight at us.

"Just a little protection," the old man chuckles to himself. "So, by the sound of it, all you're offering me is a free-for-all, and I ain't interested in that."

"Fine…" Phoenix responds, never completely discouraged. "But if you'd just listen to our reasons—"

"He doesn't want our reasons," I interject. I understand this man and his fear. When you have so very little, you are terrified of losing it. "I'm sorry to interrupt, Phoenix, but this man is a businessman, not a philosopher. Am I right, sir?"

"Maybe," he grumbles, eyeing me. "What do you have to say?"

"What Farnsworth gives you is the bare minimum you need to survive. Wouldn't you like to have more?"

"Wouldn't everyone?"

"Well, your current way of life is in jeopardy." I can tell I have his attention. "Your days of sitting here, collecting something for nothing are over. Farnsworth is ill, and he'll be getting worse. That's why we're making our move now. And unless Phoenix can get to the New World to serve as interim Principal Leader, someone else will. And that someone is power-hungry and greedy. If he doesn't kill you, he will seize your property and seal off your way of making a living because you're not of any service to him. Gas is everywhere," I explain. "You're an old man. He doesn't need you. And your boys? They look strong. They'll be sent off to the city to work in a factory."

The man looks at me, his eyes wide. He uses the barrel of his gun to push his hat further up on his head. "Go on."

"So your best option is to put something aside for your survival. But I'll bet you don't have any extra cash lying around do you?"

"No," he admits, looking at his tiny shop. "No, I don't."

"Then here's the deal. Since you know who I am, you must know I'm one of only a few remaining O's. The other three are children who, combined, can't make my weight. You go grab a funnel and an empty pint container from an old oil can or something. You fill up our tank, and I'll give you a half-pint of pristine O."

"Ronnie, no," Phoenix blurts.

"It's okay, Phoenix. I can do this." I turn to the old man. "Then you sell my blood on the black market. You'll make enough for the four of you to live for years without worrying about money one bit."

"You got yourself a deal there, little lady," the old man says greedily, and he stands, eager to get the funnel and pint.

"Gas first." It is my one stipulation.

"No way," the old man challenges. "You want gas, blood first. There's no way I'm gonna risk you taking off without paying me."

"Fine." I see no way around it. The man leaves to get the paraphernalia.

"Ronnie…" Phoenix holds my hands and speaks urgently. "I can't let you do this."

"So what are we going to do, Phoenix? Kill him?"

"No."

"Then we have no choice, because even if we wanted to kill him, which we don't, those boys would shoot us in a second."

"But Ron—"

"You've made your tough choices." I stare at Phoenix. "Now I'm making mine."

The old man returns with one of his sons who is carrying a funnel and pint. "Let's go," the old man urges.

"Okay, but we pump the gas simultaneously. That's the best you're going to get."

"Fine."

We push the bike to the front of the building and stick the nozzle of the gas pump into the gas tank of the bike.

"Can I have your knife please?" I ask Phoenix.

Reluctantly, he hands it to me. With a swift motion, I cut off a piece of my jacket and use it as a tourniquet on my arm. "You have any alcohol?" I ask the old man.

"Nope." His son looks at him. I look from his son back to the old man.

"Whiskey?" I ask.

The old man hesitates.

"You can buy a hell of a lot more whiskey if my blood isn't contaminated."

The old man reaches into his pocket and pulls out a flask. I douse the inside of my left arm with the whiskey. Without thinking twice, I make a deep cut on the inside of my forearm.

"Ugh," I grunt through clenched teeth and Phoenix moves to help me. "No. Pump the gas!"

He does as I ask as my blood flows into the funnel and down into the pint container. Even in the semi-darkness, we are incredibly exposed in the front of the store, but we have no choice. I count the seconds in my head.

"Done," Phoenix yells and I release the tourniquet. Quickly I hold my arm upright and cover the cut with my jacket. I apply as much pressure as possible. "You need stitches," he whispers.

I just shake my head. I am starting to tremble now, my teeth chattering together.

"That's not a half-pint," claims the old man.

"It's more than you need," I say, hopping on the back of the bike before the old man and his sons decide to hold us as hostages. "You'll get a fortune for that." I see the son fumbling with the blood, and he nearly spills it. "Let's go," I whisper to Phoenix. We need to get away now, while the man and his son are preoccupied. I wedge my bleeding arm between Phoenix's back and my abdomen, and I hold on for dear life. We peel out of the gas station and head for the highways of the Inferno.

****

One road morphs into another and soon more and more lanes lay out before us. I feel tiny and exposed riding on the back of the bike, but strangely, I'm grateful for the unease. It may be all that's keeping me alive. Soon we begin to pass vehicles that look shiny and new, and the passengers are no longer simply government workers. They are families with children and…pets. Gretchen was right. These people do keep small animals just for fun. I feel like we've landed on another planet. Up ahead, we see the bridge that connects us to the New World.

"There it is," I yell and Phoenix nods.

The bridge looks so much larger from our tiny bike. I've only ever seen glimpses of it from the back of a truck or those two times I flew over it. I close my eyes and push myself tightly against Phoenix as we start to cross the bridge. I open my eyes and peek out to see we are going over a wide river that flows right into a bay not too far away. That bay leads to the ocean where Farnsworth lives. I close my eyes again and feel the mist from the water splash against my face. There is such a juxtaposition of pain and pleasure in my body that I can barely stand it. All too soon, I feel our bike heading off an exit, and we officially have willingly entered the Inferno. Phoenix brings the bike to a stop and turns to speak to me.

"We're here."

"Yes."

"Are you in a lot of pain?" he asks, looking concerned.

"Only a little." I lie.

He nods, understanding. "Ready?" he asks.

"Of course not—but let's do it anyway."

"Okay. Ron, I'm really sorry for what happened back there with Brooke."

"I don't want to talk about that," I whisper.

I can't imagine spending what could possibly be my last moments on earth talking about Brooke and the things Phoenix and she did together.

"The Letting facility?" he asks.

"Yes," I say, wishing he would force me to talk about Brooke, wishing he would prove there was nothing to talk about.

I am light-headed, woozy, in immense pain, and incredibly sad. Top form to go into battle with my enemy.

The motorbike rolls ahead, but it is no longer exciting. It is incredibly scary to feel so open and exposed. Only three stop lights and we are spotted. It's terrifying, but it's also fortunate. If I'm clever, I can get us almost immediate access to Farnsworth.

Vehicles with flashing lights surround us. Slowly we get off the bike, both of us with our hands in the air. I wince when I lift my left arm. Officers with helmets on their heads and masks over their faces point guns at us. If I wanted to die, this would be the easiest way to accomplish my goal. But, I don't. It's not that I'm afraid of death. It's that I'm afraid to leave the girls without me.

"I am Veronica Billings," I shout so everyone on the street can hear. "I am the last remaining O." People begin to crowd around us and the officers look over their shoulders, uneasily. "Anyone who kills me kills Principal Leader Farnsworth directly." Murmurs are heard. I repeat myself. "I am Veronica Billings. The last remaining O. I need to go to Principal Leader Farnsworth, now!"

"Who's that?" someone from the growing crowd

asks. He points to Phoenix.

"The only person Principal Leader Farnsworth wants in his custody more than me," I shout. "Take us to Farnsworth, or you will be directly responsible for killing him."

I point at each person in the crowd for emphasis. There is murmuring and confusion among the officers. Phoenix and I stare hard at them, wondering if this is the end for us. My eyes dart from officer to officer, waiting. What I just did was a giant gamble. Finally, one summons us to a car and I exhale. We slide into the back seat, and with sirens blasting, the car moves ahead to take us to the Letting facility. Phoenix leans over toward me.

"Man, you've got balls," he whispers, smiling.

I smile back. Why not? What do we have left to lose?

****

We make it to the Letting facility in record time. Quickly, we are pulled from the back of the car and led into the facility. Someone grabs my injured arm, and I very nearly scream. I bite my knuckle, trying to make the pain pass. Although we are moved along hurriedly, we are not handcuffed or manhandled. Frankly, the officers do not seem to know what to make of us. Friend or foe?

We are brought into a large white room with white cabinets on all the walls. "Wait here," one guard instructs, closing the doors behind us. No sooner do the doors close, I start rummaging through the cabinets.

"What are you doing?" Phoenix whispers.

"Looking for supplies. And ideas." Cabinet after cabinet is filled with bandages and cotton balls. Finally, the last cabinet has alcohol. I pour some directly on my cut.

"Uh," I cry, gritting my teeth. I close my eyes and wait for the burn to pass. When I open them, I see my arm is still bleeding. "I can't be bleeding when he comes to me. He'll freak at the loss."

"What can we do?" Phoenix asks.

"Stitch me up if we can find the supplies."

Phoenix looks at me, his eyes soft, feeling my pain.

"I know it won't be fun," I tell him. "But we have to do something." At that, Phoenix starts rummaging through desk drawers.

"Glue," he announces, holding up a small bottle.

"We're going to glue me shut?" I ask, my eyes wide.

"You have a better idea?" He unscrews the cap. "It's not regular glue. It's incredibly strong. I saw someone mend a cut with it once—"

"Was that someone Brooke?"

"Yes," he admits, quietly.

"Thanks. I'll bleed."

Phoenix just stares at me long and hard.

"Fine," I cede, as I feel another droplet of blood run down my arm. "I need to save all the blood I can. Glue my arm shut."

Phoenix squeezes a thin trail of glue along my incision and pinches the skin closed. The process is painful and smells horrible, but the glue seems to be keeping my wound closed.

"Ronnie," Phoenix begins, his hands holding my arm together. "I wish you'd let me explain about Brooke."

"I don't want to hear explanations." I am

exasperated. "I want to forget it. But I can't. Because I can't get the image of you and her out of my brain. Ugh." I squeeze my eyes shut and shake my head, trying to rid myself of the image I've conjured. "See? This is why I don't want to talk about it. I don't want to spend what could be my last free moments on this earth talking about Brooke. That would be what she wanted us to do."

"I understand, but you need to know—"

"Just stop." I cover my ears with my hands. "Oh, where are they? It's taking too long. This isn't good. It has to mean Farnsworth himself is on his way."

"That is precisely what it means," Farnsworth informs us, rolling into the room. Grace is behind him, pushing his chair. She does not acknowledge me. Farnsworth looks gravely ill. He is much paler than the last time I saw him, and his lips are rimmed in blue. His hair looks stringy, and his body seems to be constantly quivering. Despite it all, he rolls his chair right up to Phoenix.

"Do you know the worst part about being me?" Farnsworth asks Phoenix. "Huh? Do you? It's that I can't hit you. Because, well, I'm stuck in this." He raises his hands slowly, motioning to his wheelchair. "And I could injure myself. Seriously. And even lovely Veronica's blood couldn't save me if I started to hemorrhage. So no matter what I'm feeling, I can't throw a punch to your gut."

I look from Farnsworth to Phoenix and back.

"But do you know the best part about being me? Do you Phoenix, leader of the Peaceful Revolution?" Farnsworth asks, smiling as he speaks. "The best part of being me is even though I can't punch you in the gut, I can order someone else to."

With that, Farnsworth nods his head, and one of his bodyguards steps forward and punches Phoenix hard, in the abdomen.

"Phoenix!" I try to rush to his side. The other of Farnsworth's bodyguards holds me.

"Oh how sweet," Farnsworth hisses. "You two seem to be getting along so nicely. Too bad I'm going to have you locked away in the Letting facility, Veronica. And too bad I'm going to have you killed, Phoenix."

I look at Phoenix, desperately.

"Well, there's no time like the present." Farnsworth snaps his bony white fingers. With that, my bodyguard pushes me forward, and Phoenix's guard drags him to his feet. We head to the door.

"Ron." Phoenix turns and looks at me. That one look tells me everything I need to know.

"Me too," I cry. "They can never have what's in our hearts."

Phoenix smiles as they push him out the door ahead of me. Despite it all, my heart feels fuller and stronger than ever. "Wait!" I turn to Farnsworth. "Wait."

"I hope you're not going to grovel, Veronica. It would be so beneath you."

"Listen to me, Farnsworth. The enemy of my enemy is my friend."

"Very cute, Veronica, but what does that have to do with anything?"

"You have an enemy, Farnsworth. Bigger than you could possibly imagine. And you and your empire will be taken down without our help."

"What makes you think I would believe that?" Farnsworth asks. "They are desperate words spoken by a desperate girl because I am going to kill her boyfriend."

"They're not," I protest.

"Listen to her, Farnsworth," Phoenix warns, struggling against his bodyguard. "She's talking about a rebel who is gaining strength and power by the second. He's already amassed large groups from the city to march into the New World. They're on their way. And you're going to need all the help you can get. You're going to need someone who understands the way he thinks and can anticipate his next move."

"And that someone is you?" Farnsworth asks Phoenix.

"Not just me. Both me and Veronica."

"So, you're going to help me now?" Farnsworth watches Phoenix and me uneasily.

"Yes. We'll help you in exchange for his freedom," I negotiate, pointing to Phoenix.

"Ronnie," Phoenix mutters under his breath. "No. What are you doing? I don't care about me—"

"He'll never let me go, Phoenix. Never. I am the only one who can keep him alive." I turn to Farnsworth. "You let Phoenix go. We'll tell you how to squash this rebel leader who will stop at nothing to overthrow you. He works with a small girl. She was once one of mine." The thought of Lulu makes me very sad. "Together they have the capability to move masses. Don't believe us?" I ask Farnsworth who's been eyeing us skeptically this whole time. "Ask someone you trust." Farnsworth calls Grace over, and she whispers something into his ear. Farnsworth looks up at us.

"It seems you speak the truth." Farnsworth's lips are pursed together.

I look at her, wondering if Grace really has heard something, or if she is simply on our side.

"Apparently I've been kept in the dark because I have been feeling so ill lately. And no one seems to know why." Farnsworth looks over his shoulder at his nurse. "I am peeved I have been out of the loop, but it seems they have all been waiting for the blood of the great Veronica Billings to save me, now, as it did once before. Way back then, when...well, before all this trouble started." Farnsworth closes his eyes for a moment. "When it was just you and me at the waterfront. Veronica, do you remember that?" He opens his eyes. Whole seconds tick by. "Veronica? I'm waiting for your answer. Do you remember that?"

"Of course I do, sir," I whisper, my eyes glued to the floor. I can feel Phoenix's stare.

"Can you promise me, Veronica," Farnsworth asks, "that if I spare his life, and we work together, can you promise me you and I will make it back to that waterfront together?"

My eyes dart to Phoenix. That is the exact promise we made each other. I look down at Farnsworth sitting there. He is pale and frail, and I almost feel sorry for him. But then I remember who he is, what he's done, and what he wants to do to us and my girls.

"No sir," I say. "I can't promise you that. But I can promise without us, you will be dead within three days."

Chapter Twenty-Two

Obviously, this is not what Farnsworth wanted to hear. I am certain of it as we stand here staring at him, waiting for him to decide our ultimate fate. My bodyguard grips my arm tighter, and I wince.

"Okay, Veronica." Farnsworth stares at me while he speaks. "You two work with me to help protect my world from the attack of this...all-powerful rebel, and in exchange, you win his freedom."

"My girls too," I demand, standing tall before him.

"Negotiating after the terms have already been agreed to, Veronica? You know I can't give up the girls. They're the last of the O's."

"They're so tiny, they have nothing to offer. You will do much better with me. I will stay here with you, as your personal donor. And I will live in your house with you..."

Farnsworth's eyes dart up at me.

"Together but separately," I explain.

He nods. He's disappointed, but he knows he'll do no better.

"In return, after we have helped you stop this rebel attack, you let Phoenix and all three girls go free. Those are the terms. If you want my blood, this is the only way to get it."

"It's not the only way," he counters. "I could force you."

"You could, but I know the reason you are feeling so terrible. And I know how to fix it. And if you force me, I will never divulge the secret."

Everyone in the room starts and begins to mumble. I'm certain I hear my bodyguard mumble the word, "treason."

"Push me, Farnsworth. Torture me. This will only grow uglier and uglier. The rebel is talking massive killing sprees. We need this to stop now. Let us help you stop the rebels, and let me help you feel better. After your world is under your control once again, you can enlist people of the New World for the Couplings. Most won't say no, they'll be so grateful their perfect worlds haven't been destroyed, and their children haven't been hurt, they'll come willingly. Then you can ensure matches that will begin to rebuild the O's. But you can't do that until everything is under control."

I can feel the disappointment in Phoenix's stare. "This is the best scenario. For everyone," I explain, looking directly at Phoenix. Phoenix offers me a small pained smile, but I know he agrees.

"Where do we start?" Farnsworth asks.

"At the end," I say.

****

Within minutes, the girls have been released to Grace's care, and I know they'll be fine with her. We are all transported by limousine to Farnsworth's house. The ride is quick, but I can see the sorrow in Phoenix's eyes when he looks at me. We jump out of the limo, and Grace hustles the exhausted, but giggling girls off to the kitchen for something she calls "ice cream sundaes," while Phoenix, Farnsworth, and I make our way to Farnsworth's conference room. The three of us huddle around a table while his bodyguards wait by the door.

"Ask them to step outside," I tell Farnsworth, and he nods to them.

They obey. I feel my heart racing.

"Your enemy is named Gunnar," Phoenix begins. "He is ruthless. For a period of time, he was my partner. We wanted to lead a peaceful revolution."

"Peaceful?" Farnsworth asks.

"Yes." Phoenix looks Farnsworth steadily in the eyes. "It was never our intention to kill you. We didn't want to rule the New World. We only wanted equality for those of us left back in the city."

"I see." Farnsworth shifts slightly in his seat. "But now he does want to rule the New World."

"Yes."

"And to do that, he plans to kill me."

"Yes," Phoenix nods, solemnly.

"So how do we stop this murderous rebel then?" Under his calm exterior, Farnsworth is clearly terrified.

"You have to speak to the people of the New World. Tell them there is danger approaching. Explain they must rally together to stop these rebels, or there will be certain death for men, women, and children."

"I see," Farnsworth utters. "What next?"

"Next, we get your word out to the people in the city. Tell them you have seen the error of your ways, and you want equality for all."

"But tell me, Phoenix. If I were to do that, how would we keep the New World running?"

"You'll have to find a way that doesn't involve blood as your primary commodity. Find another form of commerce."

"But it will never work," Farnsworth blurts. "Blood is all they know. It keeps them young and healthy."

"Appeal to their sense of decency," Phoenix offers. "Tell them they are killing children to stay youthful. Explain to them that once a world existed where blood was given to one another out of generosity and only when it was a matter of life and death. Explain we can get back to that world, one where everyone is equal."

"But they don't want a world where everyone is equal," I say, quietly. Phoenix and Farnsworth turn to me. Suddenly, what Grace had said to me makes complete sense.

"Above all, just remember who you are," Grace said the first time she helped me prep for dinner with Farnsworth. Now I remember who I am, or at least who I had been for the past seven years: a Leader.

"What are you saying?" Phoenix asks.

"They don't want it, Phoenix. They want to live in their bubble where they, and the people they love, stay young and beautiful forever. Above all, they don't want to think about anything they may have done wrong."

"So? We can't appeal to their sense of decency then?" Phoenix asks.

"Eventually, yes," I explain. "But not now when we're on borrowed time. The only chance we have to rally them immediately is to threaten to spill their blood."

"But we said peaceful change," Farnsworth interjects and Phoenix nods along.

"I know. And it will be. I'm not talking about the blood in their veins. I'm talking about the blood in mine."

"I don't follow you," Farnsworth states.

"Well, the first thing you have to do is abdicate." I stare directly at Farnsworth. "To me. They are a nation of children. And no one leads groups of children better than me."

I see the glimmer of understanding in Phoenix's eyes. "But I can't do it alone."

"Raven," Phoenix deduces.

"Raven," I repeat.

"What?" Farnsworth asks, laughing at the absurdity of the situation. Both Phoenix and I remain stoic, and slowly, Farnsworth realizes we're serious.

"Abdicate? Why would I do that?" Farnsworth asks, scoffing. I look him dead in the eyes.

"Because you want to survive."

****

We find Raven sitting on a counter in Farnsworth's kitchen. She has an enormous bowl of something in her hand, and chocolate smeared across her face. As soon as we walk in, she knows why we've come.

"You want me to help rally the people of the Inferno to fight in a peaceful opposition against Gunnar's coup," she rattles off, putting her bowl down on the counter.

"Yes," Phoenix confirms.

"Cool." She hops down and walks over to us.

Chapter Twenty-Three

After a short bout of fitful sleep, we spend the next few hours in a frenzy of prepping everyone and everything for Farnsworth's "Message to the People" and consequently, his abdication speech. Phoenix, Raven, and I work together seamlessly, and Farnsworth is so overwhelmed, he simply stays out of our way. If it wasn't all a matter of life and death, this would almost be fun. We have it orchestrated down to the last detail. I sit on a window ledge overlooking the ocean, putting the finishing touches on Farnsworth's speech, when Phoenix walks over to me. I feel him near me before I even see him.

"Oh," I say with a small start. He is standing incredibly close to me. "I didn't realize—"

He takes the pen from my hand, and I look past him to see we are nearly alone. There is only Raven, sitting cross-legged on top of a table on the other side of the room, staring at a few pieces of paper. Everyone else must have left to prep Farnsworth. Phoenix looks over his shoulder at Raven, and she gives us a big smile. She hops down off the table and clears out of the room…then we are alone.

Almost immediately, my breathing grows shallow and perspiration begins to dot my forehead. My eyes are locked on his. The yearning I'm feeling is driving me wild. Phoenix reaches up over me and places both hands on the windowsill behind me. He is looking at me so intensely, I feel naked. I blush and look away, but he takes one hand from the windowsill and places it on my chin. Gently, he guides my chin back up until I look him directly in the eyes. He has complete control now. I am trapped, cornered like a wounded animal, but yet I close my eyes and pray there is no escape.

"Ronnie," he whispers. "I don't know what's going to happen here tonight. I don't know if your crazy, convoluted scheme can work. But what I do know is I am so very proud to be working with you. You are smart, and beautiful, and loyal, and strong, and fierce. And I love you, Veronica Billings."

"What?" I look up at him.

"I love you," he repeats.

"I love you too," I whisper. I throw my arms around him and push myself toward him. We hold each other so tightly our breathing falls into time. He leans down and kisses me. One kiss leads to another and soon our mouths are locked together.

"Wait." I push him away, although, I don't want to. "I can't. I can't. Not after Brooke."

"Ronnie," he sighs. "This time you are going to listen while I explain." He holds me tightly by the shoulders, so there is no chance to get away. "I did have a past with Brooke. Yes. I'm sorry for it, now. There's nothing I can do about that. But nothing you think happened, yesterday, did. Ron, we talked and I uh…I poisoned her with your mushrooms."

"What?" I ask, much too loudly, breaking free of his grasp.

"I had to do something. I knew giving her one mushroom wouldn't kill her. It would just knock her out for a while."

"How did you find the right mushroom?" I am in awe of him.

"I saw them when I checked out the bikes. That's what took so long. You kept her talking, so I hoped some part of you understood what I was doing."

"You're sure they were the right ones?"

"I listened when you explained about the circular spores."

"How did you get her to eat them?" He looks away. "Phoenix? How?"

"I uh, I told her they were an aphrodisiac."

"You what?"

"I'm sorry, Ron. But I had to do something. And she…well…for all of her show, she's afraid of intimacy."

"You mean you two never?"

"Never. Never. I promise. We had a relationship, yes. And we did some things couples do. But no. Never that. She was adamantly opposed."

"Because of the Couplings," I murmur, realizing. "Because she was sentenced at such a young age."

"Maybe so."

"So why last night?"

"She would have poked needles in her eyes to get even with you," he explains. "She always thought I was in love with you, even way back then. That's why I never pushed her."

"But you wanted to?" I ask, feeling like I'm six years old. I feel the sweat accumulate under my arms.

"No." He shakes his head. "I knew there was someone else out there for me. I have wanted you for as long as I've been hunting you. Actually"—a small grin spreads across his face—"much, much longer."

"But you never even knew what I looked like way back then."

"Of course I did. Do you really think it took me this long to find you?" he grins again. "Really? I knew where you were. And I'm not proud of it, but I watched you every chance I had. I was so confused. I thought you were my enemy, but still I wanted you so very much."

"You're not confused anymore?" I ask. He leans forward and puts his arms up against the windowsill again, once again pinning me and holding me as his very willing hostage. It feels so good, I breathe him in deeply, trying to make the moment last forever.

"Things have never been so clear," he murmurs, leaning down and kissing me gently. This time I know it is only us, and I let his mouth open mine. His hands make their way down my back, and one of his arms wraps entirely around my waist. The other reaches up and holds the back of my head. For whole minutes we are lost—not in the New World or the Old, but in our own world. And it is exactly where we should be.

****

"Sorry, guys," Raven interrupts in a soft voice. She's come back to collect us. "But Farnsworth's freaking out."

Phoenix and I pull apart and I do the best I can to compose myself. I catch him doing the same. He smiles a smile meant only for me.

"All right," Phoenix says, smoothing his clothing. "Should we go try to pull this thing off?"

"Yup," Raven chirps, skipping ahead of us, out of the room.

"You ready?" I ask Phoenix as we walk through the door.

"It's been years, and I'm here because of you. It's not the way I expected it to be, but still…thanks to you, I'm here."

"You're going to be great," I whisper, my words choking me.

"You too," he reassures me, and just then, Grace and the rest of Farnsworth's entourage run up to us and hustle us to separate rooms to dress for the broadcast.

****

Raven and I have been brought to what was once, and may be again, my bedroom. Lilly and Violet are in their own room, being watched by someone Grace trusts. I can tell Grace is nervous as she begins setting out clothing for Raven and me. The room is so large we each have our own private space to shower and prep. Silently and without question, we each slip into the dress Grace has chosen for us. When Grace has zipped me up, I turn and catch a glimpse of Raven. She is so beautiful, she takes my breath away.

"Raven," I gasp, "you look gorgeous."

She is in a dress that is the perfect blend of sophistication and youth. The deep blue color accentuates her eyes and complements her skin coloring perfectly. Her hair is up, making her appear serious but still age-appropriate. She needs to be publicized as a knowledgeable child, and Grace has nailed it.

"Yeah? You should take a look in a mirror," Raven responds, smiling. Once again, it never occurs to me to look. I turn around and stare at myself in the full-length mirror. I am in a silk, crimson red dress, wrapped tightly at my waist and only slightly fuller at my feet.

There is a long slit up my left leg, and the top of the dress gathers from the waistline into an opened fan over my breasts. Tiny straps as thin as spaghetti hold the dress in place. Grace has brushed my hair and draped it over my shoulder. This time, she's applied makeup to my eyes and cheeks, and the shiny thing she put on my lips has color. The nails on my hands and my toes have been painted with a shiny red paint. She has pulled all focus away from my most recent injury, the cut on my inner forearm. This time I don't laugh at what I see. This time I recognize the importance of what we're doing. This time I see Grace has made me look stunning. And hopefully it will work.

Silently the three of us leave my bedroom and begin to walk down one of Farnsworth's long hallways. How easy it was when I was only trying to outsmart him. Now, I need to convince an entire population they should listen to me. It might be easier if I believed I was worthy of being listened to. I take a deep breath as we near the end of the hallway.

We step outside, and I am surprised to see Phoenix standing by the car waiting for us. He is dressed in a snug navy blue suit with an opened light blue shirt underneath and his shoes are black and shiny. He kept the slight beard, and although he looks like a tame version of himself, he is still incredibly handsome. I want to run to him, but circumstances will never allow it.

Instead, I offer a small, private smile. We walk to the car, and he stands aside to let us in.

As Raven slides in, I wait next to Phoenix and feel him breathe me in. He squeezes my hand for much longer than he should. "You look...wow," he whispers to me.

"You too," I giggle.

I slide in next to Raven. Phoenix stays at his station until Grace has made her way in. She also looks beautiful in a simple, elegant off-white suit. Then one of Farnsworth's bodyguards wheels Farnsworth out. He looks as good as Farnsworth has ever looked. He's wearing a white suit with a navy shirt, and his hair is combed just right. He has trouble climbing into the car, so Phoenix very subtly helps him. Although I'm sure Farnsworth hates it, I see he respects Phoenix for it. For a moment we're all so cordial, I forget we're playing an elaborate game.

No one speaks a word on the way to the convention center, but Phoenix sits up tightly against me, his thigh pressed against mine. It feels strong and so good, I push back as hard as I can. By the time we arrive at the center, my thigh is sore from the isometric exercise, but I don't care. We leave the car in the reverse order we entered, and are quickly whisked to the backstage area of a large platform stage. It is where Farnsworth gives his live speeches to his nation. They broadcast in the city as well, but no one there really ever wanted to watch them. I wonder if that will change now. People I have never seen before busy themselves attaching things called "microphones" and "ear pieces" to us. The microphone is so sensitive it broadcasts my hurried breathing. I have no idea how to stay calm through this.

Phoenix senses my nervousness and does his best to stay by my side. But tonight isn't about me. Tonight is about convincing a nation.

I stand backstage and look up into the early night sky. The sky here is, in no way, as clear as it is back home. Home. I hesitate to even think the word, because camp really isn't my home anymore. Truthfully, no place is. Then I look at Phoenix standing protectively close to me, and I know exactly where my home is, with him.

Raven comes up and slips her hand into mine. "It will be okay." I look at her and tilt my head. "We're doing what's right," she assures me.

I smile at her and reach down to stroke her cheek. She is so beautiful and so brilliant, but still so young. For how many years did I do what I thought was right, only to find I was completely wrong? But it doesn't matter. We're out of time and options. This has to work.

Before any of us are ready, it's show time. Phoenix, Raven, and I hold hands backstage, and I notice we've each bowed our heads, saying our own silent prayers.

Mine is easy: "Please, God, keep them alive." I repeat this over and over again until it's become my mantra.

A drum roll crashes around us, making me jump. A huge curtain opens and we step forward onto a stage that seems every bit as large as my camp grounds. The audience grows very quiet, as we stand beside the podium. I sneak a look at Phoenix and catch a nervous expression on his face. Only Raven seems unaffected by our confusing welcome. She smiles as if she was born to be here. And maybe she was. The audience shuffles and mumbles, and I have to wonder if Farnsworth has tricked us. Has he left us up here to die, both figuratively and literally? I peer out at the audience and I am amazed by these people. There are different generations standing together, but one person looks as young as the next. It is going to be nearly impossible to convince these people to give up their blood.

After what seems an eternity, Farnsworth enters the stage to a standing ovation and thunderous applause. He waves and smiles, somehow, summoning the strength to walk out himself. I am certain Grace is backstage ready with his wheelchair. "Ladies and gentlemen," Farnsworth begins. "I am afraid tonight I come to you with a heavy heart." Mumbling is heard from the people. "I am here to tell you our way of life is in jeopardy. Everything you have and know could be eradicated." Gasps are heard. A quiet ruckus begins. "The way of our world, must change. Our precious blood supply is nearly depleted. Our sources in the city have run dry."

"Secure more Couplings," someone shouts and I watch Phoenix use every ounce of strength he has to refrain from pouncing on the man.

"If only it were that easy," Farnsworth answers. "But we have run out of O. And there is no one left to match to create it." Farnsworth looks at me out of the corner of his eye as he speaks. I feel the camera broadcasting the show, close in on my face. It moves to pan the crowd, and more gasps and sounds of horror spread throughout the audience.

"We need that blood," someone else yells. The crowd begins to grow unruly, and I see the perspiration form on Farnsworth's forehead.

"I know, ladies and gentlemen." Farnsworth clears his throat. "That's why, here, tonight, I announce my abdication as Principal Leader."

The people of the Inferno draw a collective breath, and people begin to shout questions. Farnsworth puts up his hands to silence them.

"What I said before is true. You are not safe here anymore. Not only has your blood supply been depleted, but very soon a large group of organized rebels will come to attack all of us in the New World."

Shouting is heard from the people. Again, he puts up his hands, and again the people quiet.

"There is only one person who may be able to help us." Farnsworth looks at me, smiling. "Ms. Veronica Billings."

"Veronica Billings," someone cries. "She is the Leader who supplies the blood."

"Thank you, honey," a woman shouts. "I'm seventy-three." Staring at her, I would never guess she was more than my mother's age. Just as I suspected, they will never give up their blood willingly. But this is what I'm banking on.

"I ran a marathon three weeks ago," another woman squeals. "Thanks to the latest crop of blood you delivered." Spontaneous applause erupts, and I look at Phoenix. I was right. They'll never face the bad we've done. Instead, they are venerating me for doing it for them. Suddenly, they begin to chant my name.

"VER-ON-I-CA. VER-ON-I-CA. VER-ON-I-CA."

They do this over and over, until I approach the podium to speak.

"Thank you," I say, quietly. The microphone crackles, and I stand up tall. Farnsworth walks up next to me, and Raven stands next to him. For a second, I am struck by the fact that together we are dressed in red, white, and blue. I can't remember why or where I heard it, but I know those colors mean something, and somehow, for some reason, they give me strength. I focus.

"Thank you for that kind welcome." My head is throbbing. Guilt overwhelms me while I watch these people. Inside nearly every one of them is the blood of a girl I have sent to her death. "I am honored to be chosen by Former Principal Leader Farnsworth to be your new Acting Principal Leader." I pause and take a deep breath. I exhale, slowly. "But unlike him, I am not happy with the society you have built in the New World, and I have some hard truths to tell you. First, we will be attacked. Soon. When we are attacked, if you try to save yourself by banding with the rebels, they will turn on you and kill and torture your women and children."

Horrified gasps are heard. I am certain someone faints in the distance.

"Second, when they come, they will come directly for me and Raven." I lift Raven's hand in the air.

"Why should we care?" someone shouts.

"Because we are the last two remaining O's," I say, flatly. "And without us, you will have no more blood." I look out into the crowd, and I can tell by their faces this scares them, most of all. "This is why we must band together. We must stop the rebels as a team." I draw a huge breath. "And once it is over and we have survived, Farnsworth will again be your Principal Leader."

I look across them. They are so foreign to me I might as well have stepped into a civilization of spoiled aliens. Looking at them, hinging on my every word, I can't let them off this easily.

"You need to know what I did as a Leader was wrong. And what you're doing is wrong, too." Gasps are heard. I am nearly paralyzed by shame. "But I know you never meant to hurt anyone, just as I never realized what I was doing was wrong. I never realized I was—"

"A child killer?" shouts a voice from the audience. It is a voice I know all too well. And it's early.

"Gunnar," I shout and as fast as I can, I grab Raven and pull her off the stage with me. Phoenix stands at the microphone and I close my eyes, praying Gunnar doesn't shoot him dead.

"It's a rebel attack," Phoenix yells. Gunnar and the rebels let out wild calls and shouts as they march forward through the crowd. The people stand still, stupefied. They have no idea what a rebel attack means. A gunshot goes off, and I stop in my tracks. I turn back and thankfully, Phoenix is still standing. "They want to kill you and steal your way of life," Phoenix is shouting. "Lock your doors. Keep your children inside."

Chaos ensues.

"Kill him," I hear Gunnar shouting at his rebels, pointing at Phoenix. "He's a traitor. Kill him!"

I want to move forward toward Phoenix, but something is attached to my arm, pulling me back. From my vantage point behind the stage, everything looks like it's moving so very slowly. One of the rebels shoots a man standing only a few feet away from him, and it seems as if the man's splattering blood is travelling through molasses. Voices grow distorted, and I can no longer trust my eyes or my ears. I feel as if I'm watching another time and dimension. I realize the pull I am feeling is Grace. She has grabbed me by the arm and is pulling me to Farnsworth's limousine. I have such a tight grip on Raven I drag her along with me. I crane my neck, looking for even a glimpse of Phoenix, but I don't see him anywhere. Before I can take my next breath, I am pushed into Farnsworth's car and Phoenix is swallowed up by the crowd.

Chapter Twenty-Four

For the next hours, I am inconsolable. The girls and I are safe inside Farnsworth's helicopter, but Phoenix is out there, left behind, fighting the rebel attack. I have to get to him. I need to help him. My body aches to be with him, but there is nothing I can do. I have been forced to leave with Farnsworth and the girls. There is nothing for me to do except sit here, looking vapid and feeling useless. I have also deserted an entire nation of people who are helpless and defenseless against Gunnar. Yes, they stand for everything we are fighting against, but I can't help but empathize with them. After all, it was not so long ago I, too, thought our government was fair and just. It's not just Phoenix I have to get back to, it's the people who have been promised a leader.

As we fly off from the New World, I steal final glimpses of the ocean. Violet and Lilly take turns sitting next to me, placing their heads in my lap. I can barely look at Raven. I want so badly to be strong for her, to say Phoenix is smarter than them all, that he will survive, but I find it impossible to say the words. I went to Farnsworth's public address for answers, and I came back with nothing but questions.

Finally, we arrive at camp. Thank goodness. At least being in familiar territory will offer me some stability. There is no way I can take any more.

As soon as the helicopter lands, I push my way out the door and stumble across the field. I can feel Farnsworth's eyes on me, but I don't care. I fall into my cabin, and find it has been overturned by the rebel invasion. My plaques and awards have been pulled from the wall and smashed on the ground. Devastatingly, my mother's picture of the dandelion has been stolen from underneath my mattress. I feel so claustrophobic I can barely breathe. I tear at the dress I find so incredibly suffocating. I manage to pull off the decorative fan to expose plain fabric beneath, and tear off the bottom layers completely. I grab a towel and wipe my face as clean as I can. Hours have passed since the rebels descended on the Inferno. I wonder how many died. How many were children?

Thinking of children only makes me wonder about Lulu. Was she at the attack? My stomach aches knowing I am directly to blame. It will only be a matter of time until Gunnar and his troops make it to Farnsworth's house, and then it will be outright war. Gunnar knows what and whom I am protecting. He knows these three girls are the last remaining O's. There will be nothing I can do when he rallies his troops and heads back to our camp. We can only outrun him for so long.

I flop down face first on the bed and cry for what feels like an endless amount of time. I know people come to my door but I ignore them, and eventually they go away. I even need a break from my girls, because somewhere deep inside me, in the ugliest place in my soul, I resent them. I am incredibly angry I've had to protect them for so long, and in doing so, I've lost Phoenix. Besides, they are safe with Gretchen and

Margaret. Frankly, they're safer now with them than they are with me. When the tears stop, the thoughts start. I wonder about the children in the New World. I wonder about Phoenix, and what Gunnar is doing to him. I wonder what will become of us. I wonder why I was ever born. I am too tired and it is all too much to bear.

I pull myself to stand and slip out of my cabin, hopefully unnoticed. It doesn't take long before I find my mushroom patch. I pick only two, not to be tempted to do something rash and foolish. I make my way back into my cabin and lay back on my cot. Without thinking, I chew the two mushrooms, dirt and all. I need something, anything, to take me away from my thoughts.

****

When I awaken, my throat is incredibly parched and the sun is shining brightly. I have no idea how long I've been out, but I'm guessing I lost at least one full day. I am still in the short red dress that is now sticking to me. I don't care. I need answers and there is only one place to find them.

I march to Farnsworth's cabin, but he isn't there. I can tell from the position of the sun it must be near lunch time. I make my way to the mess hall, and find that it, too, was left looking like a war zone. I look around frantically, but there is no sign of Willy. My heart aches from all the loss it feels. I see Gretchen with the girls seated at a far table. She gives me a small wave. Margaret sits at the first table. She doesn't look up when she addresses me. "There's no cook," she relays, softly. "Hardly any food. Take what you want." I look at Margaret, wondering who this broken person is.

"I don't want food. I want..." and I see Farnsworth, huddled over a bowl of oatmeal, one bodyguard at his side. "You," I hiss, standing in front of him.

"Veronica." Farnsworth sounds genuinely happy to see me. "How is our new Acting Principal Leader?" he asks with a smirk.

"Cut the crap, Farnsworth." He reels from my words. "What is happening?"

"No good morning?" Farnsworth asks. "You've been asleep for nearly two days."

"What is happening with the rebel attack on the Infer—" I stop myself. "On the New World," I ask.

"It's not good." His eyes drop down to his oatmeal. He looks honestly upset. "Despite our plan, the rebels are gaining converts. I think they're just people trying to stay alive."

I nod. "Casualties?"

"Of course." He looks up at me, steadily. "But if you're asking how many or more directly, if he is one, I don't have the answer."

I nod, fighting the tears building in my eyes.

"But Veronica..." Farnsworth speaks gently, almost compassionately. "You'll spare yourself a lot of heartache if you just accept the fact he's probably dead. He was public enemy number two. There's no way they'll let him live."

"Number two?"

"Only after you." I gasp, surprised.

"But don't worry," Farnsworth assures me in his slimy voice, "as long as you stay with me you'll be fine."

"I'm not fine," I declare, looking him squarely in the eyes. "And I'm certainly not with you."

Farnsworth's eyes widen and narrow. He looks like I've kicked him in the groin.

"I'm sorry to hear that," he remarks, and I turn to walk away. "Veronica?" I turn back to face him. "It wouldn't matter anyway because I would never have permitted it…a relationship between you and Phoenix. What makes you think it would ever have happened?"

"It already did," I whisper, walking away.

****

I know what I've done is brash and stupid but my guess is Farnsworth will never survive the rebel takeover so what does it matter. I storm into my cabin and try to get myself out of the dress, but the zipper's stuck. I finally find a pair of scissors and manage to cut myself out. I know there is only one thing that will help right now. I dig up my swimsuit and stuff myself into it. Then I throw on a thin, black tank top cover and slip into my boots. Without mentioning it to a single soul, I clump down to the waterfront. I don't care who knows. Besides, not one of them, not Margaret, Gretchen, or Farnsworth would ever head down willingly. Sure, there is the possibility of a stray rebel who's stayed behind with the sole intent to kill me, but that's just a risk I'm willing to take right now.

Once I hit the waterfront, I realize there is only one reason for me to be here. This place holds nothing for me but memories, memories of Phoenix. But this really isn't about him. Or anyone else. It's about me. I strip out of my clothing and swimsuit. I stand naked on the beach, staring at the water ahead of me. Slowly and purposefully, I step one foot after another until I am waist deep. I feel the cool water divide my body in two. Half of me submerged, half of me elevated. I realize that, of everything we have gone through, this is what I hate the most, this feeling of being "halfway."

A sunny swims by and I see the sunlight reflect off his yellowish scales. It is such a perfect moment I know I am in the exact right place at the exact right time. I walk farther and farther into the lake, until my breasts are submerged. Suddenly, in the purity of the lake and this moment, I know exactly what it is I have to do. I have to make peace with myself.

I fold my arms across my chest and slowly tilt my head backward allowing my body to move with it. Soon I am submerged. Giving myself over to the lake, I allow myself to be cleansed. When I rise from the water, I will forgive myself for the sins I knowingly and unknowingly committed. Like Phoenix who rises from the ashes, I too will have my chance to be reborn. And once I am, there will be no turning back. There will be no more self-doubt or self-pity, and there will be no more excuses.

I rise, gasping for breath, and the air that hits my lungs is pure and refreshing. I walk directly from the lake to my clothes. I throw on my swim cover and scale the enormous hill back up to what used to be my camp. I move directly to my cabin and there I change into my black shorts and tank top. I lace up my boots and pack a bag with water, a jacket, and protein bars. I lace my fingers around the straps of my bag and I walk out into the sun, through the middle of camp, and into the woods. I hear the voices calling me—my girls and Farnsworth. It doesn't matter. It can't matter. That was the business of my past. The new Veronica has only one place to be.

****

I trudge through the woods for hours, doing my best to stay on the broken twigs that make some sort of a path. I am unclear where I am at all times, but I believe my heart will guide me. Hours tick by, but I refuse to stop. Mosquitoes buzz by my head, but none dare bite me. I sip water and eat my protein bars, but I take no time to rest. I am focused on only one thing and one person. It is not too long until I find her.

"Veronica Billings?" Brooke questions. "Are you incredibly stupid? Are you looking to die? Because I have no reason, Veronica, no reason at all to keep you alive."

"Yes, you do." I stand tall before her.

"I don't care about your precious special blood," she scoffs.

"I'm not talking about that. The only reason you have to keep me alive is because you love him."

"So you think I'll keep his girlfriend alive to spare his feelings? Oh, you don't know me all that well, Veronica. He tricked me. I was out cold for hours. Do you know what could have happened to my camp then? Do you? He drugged me. I can't have him, Veronica. And he's all I've ever wanted. But I'm sure as hell not going to wish you two a happy life without me."

"I don't expect you to. But you must know Gunnar has attacked the Inferno."

"That's why I'm still here." She shifts her weight from one foot to the other, uneasily.

"Okay," I say. "If we get to Phoenix, together, we'll have a chance to overthrow Gunnar."

"I don't need you," she hisses.

"Yes, you do. Because I'm the Acting Principal Leader."

She scoffs. "So I've heard."

"And...because you don't have enough troops to fight Gunnar. He has his rebels plus converts from the Inferno."

"And you and Phoenix will make a difference?"

"I didn't finish." I put up my hand to silence her, and take a step closer. "And for all your bravado, you are being overrun by Farnsworth."

"What are you talking about?" she asks, her voice low.

"I saw the Harvesters here. The first time I was here, with Phoenix. He didn't recognize them, but I did. You have been infiltrated. It makes perfect sense. It explains why you sit here, unmoving."

"Well, bravo, Veronica. So you're not as much of an idiot as I thought. So what?"

"So you don't want it. Come with me. I can convince Farnsworth to free you, and then together with Phoenix, we can convince the people of the Inferno to help stop Gunnar. We'll deal with Farnsworth, later. Leave your camp and your past behind. You can help save Phoenix, and you will be certain you will never be heading toward a Coupling house, ever again." My words sit heavily on her.

"Why would I come with you?" she asks.

"Because you want to. Because you know all the people in the Inferno are not bad. Because you want to be more than a powerless figurehead in your own camp. Because you want to be respected for your mind and not your body. Because you want to be part of a real revolution, and not play a seduction game, gathering useless troops. Convincing men to join your cause is not enough, Brooke. You joined Phoenix and his revolution because you wanted to accomplish something. Leave your feminine wiles here with all the useless men you're leading on. Abandon the Harvesters and come with me."

Again, Brooke shifts her weight from one foot to the other. She twirls the end of her hair with her forefinger.

"You're wrong," she counters, looking me in the eye. "The men I've gathered at my camp are not useless. There are some we can trust. They come with us. There is strength in numbers."

"Okay."

Brooke turns and then turns back to me. "The only reason I'm going to save him is so I can be the one to kill him."

"Fine," I mumble, wishing she was joking, and hoping she'll change her mind when she sees him. Brooke walks back to her camp. Within half an hour, she has given her troops their literal marching orders, and she has joined me, a backpack filled with supplies on her back. We are hidden behind her tent, out of view of the nearest Harvesters. She carries a shotgun and hands me one as well. I look at her, surprised.

"What?" she asks. "You think I'm worried about you with a gun? Please. I saw how pathetic you were with a gun the day you were pretending to hold Phoenix hostage." In a flash, she draws her gun and aims it at my head. "I could shoot you dead before you even think about shooting me."

I step back from her. Uneasy. "Comforting," I mumble. She seems satisfied.

"We go now," she commands, "and a few of my troops will follow. It has to be done subtly, or we will be caught. And we have to go on foot. The motorbikes are too noticeable."

"Okay," I agree, and together Brooke and I venture out into the woods, heading for the Inferno and the boy we both love.

Chapter Twenty-Five

The trip back to the Inferno to find Phoenix is arduous. There is constant tension between Brooke and me, and more than once, I am convinced she is just waiting for the perfect moment to shoot me. She never wants me to lead, claiming she knows the woods better, but I know the truth is that she cannot relinquish control. Not to me. Finally, I put my foot down.

"It's this way," I whine, sweat pouring off both of us.

"No, Veronica, it's not." Brooke rolls her eyes and trudges off in the opposite direction.

This, at least, shows some progress. It's the first time she's stopped calling me "baby-killer" and used my real name. Suddenly, she stops in her tracks. She looks back at me and tilts her head to show me something straight ahead. In the twilight, I have to squint, but then I can clearly see the brown uniform of the Harvesters.

"Harvesters?" I mouth to her and she nods. We squat down among the cover of the brush and trees, trying not to breathe. Up ahead, there are two Harvesters, walking aimlessly through the woods. They each carry a gun, but aside from that and their brown uniforms, they don't seem at all like Harvesters. Their posture is slumped over, and they appear nervous and lost.

"Converts?" I whisper, but Brooke just shrugs. "Are they yours?"

She shakes her head. One thing is certain, we will not be able to move forward without being spotted by them.

"We roll the dice," I decide, standing up.

"What are you doing?" The look in her eyes changes from anger to fear.

"Moving us forward."

I shout to them, "I am Veronica Billings. What are you doing here?"

They both pull their guns on us, but one is barely strong enough to hold his upright. The barrel flops down toward the ground. Only one keeps his gun pointed at us.

"Are you converts?" I ask. "With Gunnar's revolution?"

"Why should we tell you?" the one who seems strong asks.

"Because you are clearly lost. And he is about to die from dehydration," I point to the second boy. "And you," I point at the lead boy, "aren't far behind." They look at each other, scared and perplexed.

"It was her job," Brooke comments, stepping up. "She was the single best Leader we have ever known. She is trained to spot dehydration."

"We can give you water," I offer, and Brooke looks at me sideways. "But you must tell us who you are."

The weak Harvester is on his knees. His eyes are so sunken into his head, it looks like they may fall back into his skull at any minute.

"We were Harvesters," the lead boy admits, putting his gun down. "But there's no one left to Harvest."

I see Brooke try to shake off what he is saying.

"So what happened?" I ask.

"Farnsworth let most of us go. But there's nowhere…" he looks around the woods, his voice trailing off.

"Did you know where your harvested girls went?" I ask.

"To you," the second one replies, his voice raspy and forced. "Then after they've served their time, they are sent on to the New World. Everyone knows that."

It must be so painful for him to speak there's no way he would waste his words on lies. I give them a small smile remembering it wasn't so very long ago I, too, was this dangerous and this ignorant.

"Wow, you people really are stupid," Brooke cackles.

I pull off my pack and crack a bottle of water.

"Are you insane?" she asks. "We need that."

"A deal's a deal." I hand them a bottle. "You need to share. It's all we can spare. But there's a water source that way." I point toward the direction of the lake. "Head that way, and you should find it before either of you dies."

"Thank you," the sicker of the boys utters. They polish off the water.

"Are you planning to join the revolution?" Brooke asks, eyeing them skeptically.

"The only plan we have is to try to survive," the lead boy answers.

"I understand," Brooke responds. Then, in an instant, she lifts her gun and shoots each of the boys, square in the forehead.

"Brooke," I scream, running to the boys.

"What a waste of water," she chastises. "I can't believe you did that."

"You can't believe I did that? Who are you? You're crazy!" I lean over both boys, checking their pulses. They are both dead.

"Oh please. You didn't actually believe that story about them being 'let go,' did you?" I stare at her, still in shock. "You did? Jeez Veronica, there isn't a story you won't believe. Think about it. How far are we from the city? They're with Farnsworth. Probably part of the group that marched into my camp. You think these Harvesters just wandered up here?"

"Yes, I do think that. We're not that far from the city now."

"Oh." She looks down at the dead bodies. "Well, we need their uniforms anyway." She holds her gun to the side and begins to pull the lead boy's uniform off. The way she handles her gun reminds me of Phoenix. I stand there, staring at her. "Come on, V." I am stymied by her nickname for me.

"We're friends now?" I ask.

"Of course not. But V seems to fit you. So come on, snap to it. Help me get these uniforms off them so we can use them."

"Why?"

"Do you like to play dumb?"

"What I mean is that Gunnar has probably infiltrated Farnsworth's mansion and the Letting facility by now. Wearing the brown of the Harvesters will only get us killed that much faster."

"You think he's that powerful?" she asks, and for the first time she seems unsure of herself.

"He is exponentially more powerful than

Farnsworth. Farnsworth only has a small army and his followers of spoiled, rich people. Gunnar has legions of people seeking revenge. Nothing is more powerful than the desire for revenge. Think about how much you hate me." Her eyes dart up at me.

"That's a good point. Seems you're not that stupid after all, V."

"Gee, thanks," I mumble.

"Anyway," she stares directly at my chest. "We wouldn't have been successful, pretending to be Harvesters. You would have gotten away with it, but no one would have believed I was a boy." She flashes a tiny smile and hooks her fingers through the straps of her backpack. "Let's go."

I tighten my pack as well and step around the two dead bodies. Although it kills me to leave them there like that, I know Gunnar's revolutionaries would never bury a body, and it would be a tipoff to anyone hunting us. And, we can't afford to lose any more time.

****

As the sun sets, we trudge onward. We stop only to sleep for a few hours, and then we feel the sun rise and force ourselves to walk on. Finally, we are on the outskirts of the Inferno. This time there is no traffic. There are no families taking a drive with their pets, no people scurrying to and fro, leading their over-privileged lives. It makes me a tiny bit sad. I see the bridge up ahead, and it is completely deserted.

"There's the bridge," I whisper and she nods.

She stops to survey the situation, but I know there's no time to lose. I feel myself holding my breath and actively force it out of my lungs. I put my head down and walk directly for the bridge.

"What are you doing?" she asks, her eyes wide.

"We have no time to lose," I explain.

"We'll be spotted!"

"That's a risk we'll have to take." I push forward.

She falls in time next to me, both of us keeping our heads down, walking as quickly as possible. We make it to the highest point of the bridge without incident, but as we begin the descent down, we see trucks parked up ahead.

"Friend or foe?" Brooke whispers.

"They're all foes," I reply, and still we walk on.

The trucks don't move toward us, so they must feel we don't pose a threat. After all, how much threat could two overly tall young women carrying shotguns pose?

If they only knew.

It is not until we are directly even with the trucks that we see they are abandoned. Pure luck. The chances of lucking out like that again... I refuse to let myself think about it.

We are off the bridge and into the Inferno, and it is eerily quiet. We have another day's walk to get to Farnsworth's house, which is the only place we stand a chance of survival.

"Can we get that lucky again?" I ask Brooke and she looks at me, questioning. "Maybe we can," I mumble.

Without a thought, I break from Brooke and sprint back to the trucks. I find the keys in the second truck. "Woo-hoo," I yell, pounding my fist on the steering wheel.

"All right, V." Brooke slides into the cab of the truck. "This was borderline smart."

I smile at her as the ignition turns over. I touch

gears and knobs and the wheel. It dawns on me I have never driven a truck before.

"Do you have any idea what you're doing?" Brooke asks, gripping the seat.

"Uh-uh. You?"

"No." She looks at the dials in front of me. "I've only ever driven the motorbikes."

"Here we go." I press on the gas pedal.

The truck moves forward and stalls abruptly. Brooke falls forward and smacks her face on the dash in front of her. She scowls at me.

"Oops," I say, stifling a laugh. "Sorry."

"How about you concentrate a little harder?" she warns, pulling the gun on me. "This might help you to focus."

"Mm," I mumble, learning by trial and error. Finally, I press a lever with my left foot as I push the gear stick up. Then I ease the left lever and press down on the right. Whenever the truck makes seemingly abnormal noises, I recreate those steps and slowly, bumpily, we head out over the vast, empty highways.

"Whose truck do we figure this is?" Brooke asks. I look at her and see the gun is pointed away from me. Without even realizing it, my shoulders relax. Then I nearly stall the truck, and she shoots me another dirty look. I sit myself up again.

"Don't know." I shift into a lower gear as we go up a hill. "But we have a fifty percent chance of not being shot at."

She nods.

Thankfully, the roads are familiar and, fairly soon, we near the crossroads of Farnsworth's private drive. I pull the truck off the road and cut the engine.

"What are you doing?" she asks.

"We walk from here." I jump out of the truck and hook on my pack and my gun. She follows. Although it is amazingly abandoned, we walk through the trees lining the road to Farnsworth's house. Fairly soon, I see the huge white mansion before us. "There," I point. I have no idea what brought me here. It is the last place Gunnar would keep Phoenix, but at least it's a place to start. And if Grace is here, at least I'll have the possibility of an ally.

Somehow, we find our way to a back entrance and I begin to wonder if we are actually going to sneak inside undetected. No sooner do I think the thought, a deafening alarm goes off overhead, and bright white lights envelop us. "Drop your gun," I whisper to Brooke.

We both throw our guns into the bushes and our hands into the air. Within moments, we are encircled by members of Farnsworth's army, pointing guns at us.

"I am Veronica Billings," I declare. "Your last remaining O and Acting Principal Leader. Former Principal Leader Farnsworth is at my camp. He asked me to come. I have news."

The guards step aside and the back door opens. I watch, my eyes wide, as Farnsworth makes his way to the door.

"Ah, Veronica," he hums. "I see you've decided to join me at last. How wonderful. And by the way, don't worry about introducing yourself as Acting Principal Leader anymore. You abdicated to me earlier this afternoon. You told the people you were sorry, but you were outmatched. They understood." He turns to face Brooke. "Oh good." He smiles his white-toothed, unsettling smile at Brooke. "I see you've brought a lovely friend."

Chapter Twenty-Six

I stare, dumbfounded. "Well, Veronica," Farnsworth admonishes, "you could have arrived here much more quickly if you would have waited for me to fire up the helicopter."

Brooke stares at me, and I know if she was still holding her gun, I would be dead right now. "Come in," he tells us. "Join me for dinner."

"I don't want dinner," I snap. "I want to know where Phoenix is. Do you have him? Or do they?"

"All in good time, Veronica. All in good time." I can tell how much he enjoys my agony.

It makes me almost wish they would demand a transfusion, so I could give him more poisoned blood.

I am hustled inside to dress and prepare for dinner, while Brooke is taken to her own quarters to do the same. The preparation seems endless, even though this time I have only the choice of one dress, a long, white gown with braided straps and a bodice that hangs loosely from my breasts to the floor. No one even bothers to give me shoes anymore. I walk out into the hallway and meet up with Brooke, who looks ravishing in a floor length, black, body-fitted gown. Her hair is up, and she is completely made-up. I can't help but notice her incredible breasts spilling up, over the top of her gown. I am certain Farnsworth will notice as well. She wears heels and, in them, she is nearly eye to eye with me.

"Wow Brooke," I remark, "you look incredible."

"I know." She smiles only a half-smile. She is clearly terrified. We are taken to Farnsworth's dining room, but there is no wait staff scattered about and no food waiting to be served.

"Yes," Farnsworth mutters, walking slowly into the room. "War is hell." He motions to the empty room around him. "Everyone who was even remotely loyal to me was forced to fight. So I have nothing to offer you except…" he reaches into his pocket and pulls out a protein bar. "Dinner?" he asks. I shake my head, but Brooke snatches the bar. Farnsworth looks at her curiously. I can tell he is unable to figure her out.

"I'm wearing your stupid dress, Farnsworth," I snarl. "Where is he?" I have the instinct to reach out and choke it out of him.

"Lost all decorum, Veronica?" Farnsworth asks.

"That happens when you lose the person you love." I see Farnsworth start. I have blasphemed.

"Amen to that," Brooke adds, looking at me.

"So what's it going to be," I ask Farnsworth. "We've come all this way. Phoenix and I were here to help you fight Gunnar. We are the only reason you are alive today."

"Yes," Farnsworth agrees. "That may very well be true."

"I want to know where Phoenix is. And I don't care what you've told them. I want to offer the people of the New World the leadership I promised them."

"That's very noble, Veronica." Farnsworth doesn't move an inch. We stare at each other for what seems an eternity. My mind feels like it's drifting up out of my body. Finally, Farnsworth turns to face Brooke. "You are very lovely," he coos. I can see the tiny hairs on her arms bristle. "Ah, but I can tell you're not my biggest fan, either."

"No sir, I'm not," Brooke hisses through her teeth.

"Well, let's see if we can change that, shall we?" Farnsworth puts his arm out for Brooke to slip hers in.

"I don't think so, sir," she retorts, her voice steely.

"I would very much like to take you into the kitchen. See if there is anything left in there that is to your liking." Brooke eyes him skeptically but walks over to him. She turns back to me to see if I am joining them.

"Oh, don't worry about your friend," Farnsworth tells Brooke. "She needs some time to think."

My eyes close imagining Farnsworth will have me tied to a table in the Letting facility, waiting to be drained. Instead, he pushes open the door that leads to the outside and the ocean.

"You've always loved the water," Farnsworth proposes. "Why don't you take a stroll?"

I imagine what's out there: guns and rebels and certain death. But the coolness of the air lures me forward, and I smell the welcoming scent of the ocean. Slowly, without meaning to, my feet make their way to the doorway, and I breathe in the gorgeous night air. I look over my shoulder at Farnsworth.

"Go on." I turn back, placing one foot, then the other, moving outside until the darkness envelopes me, driving the excitement of the unknown through me.

I walk closer to the ocean, needing to feel the water on my feet, needing to be whole again. The water is incredibly calm and quiet tonight. I can only hear the smallest waves, rolling off in the distance.

"Ronnie?" I hear my name on the ocean waves. "Ronnie?" I hear it again and I turn back, not daring to think…"Ronnie," Phoenix calls, rushing forward to embrace me.

"Phoenix?" I throw myself into his arms. "How? How can you be alive?" Tears stream down my face.

"For you." His hands reach up and stroke both sides of my face. "I am alive for you." I study him and see his gorgeous face is covered with cuts and bruises. I touch one of them but he doesn't falter.

"What did he do to you?" I feel anger coursing through me.

"Nothing we need to talk about right now."

"How did you get away?" I ask.

"Gunnar isn't as smart as he thinks he is." Phoenix smiles at me. "Then I made my way here to Grace. I knew she would help me find you."

"I came with Brooke," I report.

"How?" he asks, confused.

"We walked."

"From camp to the Inferno?" He raises his eyebrows in disbelief.

"I knew you were alive. That's what kept me going."

He nods, understanding.

"And Brooke came because she wants to be the one to kill you." We share a small smile. Soon his smile dissipates. Phoenix's expression grows so much more intense. He grips both sides of my face softly, but possessively, and he leans down, kissing me on the lips. I push myself as tightly to him as possible, and he drops his hands to my waist. Our lips are locked together as he lifts me up, and our bodies press together until there is no space between us. We fit together like two interlocking pieces of a puzzle. He puts me down only so I can catch my breath. He kisses me softly now, over and over again, his lips traveling across my face, leaving gentle kisses behind. I close my eyes, giving myself over to this feeling of complete excitement and complete surrender. His lips find their way back to my mouth again, and we interlock. I wish there was something, anything, I could do to stay with him forever. There is nothing I wouldn't do.

He pulls away for only a moment, and I can see in his eyes he feels the same way. My lips are numb and my body aches for him, but the way he smiles at me tells me we are going to stop.

"Why?" I whisper, my eyes closed. "Why are we stopping?"

"Because it's my job to take care of you."

My breath catches in my throat. His words course through my veins like pure ecstasy. He takes off his jacket and lays it on the sand. He pulls me down to sit next to him, and we stare out at the ocean. He holds my left hand and turns it over, rubbing it with his hands.

"They say," Phoenix looks out at the water as he speaks. "In ancient times, men and women used to choose to be together."

"I've heard that," I sigh, breathlessly.

"And that when a man was in love he would give something to the woman he loved. And every time she looked at it, she would be reminded of how much he loved her. And she would be his, forever, no matter what."

"That's beautiful," I murmur, feeling my palms

grow sweaty with his touch.

"I wish I had something I could give you," he remarks, looking at me. "So you know how much I love you."

I smile at him. "I don't need anything to remind me of that. We just need to keep fulfilling our promises to each other."

"Like?"

"Like the promise we made to meet back at the waterfront. It's not our waterfront," I acknowledge, "but it's something."

"It certainly is, and you're wearing another incredibly beautiful dress. I have to say, I do like your choice of attire whenever you visit Farnsworth."

"Well it's not done willingly," I respond angrily and see Phoenix's mood darken. "Oh, I shouldn't have said..." My words trail off.

"No. You should be able to say anything to me. I just hate that he controls us. It shouldn't be like that, Ron."

"But he can't control what's in here," I remind him, placing my hand on Phoenix's heart.

Phoenix reaches out and takes my hand. He kisses my palm and then softly kisses my wrist. Slowly, he moves up my forearm, past my elbow, up my bicep, and my shoulder, making his way to my neck. His kisses linger there, while his fingers toy with the straps on my gown. One strap slips off my shoulder, and I feel waves of exhilaration wash over me. His hand lingers at my shoulder, before it inches across my collarbone, slowly. My breath catches. His hands and his kisses drive me wild and chills pass through my body like tiny convulsions. And then, again, he stops.

"I'm sorry," he mumbles.

"No sorry," I pant, aching for more.

"No." He shakes his head. "It's too much. Not here. Not like this."

We sit for a minute staring out at the ocean then something grabs his attention right as a tiny wave breaks near our feet. He stands and walks over to pick something up. He comes back and sits next to me.

"I don't know what they used in ancient times," he admits. "But I'm asking you to be mine. Forever."

He holds his hand open to reveal a perfectly shaped, milky white seashell. Somehow through the chaos and horror that surrounds us, we have found a moment of bliss and perfect peace. Love really can conquer all. I take the seashell in my hand and hold it to my heart.

"I've always been yours."

He leans over and kisses me, knowing what I say is true.

We sit side-by-side, staring out at the ocean, both of us content but neither of us trusting the feeling. I turn the seashell over and over in my hand. "Why is he allowing us this time together?" I whisper.

"Don't know…" Phoenix reaches up and scratches the back of his head. His knuckles look bruised and raw. "Maybe he's giving up." Phoenix smiles a charming, boyish smile.

"Right. Or maybe he's…changing?" I'm careful with my words. Too much faith in Farnsworth could threaten Phoenix.

"Maybe." Phoenix pulls me closer to him. "All I know is that I will never let him take you away again."

I sigh, snuggling closer to Phoenix, wishing it were

possible to stay with him forever. "A war is raging around us." The words I say are powerful, yet I speak softly. "My girls are alone at camp, Lulu is missing, and Gunnar may topple the New World at any moment." We both know these things, yet somehow I feel the need to say them. "Any one of those things could take me away…" Despite my best efforts, my voice breaks on my last word. I feel the tears welling.

"Hey, hey…?" Phoenix tilts my chin upward and looks me deep in the eyes.

"How did this happen?" I ask him. "Any of this? I was just a girl cursed with toxic blood, counting the days until I would see my mother again, knowing it would never happen. I loved her, and she is gone and the pain is unbearable. I would rather walk away from you now than ever feel that pain again. The pain I would feel in losing you again would be exponentially worse…and it will get worse and worse with each passing day. Can you understand that?" My eyes search his.

"I understand because it's the same for me. Don't you get it, Ron? I will never let them break us apart again. Never. Farnsworth has no recourse. He needs us."

I nod at him. "I just wish there was some way—"

"Trust me," he murmurs, placing his hand gently on my lips. He looks at me, his eyes intense and hungry. He leans toward me, tucking a hair behind my ear and the back of his hand brushes against my cheek gently. It's rough but feels so…nice. This time his hand lingers at my mouth, and I begin to kiss his damaged knuckles, one after another. His thumb is the last to brush by, and slowly it parts my lips, pushing its way into my mouth. It tastes salty and feels odd against my tongue, but I can't get enough. I begin to kiss and bite at him until his finger is replaced by his tongue.

The seashell slips from my grasp as he leans me back against the sand. It is such a heady feeling, I am spinning. I hear the crash of the waves and the rush of our breath. He lies next to me, and the feeling is so forceful and exhilarating a loud moan escapes my mouth and finds its way into his. Both of his hands are on the sides of my head and his tongue is claiming my mouth as his own. I feel his knee come to rest on the ground between my knees, my gown lifting slightly to make way. He presses against me and I am lost. I grab at the back of his shirt, trying to pry it off him, trying to pull him on top of me. My body aches, wishing his hands would find their way to…anywhere on me. My body moves against his and the feeling is…indescribable.

I feel the shift in his body as he rolls himself away from me. He sits up, breathing heavily, an arm draped across a bent knee. Before he can chastise himself for what we've done, or would like to do, I reach up and run my hands through his hair. He closes his eyes and relaxes with my touch. I hike my gown just enough to allow me to move comfortably and climb onto his lap. I face him, my mouth swollen from his kisses. He looks away, but his hands make their way to my hips to pull me closer. The connection is exhilarating. I want to dive back into another kiss but something tells me not to. Instead, I wrap my arms around his neck and push myself as close as I can.

A gentle breeze brushes against me. I lift my head to let the light wind wash over me, and I catch a glimpse of Brooke in the distance, walking toward us. My heart drops when I see she is walking purposely, her head hung low. She is coming with news. She has the answer to what's next for us and where we will go from here, and I know it's not an answer we want.

I look away, making Brooke disappear just for the moment. I wish I could just as easily close my eyes and escape all of the atrocities of our world. If only Phoenix and I could run off and start a life together. But neither of us would ever leave. There are too many people here relying on us.

Staring at Farnsworth's mansion I wonder, why us? Why were we chosen for this life? We were just two kids thrust into an unimaginable situation, one who became the strong, rebel leader and the other, the girl he fought so violently against. Somehow, these two great foes have fallen for each other and yet, this is the only thing in our crazy world that truly makes sense.

Phoenix's arms tighten around my waist. I *feel* his love for me—his protectiveness and passion. I know no matter what news Brooke brings, Phoenix and I will find the answer. Together.

Brooke is approaching quickly, and it's clear we're on borrowed time. I'm not wasting one more precious moment worrying. I bury my face into Phoenix's neck and breathe him in deeply. This is our moment of bliss, and maybe this is as happy as we are ever allowed to be.

He raises his head and kisses me, hungrily. His hands clamp on my hips, and he pulls me even closer. Lost in his kiss, my body feels things it never has before, like there's a giant magnet inside Phoenix sending shock waves through my body and drawing me to him.

Brooke stands behind us now, and there is no more pretending our future is ours alone.

I pull away from Phoenix and smile at him. The corners of his eyes crinkle as he smiles back. He nods, cups my cheek in his hand, and I nuzzle against it. We understand each other.

Even if this is all the happiness we are ever allowed, it will be enough.

A word from the author...

Originally from NYC, I have a fondness for cities and all that is gritty. I have a soft spot for flawed, passionate female characters, and although I enjoy writing NA/YA, my first novel was steamy women's fiction. I began my writing career as a playwright, which is probably why I love writing dialogue. My other loves include (in no particular order): coffee (although sadly, it's now decaf); yoga; Luna bars (I am petitioning them to bring back Chocolate Raspberry!); running in my neighborhood; Hemingway; Bukowski... and, above all, my husband and my girls.

~*~

You can learn more about Cathrine and her writing at:
http://www.CathrineGoldstein.com

Thank you for purchasing
this publication of The Wild Rose Press, Inc.

If you enjoyed the story, we would appreciate your
letting others know by leaving a review.

For other wonderful stories,
please visit our on-line bookstore at
www.thewildrosepress.com.

For questions or more information
contact us at
info@thewildrosepress.com.

The Wild Rose Press, Inc.
www.thewildrosepress.com

Stay current with The Wild Rose Press, Inc.

Like us on Facebook

https://www.facebook.com/TheWildRosePress

And Follow us on Twitter
https://twitter.com/WildRosePress